The Stone Ship

The Stone Builders #2

By

John Lars Shoberg

Dedication:

To Trudy

ISBN 978-0-9863301-7-9

Print 1 - May 2021

MoonPhaze LLC, 613 del Pilar Dr., Groveland FL, 34736

MoonPhaze.com

Table of Contents

The Stone Ship

Prologue

Captain Constance Young, commander of the UEF *Resolute*, thumb activated her cabin door. She leaned against the corridor wall, pushing away her exhaustion, while watching the door dissolve into a passable energy field. It had been a double bridge shift. The last 16 hours she'd been delegating work to her numerous science teams. Surveys had to be completed before they could drop into the newly discovered Vanera solar system and explore its planets. *Before the fun can begin*, she told herself.

"Twenty-eight more days," she said as she stepped into her cabin, staring at where her bunk folded against the side wall. Sliding one foot in front of the other to get over to its controls. "Twenty-eight days to map this Oort cloud, I suppose someone will have another name for it by morning. Damn big one, too. Lots of rocks! But I suppose we can't have any of them following us into the system. Well, that's tomorrow's problem." She pressed the wall panel and her bunk folded down invitingly in front of her.

"Ma'am," came a voice from the wall. "Is there anything you require?"

"Not tonight, Jeeves. Just kill the lights." As the room gradually darkened, she unbuttoned her uniform's collar, fell forward onto her bed, and sank away from any decision-making into sleep.

* * *

"Captain to the bridge." The lights in her cabin sprang to full brightness. "Captain to the bridge," was repeated as Connie rolled off her bunk into a seated position.

She took a couple of deep breaths to calm the wakeup rush she felt, then a couple more to keep herself from falling back onto her bed. "Jeeves, time?"

"Oh three hundred, Ma'am."

Damn, I thought I had everything running on autopilot, she said to herself so her virtual steward wouldn't interpret it as an instruction. *Only three hours sleep.*

"Jeeves, voice channel."

"Right away, Ma'am."

She blinked her eyes against the harsh light and took a couple more deep breaths, *you can't command others until you have command of yourself.* Then responded, "Young here. What's the crisis, Mr. Hamilton?"

"If you could come to the bridge, sir?" She only let her automated butler program call her Ma'am. "I'd rather Mr. Shearing explained."

"How long was I asleep?" She raised her gaze to the imaginary spot in the ceiling she had assigned for Jeeves, with the bridge channel still open so her Second Officer could hear the response.

"About three hours." Mike Hamilton answered from the bridge right on top of Jeeves' reply.

Damn, he knew. I guess whatever Shearing found in his sensor sweeps must be important. "I'm on my way, but you'd better have my coffee waiting for me when I get there. Young out."

She pulled her slept-in tunic over her head, walked over to her closet and tossed it in the hamper. She stepped through its yard long racks of hanging uniforms, working ones on her right and dress uniforms on her left, and into her personal head where she splashed enough cold water on her face to shock it into control. Then proceeded back through her single step closet into her main room, pulling a new tunic off the working rack as she went. The hanger was still wobbling from side to side as she slid the tunic over her head and ignored her unstained pants.

* * *

"As you were. Well, Mr. Hamilton, what's your big surprise?" Connie asked as she stepped across the threshold onto her bridge, knowing the hatch would form behind her again as she took her fourth step into the large circular control center of the *Resolute*. The Helmsman returned to her station forward of the Command Chair. She and the new weapons officer were hitting it off, according to the reports she'd been receiving. *Bobbie's not fragile*, she thought, *she knows what she's doing.* And pushed the thought from her mind. Besides, there was nothing for a chauffeur to do right now. Until they finished this outer system survey, the ship was on orbital autopilot.

"Mr. Shearer, the Captain is here now. What do you have to report?" The Duty Officer rose from the Command Chair, gestured over to the sensor banks on the right side of the bridge. He met Connie half way there, handing her a large cup of latte and walked with her over to the lone operator monitoring it on this, the Third Shift.

"Mr. Shearing, how many consecutive shifts is this?" the Captain asked, dropping her hand on his shoulder.

He looked up at her, she could see the dark lines forming under his eyes that her voice was denying. "I got down to the mess for an espresso about an hour ago."

"I had to call him back when that sensor," Mike pointed to the three-by-two-foot box sitting on the ledge of Will's station with several wires patching it into the main sensor grid of the *Resolute*, "started beeping."

Connie squatted down to bring the box to eye level. "Is that the spectroscope you built back on Ranklin?"

"Yes, sir." Lt. William Shearing had been the Science Officer aboard the Ranklin Space Station while Commander Connie Young was in charge. Working closely with the Harmony Science Center there, they had constructed this sensor to help them track down all the stone structures buried throughout the planet.

When she nodded, he continued, "I installed one into the sensor banks here. Mr. McStron okayed the installation." He pointed to one of his readout screens, the only one that was pinging. "It's registering Dr. Carpenter's electrostone."

Chapter One

"Using what we believe to be a snippet of sung verse, which I would like to thank Dr. CeSonta Cowloom of the Harmony Science Institute for." Rajai Pashine, who recently received his Doctorate for his analysis of the artifacts he and other members of the Harmony Science Institute discovered on the Human/Wassaran colony of Ranklin, stood behind the podium and clicked on a slide showing a new stone-like page with inscribed marks embossed into it. "Wassaran hearing being what it is, he was able to point out the verse to us human listeners. Based on that verse and these text passages, I believe the ancient Ranklinites actually called themselves: Torvons"

"Isn't that a bit presumptuous?," Dr. Laudrum bellowed from his seat in the third row of the auditorium for the fourth time in this hour-long presentation. " You **may** have a presumed snippet of vocabulary, which we can't hear but the Wassarans claim to, from the several hours of recordings that you found in your **private** find. A find, I might add, that Earth-based science institutes have been barred from participating in. But after all your precious modulation, what I heard could just as easily be interrupted as an attempt at *a cappella* music. Vocal tone production, if it was even done with a Ranklinite voice! Which brings into question the entire vocabulary you **invented** for the ancient Ranklinites?"

"If my theory is correct, the Torvon language is a lyrical, almost sung language."

Rajai's mentor, Dr. Martin Carpenter, sat in the same row as this heckler and watched as Raj came around the podium and over to the edge of the stage. While the acoustics of the small auditorium allowed his friend to give his presentation without the need for a PA system, he knew Raj enough to know when he was trying to calm someone down, usually himself. He could tell this Reginald Laudrum had rattled Raj.

"I assure my esteemed colleague," Rajai continued in a quieter voice.

"One month after being granted his degree, and he presumes to be our equal," Dr. Laudrum stood up from his seat and gestured around to the remaining people in the room. He began working his way to the aisle. He bulled his way past the only other person in that row. Rajai's lecture, having been scheduled only two days earlier when he and Martin had found they would be on Earth a week longer than they'd expected and would be able to attend this symposium, had drawn merely enough to fill a quarter of the seats in the 100 seat auditorium. Many of those had already left after Dr. Laudrum's third interruption. "Well, I, for one, have had enough of this drivel. Good day to you, sir." He growled down at Martin as he banged past him, "Deal with your upstart student." When he got to the main aisle, he turned and headed to the back entrance of the large room. He tossed the research paper, which each attendee was given when they arrived for the presentation, over his left shoulder. "And you can keep these inept findings."

"If you would have just let him talk," Dr. Martin Carpenter said quietly to no one, as he rubbed his knees.

"House. Lights," Rajai called to the computerized control booth. As they came up, he could see the handful of scientists left. His last minute addition to the Interstellar Xeno Conference here in Berkley hadn't gone as Martin had said it would. But about what Rajai had expected. "I guess that wraps up my presentation. I'd like to thank you distinguished gentlemen for staying with me."

Martin made his way to the front of the auditorium, but not before a couple of professors from the Peruvian Explorers Foundation, who had been sitting in the front row, had gotten up to the stage. Rajai at first sat on the edge of it, but jumped down to talk to them.

Before Martin could join in the conversation, he heard the back doors open again. "I thought everyone else had already left." He turned to the noise.

Two men dressed in blue UEF uniforms marched down the central aisle, removing their caps and tucking them under their arms. Martin looked over at Rajai. The conversation he'd been having stopped and the visiting professors headed for the other aisle to leave, moving faster as the UEF men got closer. Martin was almost up to his former student when the lead officer held out his hand to Rajai.

"Dr. Carpenter, may we have a minute?" the lead officer said.

"I think there is some confusion," Raj began. "I am not Dr. Carpenter."

"I am," Martin announced as he stepped beside his friend. "What exactly do you fellows want?"

"Dr. Carpenter," the officer turned so his hand pointed at Martin. After they shook hands, "Could you please come with us?"

"And why should I do that?" He stared hard at the collar of the officer speaking, "Colonel?"

"Colonel William Frederick, sir. Captain Constance Young, commanding the UEF *Resolute*, has found something orbiting the newly discovered Vanera system. Something she specifically asked for you to look at. She's requested you join her on the USF *Resolute* to confirm her find."

"Raj, you'd better get your notes and computer." As his protégé went up the steps to the stage podium, Martin continued, "How soon do we have to leave? And how far away is this system?"

"**We**?"

"Connie, Captain Young, was on Ranklin when we discovered the Torvon colony. So if she's asking for me specifically, then they found something related to them. And Raj knows as much as I do about them, so he's coming with me." As his student came back down, Martin draped his arm around the younger man's shoulder. "So again, when do we have to leave and where is Vanera?"

"795 by 1156 galactic, about a two-week trip from Earth," announced the second officer. "Sir, the car is waiting."

"You'll be leaving immediately. We instructed your hotel's staff to pack your things and have them delivered to Vandenberg. You're scheduled to liftoff," the officer consulted his watch, "in just under three hours."

"I guess..." Martin caught the back door to the auditorium move. The Peruvians were still collecting their things from where they had been sitting and no one else had come in, but now it was closing. "...we can't argue with your efficiency. If you gentlemen would lead the way."

* * *

The driver of the deep blue limousine with United Earth Force plates closed the passenger compartment door as Rajai settled into his seat. After which he nodded to the overseeing Sergeant in the forward vehicle and walked around to take his position behind the vehicle's override controls. "Sergeant Rogers is indicating his readiness to proceed," he then announced to his passengers.

"Tell him to proceed, Specialist. And give us some privacy."

Martin felt the car move forward as the window between the two sections darkened until he could no longer see the driver. He watched them pull away from the University's convention center as the windows went black also. As they grew darker, the overhead lights compensated for the missing sunlight, until it was now as bright inside the limo as it had been in the California sun.

"I think you should read this." The Colonel set his cap on the seat beside him and picked up a folder, handing it to Dr. Carpenter. "It will explain everything Captain Young sent us and why she is asking for you. Dr. Rashine, we'll have another copy of this report ready for you before liftoff."

Martin reached across the three feet separating him from Colonel Frederick's hand and collected the blue binder. It was a three-ring binder, inside was almost an inch of papers, each one stamped in red "Top Secret".

Martin felt his eyebrow drop at the discovery. "You received clearance before I arrived on campus," Frederick explained. "Lieutenant Okeke will have started the process to get your clearance, Dr. Rashine."

Martin lifted his gaze over the binder.

"We can't very well have your assistant accompany you unless he has the proper clearances."

"Colleague, not assistant!"

The Colonel leaned back against his seat. "Either way, we'll know before liftoff if he's allowed to read those reports."

"He is now!" Martin slapped the binder closed and handed it to Raj. "I need him, Connie needs him, and that means you and your superiors need him. So make your clearances happen before we leave this car."

Colonel Frederick began reaching across to collect his materials.

"If he doesn't go," Martin said, "I don't go!"

The Colonel leaned back into his seat and tapped his collar. "Mr. Okeke, expedite that clearance for Dr. Rashine."

"I can wait, Dr. Car..., ah Martin." Raj passed the binder back to Martin.

Who made no move to take it from him. "I need your opinion of this data, not your interpretation of what you think I saw in it. You know how I mumble when I read and I know you know how to listen to that mumbling. I want you to have the first look."

"Then I guess we wait for my clearance." Martin saw his friend's head turn towards the gun, not usually carried anymore by military personnel on Earth, strapped to the Colonel's hip.

Martin nodded his understanding. "I guess we do." They all relaxed back against their seatbacks with the closed binder on Rajai's lap. "So, Colonel, what kind of ship are you sending us in?"

* * *

"Would you gentlemen care to watch our liftoff from your cabins or the bridge?" Captain Sokolov met them at the walkway across the launcher leading into the UEF *Hermes*. He wasn't wearing the ground based uniforms Martin had seen throughout the military base, he had on black slacks and a blue tunic. He gestured for them to enter and followed behind them. "Your clearance came through, Dr. Rashine."

"Thank you, Captain," Martin said before Raj could speak. "I've never used the linear accelerator launcher before, always used the space elevator. We don't have a civilian equivalent: I'd love to watch things from the bridge. Raj?"

"If it's alright with you, Martin, I'd like to go over Captain Young's notes, now that I'm allowed to view them." He hugged the binder to his chest and tapped it once.

"All work, no play! But I understand. I'll catch up with you after we've passed the moon."

As they crossed the threshold of the bullet-shaped ship's hatch, Captain Sokolov instructed the marines meeting them there, "Take Dr. Rashine to his cabin, then report to me on the bridge."

"Yes, sir," the two said in unison, then turned on their heels. One led the way down the narrow corridor while the other slid in behind Rajai to bring up the rear.

"Shall we proceed to the bridge?" Captain Sokolov motioned in the opposite direction with his hand.

"After you, sir." Martin fell in behind the *Hermes'* captain, forcing himself not to constantly duck in the corridors that were just an inch taller than he was.

Captain Sokolov came to a door at the end of the corridor, spun the wheel on the hatch before he was able to push then pull it towards them and pivot it against the wall it was hinged to.

"Small courier ships like the *Hermes* can't spare the extra power to have those new programmable matter doors the new cruisers do. We use every ounce we produce to get from point A to point B. We just do it twice as fast as they can." He motioned Martin to step through and followed him, keeping his hand on the door to swing it back into place before securing it again. "Number One, are all systems secured for sled-lift?"

Everyone on what Martin assumed was the bridge was dressed in matching tunics to the Captain's. So far, only the marines he had met earlier were dressed differently; they had a bulkier beige shirt on. A woman stood up from the central chair. "Captain, everything is secured for lift-off."

"No, stay as you were. I'll be escorting our guest, you handle this launch." He turned to the empty seats at the far left of the bridge. "We'd better get seated. It's smoother than the old chemical launches we used to do, but this thing still packs a real kick."

"Pilot, please inform flight control," she instructed the man sitting with his back to her in front of a board of computers displaying data Martin couldn't even begin to guess.

"Aye, ma'am. Launch Control, this is the UEF *Hermes*, ready for catapult initiation."

"All systems go on this end. Launch in T minus one minute."

Number One pressed the intercom button in her chair's right arm. "To all hands, prepare for launch." She kept the circuit open for everyone to hear Flight Control's countdown.

"Three, two, one. Godspeed, *Hermes*."

Martin was pressed back into the bucket-style seat he and Captain Sokolov were occupying. He stared at the bridge's view screen, as the small spaceship was alternately pulled then thrown down the rail track. After a mile and a velocity of 500 MPH, they began to ascend on a track that was almost vertical. After gaining still more velocity and reaching the end of the steel track, Martin could feel the engines in the rear of the ship ignite and push them even faster through the clouds, the darkening blue sky, and eventually, into the blackness of space.

"I have scheduled a refueling stop at the L-5 space station before beginning our de-system climb, Captain."

"You're prepared as ever, Number One. Have you informed the crew that there will be no stretching of legs on this stop."

"They know we are in a hurry, Sir."

Captain Sokolov turned to Martin. "We'll do one orbit of the Earth to pick up escape velocity before proceeding to LaGrange Point 5. It'll take us a couple of hours to get there. Then we pivot 90 degrees and burn our way out of the solar system's elliptical plane. Once the system's gravity well is reduced, we can use our FTL engines. Then it will be on to Vanera to meet with the *Resolute*." He rose from his chair. "I suppose I had better show you how to find your room and the chow line."

Chapter Two

LeRena Harrod stood at the bottom of the loading ramp scanning the boxes of supplies being led into the new Harmony Science Institute space ship. She had received word just yesterday that the UEF Captain of the *Resolute* wanted the original team from their archeological dig, to help in something she had found around a new solar system she was exploring. LeRena trusted Connie, she had helped save the Ranklin colony back during her people's takeover and the subsequent Earth Purist uprising. Besides, her entire institute wanted another crack at understanding Ranklin's original colonists.

"Medical supplies, Stores," she read off her tablet's readout of the pallet's scan code. "Take this one to the cargo hold. Hopefully, we won't need it."

"Sure thing, ma'am, " the laborer said as he pushed the gravitationally suspended pallet up the ramp.

The Harmony Peace Force Chief, Sergey Lunkin, strode past the next pallet and dropped a duffel bag next to LaRena.

"Sergey, what can I do for you?" LaRena tapped her recorder, readying it for the next load.

"I want to go with you." He stood straight up, even getting on his toes, so he could almost look LaRena in her eyes.

Almost, but the Wassaran leader of the Harmony Science Institute still had to look down on her friend. "You have duties here on Ranklin and a son to watch over."

"Noaljak can handle the Peace Force while I'm away. Ever since we routed Marco and his thugs, things have been quiet. Everybody respects each other. And Thomas said he'd watch Vlad. I've got a couple of years of leave coming, and it's been over a year since I've seen Connie."

LeRena turned and scanned the next pallet. "Food, Perishables. Get these to the freezer in the galley." She turned back to Sergey, "How did you find out we were meeting her?"

"It's my job to keep tabs on our community. Your brother-in-law Bill told me. He thought he was done with infants until you dropped LaGena off with your sister. I got all the arrangements made this morning. Everything I need is already packed."

She tapped her tablet a few more times, stared at the results, then turned back to Sergey. "Okay, get aboard. Michael can assign you quarters."

"Thanks, LaRena." He grabbed his duffel bag, slung it over his right shoulder and quick-timed up the ramp.

Michael was just coming up in the lift as Sergey started looking around the loading dock. He walked over to the rising platform before Michael had time to lift the safety bar out of his way.

"Step in, Sergey." Michael held the bar up as Lunkin stepped onto the lifting platform, dropped his duffel onto the metal grid and took a wider stance before Michael could replace the bar and lower them down to the ship's cabins.

"I just got a message from the boss. She said I need to get you a bunk, it looks like you're going with us?" Michael turned the bar, locking it in place and activating the lowering mechanism.

"I haven't seen Connie in a while."

"Sounds like a good reason to me. One of the laborers, Peter Tsai didn't want to go on this trip anyway. Up for some grunt work?" As the lift reached the bottom of its shaft, the safety bar automatically rolled back to its unlocked position. Michael lifted it out of their way.

He motioned Sergey off the lift and dropped the bar back into place as he stepped off. "If you'll follow me, we have a spare cabin right down here."

"I can share, if that helps?"

"This bottom floor of the *Venture* is living space."

"When did you guys name this *Venture*? You only got it last month."

"Yesterday. The boss lady said we had to call it something other than 'the ship' if we wanted to take it on this mission. I suggested we name it after the main character in a series of Arthur Conan Doyle books I was reading, but they decided to name it in honor of a lost American Space Shuttle. In the end, it amounted to the same thing. Here we go."

Michael stopped before a door with a blank white card in the eye height letter holder mounted to it. He pulled the card from the holder, took out his tablet, punched a couple of icons, and waved the tablet over the door knob. When he heard a click, he put his tablet away and opened the door. "This one is yours." He took a tablet out of the desk just inside the cabin and handed it to Sergey. "Here's your tablet. Get unpacked, then report back to LaRena. You'll have to pick up the slack if we're losing Peter."

Sergey threw his duffel on the bed and turned around to offer his hand. "Thanks, Michael; seeing Connie again means a lot to me."

Michael took the Peace Officer's hand. "Then I guess we get to work you twice as hard," as he shook it. "Better get moving, LaRena wants to lift off by dusk. You know where the dining hall is, right?"

*   *   *

A dozen pallets later, Sergey was excused from duty. As it was still an hour from lift off and the hatches to the outside were sealed, he spent the time catching a quick nap in his cabin.

The next thing he knew, Justin Davis' voice was announcing through all the speakers in every room of the *Venture*. "Now hear this. We will be switching to artificial internal gravity in ten minutes in preparation for external gravitational reversal. Those wishing to view our launch should proceed to the viewing lounge outside the dining hall at this time. Repeat. We will be switching..."

Gravitational drive was a new technology, and Sergey had never seen it used to power a spacecraft off a planetary body. He had to watch this. He swung off the bed, headed for the door grabbing his tablet on the way. It fit neatly into the pocket in his right leg tailored to hold it. Without the tablet in the cabin, its lights winked out as his door closed.

Sergey was waiting for the lift to arrive when a wave of dizziness hit him. It passed in a second as he felt lighter than before. "They've already switched to artificial gravity. Hurry up, lift."

Wiz CeSonta Cowloom and Dr. Daisy Lawton joined him waiting for the lift by the time it finally arrived. Sergey knew the Wassaran to be the Institute's Chief Geologist, while Dr. Lawton, who stood three feet under Cowloom, was a member of the Xeno-research staff. "Do you think they will be needing a paleontologist on this trip, Ms. Lawton?"

Cowloom lifted the bar as the lift stopped. "I requested Daisy's presence, Chief Lunkin. After our last study of the ancient Ranklinites, I thought her skills could come in handy."

"I think Ce couldn't bear to be parted from me," she said squeezing the Wassaran's left arm. Her head came up to his elbow.

They stopped and Sergey lifted the safety bar for everyone to exit. They followed several other members of the expedition as people rounded the outside to the work areas and through the dining hall to the large windows looking onto the corn fields that the spaceport bordered. There were no chairs on this observation deck, so the two dozen members of the expedition stood around, waiting for liftoff.

Justin's voice came over the PA system again. "Commencing assent in five, four, three, two, one."

The circular ship, larger than the main work labs of the Institute that owned it, reversed the polarity of gravitational particles and slowly started to push itself away from the planet's gravitational field. Slowly at first, but gaining speed as it went, until by the time it left the light blue of Ranklin's atmosphere for the blackness of space, it was travelling at seven miles per hour, or escape velocity.

Finally, I'm on my way to see you again. Sergey thought of Connie as the smaller of Ranklin's moons sped past them.

Chapter Three

"Chief, are we ready to move out?" Lieutenant Kalifa Attah looked across to the object that sat against the rocky asteroid outside the magnetic atmosphere shield currently keeping the shuttle bay pressurized. *I can't even call it a metallic object, it's just a rock*, he said to himself. Captain Young had maneuvered the *Resolute* to within twenty yards of it, with the asteroid on its far side. They were almost the same size. Whatever this object, this cylinder was, its sixteen-by-twelve-foot frame was going to barely fit on the salvage sled they were preparing to secure it to.

"You heard the Lieutenant," came the voice of his Crew Chief, Leo Fitzsimmons, over the suit intercom. "Buddy up, secure your lines and take hold on this sled." The six men making up the salvage team quickly attached a line between the three pairs of them. Then a member of each pair attached another to the sled itself. In a staggered sequence Kalifa heard six "Ready, Chief" announcements before Fitzsimmons pronounced them ready to go.

Kalifa called up to the control booth in the back, "Go for decompression." A hissing noise filled the room. As more of the air was removed for storage, the hissing noise became softer until it was not enough to register on the environmental suit's speakers.

"I'm dropping the shield, Lieutenant," Kalifa heard through his suit radio.

"Acknowledged, Control." He pulled his gaze away from the source of his speculation and waved his men forward. "Then let's get to it. Chief, get them over to the package." He took two steps and was outside the ship. He ignited his maneuvering thrusters and flew over to his objective. He took a position standing on the asteroid so he could look lengthwise over the object they were to retrieve. Fitzsimmons joined him there a moment later.

Rather than attempting the delicate balancing of six separate thrusters, spaceman Michaels operated the thruster controls of the salvage sled and the rest of the team held the hand holds and went along for the ride. They brought the sled up against the object lengthwise before the second man of each team thrust over to the asteroid and secured themselves. Each drove a piton into the rocky surface with another line attaching them to it.

"According to the Captain, we can't drive anchors into the object," began Kalifa. "We're going to have to run straps around the object to secure it."

Chief Fitzsimmons called to his men, "Locate gaps between the object and the asteroid. Gaps large enough to run the push rod through."

After the third, "I'm not finding any, Chief.", Fitzsimmons turned to his commanding officer. "Deploy the spreaders, Chief," he commanded.

"Michaels, get your spreader between the object and the asteroid. Minimum pressure."

Aye, Chief." From his tool belt, Michaels unclipped a device that looked like a clamp with long jaws and a small motor mounted on the end. He pushed the jaws into a short, small gap in between the two objects, about half the length of the six inch jaws. Not being satisfied with the fit, he extracted it and found another gap that allowed the jaws almost full entry. He gave a single tap to his arm mounted electronics package, where the controls for the spreader were virtually displayed, and the motor began turning the screw. After a few seconds the motor stopped as the resistance it faced was greater than the force it was providing.

"Permission to increase pressure, Chief?"

Kalifa answered instead. "At your discretion, Spaceman. One increment at a time though, I don't want this thing flying away before we get her secured."

After the third tap on his panel, the two objects began moving apart. A metal bar with a nylon strap magnetically attached came through from the other end. Michaels pulled the bar though and handed it to one of the men at the base of the sled. They attached it and ratcheted the strap tight. Michaels powered down the spreader and grabbed it before it could fall between the two objects as they continued to move apart.

As the two continued moving away from each other, more gaps formed and two more straps were applied. When the object began to drift away from the asteroid, Michaels used the sled's thruster to push it back against the rock, until they had a chance to inspect their connections.

"All secure, Chief."

"Then let's get her back to the *Resolute*, Chief," Kalifa said as he powered up his thrusters, flew half way back to his ship, turned and watched the crew maneuver the package away from the rock and head home.

* * *

"This is the thing you pulled off that asteroid?" Captain Young stared at the cylindrical rock her salvage team had brought into the *Resolute's* landing bay. Across the magnetic curtain, she tried to study their find as the bay doors moved their way closed.

Lieutenant Attah, still wearing his environmental suit and inside the section of the bay that was still in vacuum, directed the sled to bring the artifact into his ship. "Sir, this is the object Mr. Shearing directed us to." He switched from waving his arms to pushing them to the floor. The operator of the sled lowered it, then held up his hands clenched together indicating he had shut the unit down.

As the bay doors came together, Connie, Commander McStron, her First Officer, and Lieutenant Shearing began to hear a faint hissing. The hissing grew louder as more air filled the chamber. The next step would be for the area to be scanned for radiation or harmful pathogens. Another ten minutes passed before an "All-Clear" klaxon sounded. The men inside doffed their space helmets and began storing them as the magnetic curtain was turned off.

"Mr. Shearing, please confirm that this is a Ranklinite creation."

"Yes, sir." He picked his case off the floor, slung its strap around his neck, pulled a ten inch wand out of its side, and began waving it around the object.

"What do you make of this, Number One?" Both she and McStron crossed the deck to get a better look.

17

"Twelve foot wide cylinder, about sixteen feet in length with three tubes emerging from the far end, each pointed in a slightly different direction." As they walked around to the rear of the sled, Lawrence tried looking into that tube. "It looks like it has a couple of small holes in the back end." He stood up and faced his Captain. "They could be feeder nozzles for whatever propellant drove this thing?"

"So what's your conclusion?"

"It's too small to be anything other than an escape pod."

"I concur." She turned and spoke more loudly." Everyone spread out. Look for anything that looks like a hatch." She walked over to where the supervisor of the salvage was stripping his environmental suit and stowing it in its locker. Lawrence was right at her shoulder.

William Shearing sheathed the wand in its case and approached Connie. "Captain, this is definitely the object giving the signal from my scanner." He patted the case he was carrying. "And if it is Ranklinite, there may be no hatch to find. Their control of electrochemical construction was amazing."

"They could make a hatch and seal it at will, I see your meaning, Mr. Shearer. There isn't a lot more we can do until the science teams get here. Resume your post on the bridge, Mr. Shearing." She turned to the approaching salvage supervisor, "Mr. Attah, a word."

"Ma—" she threw the Lieutenant a scowl, "Sorry, sir."

"Get this area secured. Assign teams to assist our science division in working with this object until the Ranklin teams get here. But under NO conditions allow anyone to try cutting into that thing."

"Sir, if I may ask," Her look gave him a go-ahead, "You and Lieutenant Shearing kept referring to this thing as a Ranklinite artifact, now you're talking about a Ranklin science team. Do we know these people?"

"A Human and Wassaran colony on the planet Ranklin discovered an ancient race had inhabited the planet before our two species ever met. Instead of calling them "These Old Guys", they have been referred to as Ranklinites. At least until someone comes up with a better name. The Harmony Science Institute is sending a vessel with the scientists that did the original investigation of these people. They had some weird science I couldn't understand, just accept. The Ranklinites used a stone construction system, this thing could easily be an escape pod. So until we know what's inside or at least how to safely open it, I don't want anyone poking holes in it."

"Thank you... Sir." Connie heard him almost make the same mistake but he caught himself at the last second. He turned on his heel and called out to his teams and began issuing instructions.

"I think we should head back to the bridge, Number One. We still have a mapping mission to complete."

*　*　*

"Sir," Lieutenant Shearing called out as Captain Young and Mr. McStron were announced onto the bridge. "I'm detecting another Ranklinite signal."

They veered over to the sensor console. "Could you be picking up a signal from the piece we have in the landing bay?" McSton asked for his Captain.

"No, sir. I'm currently tied into our external sensor array and it is coming from somewhere approximately one mile from our location."

"And you didn't register it before?" McStron placed his hand on the back of Shearing's chair and bent over to look at the range finder displaying the new object's location.

"I probably did, but the two signals were on the same vector, and the pod we collected masked this new one."

"Well, I guess we have another object to track down," Connie said as she turned to her Helm officer. "Mr. Brown, let's move the *Resolute* forward a mile." She then leaned toward her First Officer. "At this rate, we won't even get the outskirts of this solar system mapped." She straightened back up, "Helm, at your discretion."

Chapter Four

Reginald Laudrum banged open the door to Berkley's Engineering workshop. "You've had that fragment for over two weeks. Haven't you found something about it we can use to build a detector?"

"It's not giving off any electromagnetic signals," Bart Higgins, Head of the Department, said over his shoulder, not bothering to look up from the microscope monitor as he moved the viewing angle from side to side on the slice of stone he had in its lens. "I've had the Chem department run an analysis and there are no unique elements present."

Laudrum stopped his pacing behind the Engineer's chair, "You let that fragment out of your sight?" He tried to swivel the chair around, but Bart had his feet firmly planted, having experienced Laudrum's outbursts before.

His resistance didn't matter, he'd lost his spot on the stone slice and would have to start the search over again. Preferably after locking Dr. Laudrum out. "Reg, the more you burst in here and demand results, the less time I have to find them. You've just ruined an hour's work. Science takes time and patience."

Just as he finished talking, a ping sounded from across the room. Dr. Higgins quickly stood up and crossed the room to the bench with several different sensing devices on it. Only the radar screen was active, it had most of its guts spilled all over the bench with clips and twisted wires holding pieces together, but it was pinging. Then it stopped.

"That's the frequency!" Bart stopped the scan of the instrument and dialed it back to the last one it had been transmitting. The pings started again.

"There's your detector!" He straightened up and faced the archeologist who had brought him the small sample of the

Ranklinite stone. "We're not looking for something the rock is giving off. We're looking for a radiofrequency the rock absorbs."

"Get that thing pulled together. Have several of them ready to go by the morning." Laudrum had turned and was heading for the door. "I'll have a research ship ready to leave by 0800 hours. We're going to," he had to stop and think for a minute, "795 by 1156 galactic, where that new system the UEF discovered is, and see what we can find before the Harmony Research Institute can."

He was out the door and off to pester someone else. Bart could hear him yelling commands as he walked away. Now it was his turn. He called in his research assistants and gave them instructions on how to build the detection devices and left them to knock out as many as possible while he packed for the trip to Vanera.

* * *

Dr. Laudrum stepped into his office, planning to finalize the flight arrangements, only to find three people occupying it. One short and wide, cracking walnuts with his right hand and dropping pieces of their shells on Laudrum's floor. The second, just over six foot tall, was browsing the books Laudrum had on his shelves, pulling them down one at a time and piling them on the corner of his desk. The third visitor was sitting behind his desk in Laudrum's own chair with his feet resting on a grant application Reg had been preparing for over a year. The three people who had put up the money to finance his trip to get a jump on the Harmony Research team.

"Andreyev, Dortello, Belinsky; gentlemen, I was just about to call you." He walked around his desk and pulled the third man's feet off it, then lifted the back of his chair to dump him out of it. He sat down, straightened up his grant proposal papers and slid them into his top drawer. "Dr. Higgins has finally cracked the problem. We'll be leaving at 0800 hours tomorrow morning."

"Then it is a good thing we never unpacked since arriving in this warm climate," said the tall Myles Andreyev.

"We wouldn't want you to make the trip alone," the shorter Enrico Dortello said after spitting out the shell that had clung to the walnut he had tried eating.

21

Laudrum watched it hit the floor just short of his filing cabinet. "Must you?"

"I like walnuts, the way they taste, the way they splinter as you crush their attempt to keep you from them. I sent a case of them over to the ship when we got here."

"Marvelous!"

"We need to see exactly what we've paid you for," Ivan Belinsky said as he opened the door to Laudrum's work room. He closed it after seeing the lights were off. "You bringing anyone else?"

Laudrum turned his chair to see what his second Russian financier was doing. "Just a couple of lab assistants who can double as pilots."

"Then we see you in the *Yuri*. I assume you have her prepped and ready for takeoff." He leaned over Laudrum's desk to look him in the eye. "It is good to be ready," he added as Laudrum nodded in assent. "Gentlemen, let's let our employee prepare himself for the arduous journey we begin tomorrow." As they filed out the door, Andreyev turned back to look at Laudrum. "See you in the morning."

Laudrum felt a chill as if he had just received a threat.

Chapter Five

"Gentlemen, it's good to see you again." Captain Young met the two boarding scientists as they stepped through the connecting lock from the *Hermes* to her own battle cruiser. On her right was a tall man with Commander pips on his collar and to her left was a shorter officer with an Ensign rank insignia. Connie held out her hand momentarily, then withdrew it when she noticed the baggage the two of them were carrying. "Ensign Jacoby, take their bags to their quarters and wait for them there."

"Yes, Ma'am"

"Grrrrr," Rajai heard a growl coming from Connie.

"Sorry, sir. It won't happen again, sir."

"See that it doesn't. Now off with you."

Raj hurried past the waiting officers and deposited his suitcases on the gravitational pallet parked behind the greeting party then turned to help Martin. His friend quickly set his own luggage on the pallet also, before Raj had the chance. Then Ensign Jacoby took off down the connecting corridor.

"Raj, you're not my assistant anymore," Martin said as the pallet moved towards their rooms. He turned back to the waiting officers and held out his hand. "Connie, it's good to see you again."

"Hold that thought." Connie stepped up to the wall, swung the hatch across to the other ship closed and sealed it, then pressed a button on the panel next to the hatch. "*Resolute* commanding to *Hermes*. Your passengers have arrived safely and the airlock is sealed. Have a safe return trip."

"Affirmative, *Resolute*. Good hunting."

She turned back to her visiting scientists. "This is my First Officer, Commander Lawrence McStron."

The taller man offered his hand as well. "Pleased to meet you gentlemen. Connie talks highly of the work you all did on Ranklin. I look forward to seeing what you guys can do out here."

"I hope we don't disappoint you, Commander." Martin shook the offered hand first, followed by Raj.

"You two must have had a grueling ten days cramped up in that courier ship. But if I remember correctly, you're going to want to see the artifacts before you'll be able to get any rest." She motioned with her left hand for them to proceed in the opposite direction their luggage had gone.

"Artifacts," Martin replied as he looked from the direction Connie was indicating back to her, then to Rajai.

"I thought there was only the one," Raj responded. Then they both turned to stare Connie in the face.

"After we got the first one aboard, Lieutenant Shearing, you remember Mr. Shearing? He discovered a second one. We've got it secured outside the ship. It being too large to be brought aboard. You probably would have seen it had you been traveling in something other than one of those small courier ships, something with more view screens than on the pilot's console. Would you like to have a look at the first one we found, the one we **can** get into our landing bay?" She again motioned with her hand for them to proceed.

* * *

The entryway to the landing bay also had the potential to open into the vacuum of space, so unlike the interior doors of UEF vessels that could be turned off to pass through them and have their atoms reprogrammed to be solid form again, Commander McStron had to turn an actual wheel to disengage the metal bars holding a five inch steel door in place across the entryway into the landing bay.

Once he had pulled it inwards and against the right corridor wall, Connie stepped through and gestured across the bay to the large stone object at the far end. "Gentlemen, there's what we're calling the pod."

Both Martin and Rajai stepped over the hatch's threshold and walked straight up to the stone cylinder. "Martin, this looks newer than the structures on Ranklin." Raj walked all around the object.

Martin walked up to the front end of the cylinder and ran his hand over the spherical dome projecting from it. "The stone feels different too." Then he balled his hand and rapped his knuckles on it. "Sounds hollow. Captain, has anyone tried to get inside this thing?"

She walked up to the two of them and stood with her hands clasped behind her back. McStron stayed behind to close the hatch and await their return. "When we couldn't find an obvious hatch, I thought it would be best to wait for the experts to get here."

"I'd hardly call us experts," Raj said, coming back around to join Martin. "We've just been guessing our way through this."

"You've been making some pretty good guesses. Raj, feel here." Martin reached over to Raj with his right hand, keeping his left against the side of the cylinder. As Raj placed his hand where Martin moved his away from, "Do you feel that?"

Raj closed his eyes for a moment. "It could be lettering." He moved his fingers left and right against the side of the dome. "Yes, it feels like the Torvon word for doorway." He ran his fingers above and below the indentations. "There's a pinhole here also. What was the current we applied back on Ranklin to get the liquid stone to solidify?"

"Damn, I don't remember. It was Mike, LaRena's husband, the architect, who worked that out. Did he ever publish those findings?" Martin turned back to Connie as Raj shook his head. Mike wasn't the kind of guy who would publish something like that. "What's the ETA on the Harmony team?"

"They should be arriving tomorrow. They've got one of the new ships with the new gravitational drive engine. It's a lot faster than either the *Resolute* or even the *Hermes*. The only reason you got here first was that we contacted you a week before you requested them."

"Can we get word to them, to Michael? See if he has the key to opening this thing?"

"It would probably be just as quick to wait until they get here. But don't you want to see our latest find, first?"

"Something bigger than this?" Raj turned back to the cylinder and spread his hands wide to mimic its size.

"Oh, yes. If you would like to follow me?"

She led them across the ship, from the port to the starboard side. They stopped at the viewing lounge adjacent to an airlock there. "This is the starboard recreational center, though it's closed right now because of that." She pointed to the large glowing object outside the panoramic viewports.

There sat a large asteroid with the sheen of a force field surrounding it. The asteroid appeared to be oddly egg shaped, almost like it was two different objects slammed together. One end oblong with a pot marked texture and the other much larger, more like a sphere cut in half, then slammed onto the rest of the rock. And it was smooth!

"Can we get out there?" Martin could almost hear Raj salivating over this find.

"Martin, was this what it was like when you discovered those storm drains back on Ranklin?" Raj took a step closer to the viewports and laid his hand on the transparent aluminum separating him from his dream.

"Only more so, Raj! I had no idea where they would lead me. Now I have a pretty good clue."

"Number One, are the environmental suits serviced for our guests?" Connie said over her shoulder.

McStron was still hovering right behind his Captain. "Ready and waiting, sir."

"Then let's not keep our guests waiting. If you gentlemen will follow me." She motioned out of the lounge and back into the corridor.

*　*　*

McStron adjusted the suits of the two scientists, then twisted their helmets into place. He activated their air supplies, and checked the readings from their forearms' computers. He touched his ear to activate his radio link to inside their suits. "Can you gentlemen hear me okay?"

"You are coming in loud and clear," Raj said. When McStron didn't reply he looked at the ship's first officer and nodded his helmet. Which took moving his chest to get the thing to go up and down. He could move his head freely inside but he didn't know if McStron would see that subtle of a movement.

26

He felt McStron press something on his right arm, the opposite one from his computer interface. "Try talking again, Dr. Pashine."

"Is this thing working now?"

"Loud and clear, Dr. Pashine. How about you, Dr. Carpenter?"

Raj saw his friend pressing the same button as McStron had. "Loud and clear."

"Follow Captain Young's instructions about tethering while out there. If you lose contact with each other or the ship, you have thruster packs attached to your back. Press this button on your arm computer and the maneuvering interface will be called up. Up, down, right, left are based on the position of your body, not your surroundings. And the center button is your forward control. The longer you press them the faster you'll go. Releasing them will stop their discharge, but not kill your momentum. So if you have never done this before, be very careful about how hard you use your maneuvering pack. Finally, if you feel unable to get back to the *Resolute*, slap your palm over the entire panel." He adjusted a few virtual buttons on the interface. "I just rigged your panic button to interface with the Captain's unit, giving her control over your thruster pack. Never fear, we'll get you boys home."

The First Officer turned, as he heard a metallic footfall behind him. Captain Young came around the bank of lockers where she had been suiting up. He checked over her suit before announcing, "Everything looks good, Captain. Are you ready to proceed?"

"Have you shown them the thruster controls?"

"And how to link them to yours in case they can't get the hang of it, Sir."

"Gentlemen, are you ready?" she asked.

Both men gave a thumbs up. When Raj looked over to Martin, he could see his grin reflected on his mentor's face. This would be the first time either of them had done an actual space walk.

"Then the airlock awaits." Connie lead the way out of the changing room, into the corridor and over to the adjacent airlock.

Raj watched McStron swing open the door. They stepped over the raised threshold and into a smaller room. Connie pulled a safety line from a belt hard pouch and attached it to a bar above the outside hatch, then she motioned for the others to do the same. Raj heard the inner door clank shut through the helmet speaker.

"Evacuating the chamber now," McStron said through their helmet radios. After a couple minutes of slowly diminishing hissing. "Okay, you're clear to open the outside hatch. Good luck."

Connie worked the panel that released the door locks, then pulled the door into the airlock and swung it to the right on its hinges. "Dr. Carpenter, attach another safety line to me. Dr. Rashine, you connect another to him. Once you've done that, release the ones you have connected to the chamber, they will retract back into their pouches. Let me thrust us to our first position."

"We're not floating," Martin said.

"You're still within the artificial gravity field of the *Resolute*. Once we're outside this hatch, you will be. So after I step out, I'll need both of you to step onto threshold and jump away from the ship. That's why we rope ourselves together before stepping out."

She stepped onto the metal edge of the hatch with her right foot and pushed off with it. After she floated far enough away that Martin's line straightened out, he jumped out also. Raj placed one hand on either side of the hatch, pulled both of his feet onto the metal ledge, and as his line to Martin began to tug at him, he pushed away with both feet.

Almost hitting his helmet.

"Too much upward momentum." Connie thrusted over and grabbed the line between him and Martin . She pulled him back. "It's not like working under gravity out here. Every move has a cost. You have to be mindful of everything out here."

"But what a view." Raj hear Martin exclaim. "So much better than a mere view screen." Raj watched him grab his line and pull himself around to look from deep space to the asteroid they were out here to inspect. "Damn, that thing's big. Connie..."

"While we're on an open channel, please use formal methods of address."

"Oh, sorry. How big is this thing, captain?"

"Approximately 120 feet in diameter."

"Are we able to get inside?" Martin asked.

"A lot of the other side is blocked by the asteroid, but there is more than enough open area to get inside it. We established the force field so we could maintain a working atmosphere inside the structure. It's accessed by a different airlock. I've had a doozy of a time keeping my own science teams out of there until you guys got here."

"Maybe I should meet these science teams. We're going to need all the help we can get exploring that thing. Right, Raj?"

"I want to go inside."

"You getting space sick?"

No, inside that," he pointed at the thing hugging the asteroid.

Chapter Six

Lieutenant Attah, who had been in charge of all salvage operations and had been called in to help, stored Rajai's environmental away and took him to another section of the locker room to get him kitted up for a shirt-sleeve inspection of the asteroid find.

Martin, with McStron's assistance, hung his environmental suit up for refurbishing next to Rajai's. After Connie came back from the woman's side of the changing area and hung hers up also, she led them to a conference room. This interior door simply dissolved to allow them to enter the room.

Inside, Martin could smell the coffee service against a side wall before he noticed the oval table in the center of the room with five of its dozen chairs occupied. Everyone stood up as they entered the room. *When the Captain entered the room*, Martin mentally corrected his observation.

"Everyone, please take your seats," Connie said as she went to the chair at the head of the table and deposited her electronic tablet there. She turned to the cart with the coffee service, grabbed a cup and filled it from an urn emblazoned with the emblem of the UEF *Resolute* on it. "Dr. Carpenter, coffee?"

Okay, she wants to keep it formal in front of her crew, Martin realized, *I can live with that*. "Black with one sugar, please." He took a seat next to the one Connie had set her command tablet in front of.

She placed a fine, white porcelain cup and saucer, both decorated with the *Resolute's* emblem, in front of Martin. She deposited a similar one in front of her seat and sat down. Martin took the spoon from the side of the cup and gave his coffee a stir, then lifted a spoonful of the beverage to his lips to test its temperature. It was ready to consume, so he lifted the cup and took a small swallow.

"Dr. Carpenter was the lead scientist on the discovery at the Ranklin colony. He is currently Earth's leading expert on the Ranklinite culture. Which is why I asked him to join us in our investigation. I expect everyone to treat him as our lead scientist on this endeavor. He'll be running point on this one.

"Dr. Carpenter, I would like to introduce our own team of specialists aboard the *Resolute*. You've met Lieutenant Attah, our salvage expert, he's the one taking Dr. Rashine on his tour. This is Lieutenant Karl Wilhelm from Engineering, Lieutenant Achachak Brown from Astrophysics, Lieutenant Marsha Smith will be your Chemist, Dr. Marcus Williams is keeping a medical eye on everyone and Lieutenant Edward Chen is acting as our Archeologist."

"You have an actual archeologist aboard a warship?"

Connie looked over to Chen. "Sir, I am normally the C shift weapons officer, but my degree from the academy is in Archeology. I'm the closest thing to an archeologist the Captain has."

"Everybody onboard a UEF vessel has secondary skills, Dr. Carpenter. We can't bring the entire Harmony Science Institute with us out here." Connie sat back in her chair and folded her hands in front of herself. "Lieutenant Chen, you begin the briefing."

"We've only done a cursory inspection of the object, pending your arrival. We didn't want to disturb anything, so we haven't gone inside yet. As you can expect of something exposed to the vacuum of space, we've found no loose items inside the structure. It looks like the shell of a habitat of some type, but one with about one-half Earth gravity. But Lieutenant Wilhelm can address that better than I. There does seem to be some dust accumulation due to the thing's gravity, Interstellar dust, we are assuming. We haven't collected any for analysis yet. Isn't that right, Lieutenant Smith?" When she nodded, Chen continued, "I have been looking forward to working with you since the Captain told us you were coming. I reviewed all of your and Dr. Pashine's papers in the last week." Chen, who had been leaning on the table during his presentation, now sat back into his chair. He was just slightly shorter than the rest of the UEF officers lined up in their chairs.

Karl, who was sitting next to him, began. "As you are aware, all known space vessels use artificial gravity technology. They provide the passenger with a connection to the floors of the vessel they are traveling in. Once you are outside the vessel, the simulated gravity ceases. You can turn the generator on and off at will. When you do, the simulated gravity also ceases.

"Not so with the structure outside. It appears to be held to the asteroid by its own gravity field; as Lieutenant Chen mentioned, a gravity of one half gee. And that is maintained throughout the structure. Not just the floors. The walls and ceilings also exert the same pull. We're waiting to go inside and see if there's an active mechanism to account for this."

Martin looked over to Connie, then back to the Engineer. "Could it be something that has just not worn off yet?"

"Artificial gravity doesn't work that way. It's either on or off. The effect doesn't seep into the material it's projected on."

"Lieutenant Brown, what did you come up with for an age estimate?" Captain Young kept the meeting moving.

"If we assume these items are some type of debris, and from the same event—" she began.

"Event? What kind of event?" Martin leaned forward, balancing his arms on the conference table.

"We have no idea at this point, it's just a point of speculation. Dumped cargo, exploding space vessel, really, anything. We had been hoping you would have some ideas that we haven't thought of." As Martin leaned back into his chair, Achachak continued. "Based on the relative positions they were found in and the orbital speed of this belt of asteroids, I'd say they've been sitting here for at least three hundred years. We have no way to determine the amount of time they'd been drifting before arriving in this system. Or, for that matter, from where."

Martin whistled at the conclusion.

"Lieutenant Smith?"

"Yes, captain. We managed to collect a small amount of the dust accumulating inside the structure, and as Lieutenant Chen said, its analysis determined it to be simple interstellar dust. I did manage to get a scrapping off the edge of the object and ran an analysis of it based on the finding of your Dr. Justin Davis. The atomic composition is very similar to what he found, but everything is arranged differently; same elements, but new compounds. They appear to be using less material to achieve the same structural integrity."

"I need to get a look at that beauty," Martin said.

"Once you do, I'd like you and your co-worker to come by my sick bay for a check-up. And in the mean time, wear one of these." He passed a small round chip to Martin, who turned it over to look at it. "It'll stick to your clothing." He looked over at Captain Young. "I'm assuming Lieutenant Attah gave one to Dr. Pashine?" When she nodded, he continued, "It's okay to wear a suit over it if you need to, we need to know what your body is being exposed to. We haven't detected any harmful radiation from the object, but I found you can never be too careful. Captain, with your permission, I'd like to get back to sick bay, where I'm probably needed more than in this briefing." He rose from his chair before the captain could respond.

"Dismissed, Doctor. In fact, I think we're probably done here. Good work, everyone. Dismissed." As they started to leave, she added, "Mr. Chen, please stay. I was wondering if you could take Dr. Carpenter on a tour of our little object?

"Yes, Sir," he responded cheerfully, gestured towards the door.

Martin rose from his seat, reached down and drained the last few swallows of the coffee in his cup. *The trip on the Hermes must have hit me harder than I thought*, he internalized, *That's good coffee.*

Chapter Seven

"While we call it a "shirt-sleeve" work environment, you'll still be wearing a pressure suit." Lieutenant Chen opened the locker and pulled a light jumpsuit out and handed it to Martin.

He took off his suit coat again and stored it in an empty locker. Then stepped into the legs of the suit and pulled them over his pants. After he zipped it up the front, Chen handed him a two inch thick, three inch wide belt to strap around his waist. Martin, being a little thicker than most of the UEF crew, needed an extension to make it around his waist.

"It's in case the force field around the asteroid fails. It won't protect you from long exposures outside, but it should get you back to the ship. Once you don this helmet," he handed Martin a clear plastic sphere, "just clip it to your belt here." He touched a clip mounted on the right side of Martin's belt and pressed a couple of buttons on it. "Once that helmet seals in place, your air supply is automatically activated. You have enough chemicals in that belt to generate twenty minutes of breathable air. But don't delay out there, head straight back to the ship if something happens. You're wearing a pressure suit, not an environmental suit. There are more things in the vacuum of space that can kill you than just loss of air. Get straight back to the *Resolute* if the field drops."

"Does it fail often?"

"We've used it over a dozen times without incident. I've yet to hear about a failure elsewhere. But one would be too many, hence these precautions. Normally, we use these suits to work on areas inside the ship where an inert atmosphere is required.

"If, and I say if, you encounter explosive decompression, press your belt buckle before donning your helmet. It will fire a magnetic line that will find the nearest magnetic object and secure you to it. We've got a lot more features built into that thing, but you won't be going into any overheated Argon environments this trip."

Martin spun around slowly. "Everything look okay, then?"

"Let me clip these guys to your shoulders and I think we'll be ready to go." Chen attached a video camera to one shoulder and a light source to the other. Then he picked up his own helmet and snapped it to his belt before heading back out the hatch to another airlock.

* * *

The gap between the *Resolute* and the asteroid was spanned by a programmable matter bridge inside a corridor the force field projected to the rock. As he walked through it, Martin could see the cables running from the ship to the rock and the rods holding it in a stable position relative to the ship.

Chen stepped out onto the asteroid's surface without missing a beat. Martin stopped momentarily to try and figure out the best way to step up onto the steeply upward sloping surface.

"Don't push up too hard," Chen called back. "Not much gravity at this point."

Martin put his foot on the rock face that was eighteen inches above the connecting bridge and pushed down with it. Almost catapulting him off the asteroid, if Chen hadn't grabbed him by his belt.

"It'll be easier to control yourself inside the artifact. The gravity in there is almost as much as in the *Resolute*."

"Thanks." Martin took a few more deep breaths.

"Ready to move on?"

"Easier, you say?"

"Just take small steps until we get there." Chen pulled a line from his belt and hooked it to Martin. "Just walk like I do."

Without the screening of windows and magnetic fields, Martin saw that this artifact had the same colors, sheen and texture as the one sitting in *Resolute's* landing bay. They were definitely different than the stone structures he had uncovered on Ranklin.

He stopped his progress towards it to try and take in the big picture of this hollow shell. It was twice the height and width of the *Resolute*, and where the *Resolute* had an oblong shape, this

35

thing was spherical. *Well, at least semi-spherical*, he corrected himself.

Inside of it he saw what could only be described as floors, decks, some type of walking surfaces. All at a slight angle to his upright position on the asteroid. Yet all parallel to each other. Over a dozen levels of these things, all evenly spaced except for the center level which had a gap three times the size of the others. And was open all the way to the other side of the structure, no walls cutting off Martin's view of the interior.

Raj stood waving at him from the floor of that open space.

Martin waved back. "Chen, there's Raj." They quickly climbed the rest of the rock over to the artifact. As they did so, Martin noticed a pull towards the artifact affecting his walk.

"Martin, take a look at this! I'm finding what appears to be labels all over the walls." Raj rubbed an area to the left of a large hole in the side wall of the structure.

Martin gave a cursory look at the marks, then moved over to stare down the opening. It appeared to be around twelve feet in diameter and ran about twenty feet before emerging into space.

Martin looked back at the markings and asked, "Those don't happen to translate into Escape Pod, by any chance, do they?"

"I've been so delighted to find more Torvon words, that I forgot to actually read them." Raj had to stop and think for a moment. "This is a designation for some kind of craft or missile. It translates to: Forward A1B1."

"Sirs," asked Chen squatting down by the floor, "would you have a look at this?" He pointed at what looked like a short wire attached to the wall about three inches from the floor.

"That plug on the end," Martin began.

Raj finished his thought, "Looks about the right size to plug into the hole we found on the artifact in the landing bay."

"Do you gentlemen think what we found was an escape pod?" Chen asked. He stood up and looked around the area they were standing in. "And if so, where are all the others?" There were five empty holes on each side.

"Whoa," Martin looked up and down in the space he was standing in. "Let's not jump to conclusions." He walked over to where he had entered the structure and looked at its edge. Where he was standing, it was a good twenty feet thick, like the hole indicated.

"Why is the edge so smooth?" Chen had walked up behind Martin, staring at the same edge of the structure.

Martin turned to face Chen and just gave him a puzzled look. "How do we get to the upper levels?"

"There appears to be a shaft at the far end." Lieutenant Attah walked up to where everyone else was standing. "With what looks like a ladder mounted to the side of it."

"Or we could just jump," Raj said, then proceeded to leap straight up, do a somersault and land feet first on the ceiling. "The gravity appears to be localized to each of the floor plates here."

"The walls also," said Kalifa. He was now standing on the wall next to the 'A1B1' hole, walking up to the ceiling. "It's the oddest phenomenon we've ever encountered. It's like every piece of this thing has had its natural gravitational force enhanced."

"It would go a long way to explaining why this thing is still exerting a gravitational pull after being unpowered for three hundred years," Chen observed.

"Martin, you have to get up here." Raj was calling down to them from the floor above, apparently having climbed around the outside edge to gain access to the upper level. "It's not wide open like down there."

"This place does feel like a hanger bay," their salvage expert said.

"But for what?" the UEF engineer asked. "Did you see any way the front could be opened?"

"Raj, see if you can find that shaft Lieutenant Attah pointed out and meet us in the front section down here." Before he looked away, he saw Raj's foot appear over the edge of the upper floor. "I said, use the ladder. Safety first on a dig, no matter where it is."

"Yes, Dr. Carpenter."

At least he's overcoming the insecurities he had on the Ranklin dig.

They examined the convex surface of the far forward wall. There was the same amount of dust on it as the floors around it. As they brushed the dust aside to feel for any of the indentation marks they'd found elsewhere, the dust simply settled back against the wall in a very slow fall.

"Lieutenant Chen, can you collect some this debris for analysis? Do we have any sample collection bags in these things?" Martin stopped, stood straight and shook his hands. The dust he had accumulated fell away and back to the wall. "I'd hate to think we missed anything by assuming all this is from after the event."

He looked over to the two naval officers rotating their belts to get into a back pouch. "Lieutenant this and Lieutenant that is getting a bit long. Do you guys have another name I can call you?"

"Ed," Chen said, "but not in front of the Captain."

"Kalifa, but my friends call me Kali. When protocol allows."

"Then I suggest you gentlemen keep me away from any protocol situations. I hate titles. Even mine, please call me Martin."

"And me Raj," came from the opening in the ceiling they had decided earlier was for an elevator. "I finally found you guys. I took a few wrong turns getting here. There are several rooms up here, many with doors closed when whatever happened, happened; since they still have stuff in them." As he stepped onto the ladder, "What have we got here?"

"Nothing," Martin said. "No seams, not that I was expecting to find any of those, no labels, not even any small holes that we can find."

"You know, Martin," began Kalifa. "If this was a hanger bay, they may have controlled things from somewhere they could secure during periods of decompression. A control room we can't see."

"Or that may have been destroyed with whatever happened here," Edward finished the thought.

Raj tried jumping the last six feet to the floor and ended up on the wall instead. One step above the floor, so he finished by walking down. "That felt odd. Nothing on the wall? Do we have anything to put this in?" He handed over what appeared to be a bound pair of socks. "I know we shouldn't disturb anything until we can catalog everything but I believe we need to know exactly how old this thing is. And this was the least disturbable item I could find for carbon-dating."

"Take that back inside, would you Kali?" Martin asked, handing him the now-bagged item. "Take some of these dust bags with you and see what your chemists can make of them."

After he and Edward handed their samples over to Kalifa and he secured them in a large pouch on his left side, Lieutenant Attah headed back to the end of the structure and Martin headed for the ladder. "I say we do a cursory survey of those rooms Raj found. Got your camera, Ed?"

He opened a pocket just below his ribcage and extracted a small three by six by one-quarter inch device. "I have this," then he patted a small box mounted on his right shoulder, "if the ones we have on our shoulders aren't good enough. Yours have been recording since I activated it back in the changing room."

"Kali told me about mine as we suited up."

"I'm glad other people are thinking around here, I seem to have forgotten enough basics. Raj, could you lead the way?"

* * *

They emerged from the shaft into a 'T' style corridor. The one that ran towards the front of the structure went for only a few feet, the one running perpendicular to it disappeared into the darkness and the one running away, faded into darkness but there was a light much further down. They decided to explore that corridor. "Probably ends in the back opening of this thing, like the parallel one I explored earlier," Raj said, pulling Martin fully off the shaft ladder.

"Then I would suggest we explore in that direction." Edward walked up to the first door he came to.

"Be careful opening that." Raj quickly came up behind Chen and dropped his hand on his. "In some of the rooms the contents had been pulled against the doors."

"In or out, Raj." Martin finally caught up.

"Push the metal button in and slide the door to the left, into the wall. I had a couple of rooms spill things out on the other side."

Lieutenant Chen depressed the round silvery object on the dull red metal door. It went in as far as it had been sticking out before.

Pushing the quarter inch hole to the left, the whole door slid into the wall.

Nothing tumbled out of the room. Nothing was sitting just inside for them to step over. "This room must have lost pressure slowly when the event happened. We really need to find out what 'The Event' was so I can stop calling it 'The Event'." Martin shined his shoulder-mounted light into the room and stepped in.

"This looks like a crewman's quarters," Edward said as he entered behind Martin. He shined his light over at the bed in the right hand side of the twelve by fourteen foot room, then over to the desk mounted on the far side, and turned to illuminate a ledge running across the left wall with a few items on it.

Martin walked over to examine the items on the ledge while Edward looked over the stuff on the desk. There was what looked like a comb, with a few strands of desiccated hairs still in it. *I'll leave that for later*, he mentally noted, *probably fall apart if I touched it now.* There was a small bag sitting next to it. He almost kicked the chest that was on the floor, before noticing it was there. "Raj, it looks like we've got some personal items here. We can finally start piecing together how they lived."

"Gentlemen, this looks like a clothing rack here in the corner." Chen shone his light on a rack with several sets of clothing dangling from it. One that was protruding from the wall. "I'm seeing several sets of the same style here. I think we found their uniform."

"And this looks like an entertainment center," Raj shined his light on the wall to the right of the door. Another ledge was built about waist high with what they had discovered to be a Torvon recording machine on it. Above that was a large rectangular box built out from the wall. "Notice how it's in line with the bed."

"Raj, did you notice any of the bars paralleling the ladder like we found on Ranklin?" Martin was still looking at the clothing rod.

Raj turned to look over to his mentor. "Now that you mention it, I haven't seen any of those poles mounted around here."

"There doesn't seem to be the dust in here as in that open area," Edward said before poking his finger to his ear. "Yes, Sir." Then announced, "That was Dr. Williams. I need to get you

gentlemen back to sick bay. He says we've been out here long
enough, for today, at least."

Chapter Eight

"Hey, Doc," Myles Andreyev climbed up the short stairway onto the *Yuri's* bridge, still working his toothbrush inside his mouth. Between his accent and the muffling of him having it there, it took work for Laudrum to hear him. "When we getting there? This treasure you sold us on."

"If we had wanted to risk UEF interdiction, we would have been at the system by now," Laudrum explained, *for the third time*. "We've spent an extra day bypassing the Vanera system to stay out of sensor range of the *Resolute*. We've coming up on the far side of the system so we can use the planetary objects within it to mask our presence."

"Yeah, what he said," Ivan Belinsky belched a response while wiping the peanut butter off the hand his sandwich had gotten it on, onto the arm rest of the co-pilot's seat he was 'keepin' warm' for Mary Davis. She and Ron McNamara were the two graduate assistants Dr. Laudrum had brought along.

Reginald glowered at the stain the brute of a man had left. He pulled a rag from a lower pant pouch and wiped as much of the grease as he could from the plastic arm rest. "Have you no respect," he mumbled before turning on his main financier. "We'll be at the inner edge of the system's Oort cloud in another eight hours. Then we sit there for the five hours it'll take Bart and Ron to map this system. We have to locate somewhere in it that we're likely to find Ranklinite," *I am not using that upstart Pashine's word for them*, "artifacts that the UEF expedition isn't already at."

"Then we grab the stuff and get out of there," Belinsky said, then brought his sandwich back to his mouth for another bite, dropping more crumbs on the cockpit floor.

Reginald shook his head at the mess. "No. Once we have found a dig site and have laid claim to it, they cannot take it away from us."

"They got bigger guns," Belinsky continued to drop chunks of his crumbling sandwich where Mary would have to rest her feet.

"**They** have to obey certain rules. Unless we invite them in, ask for help, they have to stay away from our find. Especially that smug Dr. Carpenter." He walked over to the locker on the back of the small control room and took a hand broom from within it. "And you can clean that up before our pilot gets back." He shoved them into Belinsky's lap before turning and walking back to his sleeping cabin.

Chapter Nine

"It's good to see you again, boss lady," Martin said as LaRena Harrod stepped into the entry corridor of the *Resolute*. He offered her his hand since he wasn't comfortable hugging someone as tall as a Wassaran.

"Not anymore, Martin. We had an election just after you left for Earth. Aaron is the new administrator of the Harmony Research Institute. I needed more time with the twins."

"And how are they doing? I had to leave before they arrived."

Michael came around his wife. "They're a handful. Crying like humans and eating like Wassarans. We can barely keep up. I haven't completed any designs since they were born. I'm glad your sister agreed to take care of them while we're gone, Honey." He offered his hand to Martin.

"Let's get down to the conference room. Connie, oh we have to call her 'Captain Young' if any member of her crew is around," Martin whispered to them. "No luggage? You guys staying aboard the *Venture*?"

"Keeps us closer to our labs," Justin Davis said as he emerged from the transfer corridor and fell in behind.

"Con—, I mean, Captain Young, has a welcome party scheduled so you guys can meet your UEF counterparts. We've got a lot of work to do here. Possibly more than we had back when we first found the Torvons."

"Any ideas yet on the age of the find?" CeSonta Cowloom asked as he caught up.

"We've actually found organic artifacts this time. According to radiocarbon dating, these things are only a hundred years old."

Aaron Fuller quick-stepped up behind Cowloom. "That means their species may still be alive somewhere!"

Martin pressed the wall button and the door to the conference room disappeared. As they walked in, several members of the

Resolute crew were milling around where the conference table had been and a food buffet was set up against the far wall.

Cowloom began to drift in that direction when LaRena caught him by his arm. "Cowloom, do you really want to go down that rabbit warren again?"

"Rabbit hole, dear," her husband corrected her. "It's rabbit hole, not warren."

She turned to Michael, "Whatever," but smiled at him all the same. Then turned back to Cowloom, "You finally lost that hundred pounds you put on two years ago. Do you want to go through all that work again?"

"LeRena, Michael, CeSonta, it's good to see you again." Captain Young was making the rounds, greeting people. "How is everything back on Ranklin?"

"Everything's good, the twins are healthy little children," LeRena said, looking over Connie's shoulder.

"Meaning they're screaming all the time," Michael added.

"How's Sergey doing?"

"You could ask him yourself."

"Connie," came the voice of the man who had walked up behind Captain Young.

She turned at the recognition of it. Sergey wrapped her in his arms before she could resist, then she melted into and returned his embrace.

"Hey, get a room, you two," said Justin Davis as he walked past, heading over to the buffet.

After a couple of minutes, Connie got her hand between the two of them and pushed away from Sergey. "I still have host duties," she said in parsed words, still trying to catch her breath. It had been over a year since they had seen each other. "But stay with me. Since you're here, I can finally talk to you without UEF censors. Let me get all the introductions made and we can go to my cabin."

"You're the boss, I mean captain," he said, grinning. He placed his right hand in his left behind his back, as that was the only safe place for them right now. He stayed one step behind Connie as she made her way through the room calling each of her science team to meet their counterparts from the HRI

About a half hour later, even though they hadn't gotten to everybody, they slipped out with only Connie's two bodyguards knowing they'd left.

* * *

Looking over the sea of blue uniforms, sprinkled with various civilian dress, Martin found Lieutenants Chen and Wilhelm in the middle of the room talking with Justin. "There's a couple of people you need to meet." He lead the four of them through several bodies of conversations until they got close enough that Justin and Ed made room for them.

"Martin, Raj, found anything I can sink my analytical teeth into?"

"Check with the Chem section. I gave Lieutenant Smith a few samples yesterday."

"I'm afraid Marsha is too efficient," began Karl. "I think she's got the reports filed already."

"Have you seen them? Do you know what's she's found?" Raj was never comfortable at parties, Martin remembered. He always loved puzzles, but never puzzling out human behavior.

"The dust samples you brought back matched the composition of the rocks in this Oort cloud. And that scrapping you gave her, well, this old engineer can't follow the formulas she reported. But maybe you will." He pulled a computer tablet out from inside his dress uniform jacket and handed it to Justin.

"Actually, the real analysis begins when we get that capsule opened."

"Then you're sure it's an escape pod?" Karl continued.

Martin noticed a few more people began drifting over to them as he mentioned the capsule. "That's only a hypothesis at this point. But if Michael here can get that thing open, we can see for sure."

"Get what thing open?"

"If you gentlemen will follow me," Chen said. He led them through a parting crowd to the left side of the room where a video monitor was built into the wall. Lieutenant Attah had beat them to it and had already called up a camera feed from the landing bay.

"We brought that aboard about two weeks ago," Kalifa began. "This was what you wanted to look at, wasn't it, Edward?"

"We still don't have any idea how to get into it," Karl took over. "The Captain said you guys might know a way, so we've avoided trying to cut into it."

"Yesterday, Raj found a label for doorway on the front end of the capsule."

"The stone has a slightly darker ring running around most of that end as well as a quarter-inch-size hole under the label," Raj finished explaining.

"Michael, what was the electrical parameters you used to initiate the electrostone's transformation back on Ranklin?" Martin asked what everyone who had been already working on the artifacts wanted to know.

"Nothing special. I just took a couple of leads out of a lamp and used the Harmony electrical grid."

"And we never thought to run any desolidifaction tests." *Stupid me, I should have thought of that*, Martin thought. "Karl, aaa, Lieutenant Wilhelm, can you assemble a team of electricians and see what we'll need to liquefy a small piece of the artifact? Lieutenant Attah, can you get him a sample to work with? Lieutenant Chen and I will go with you and find the least important place to get it from. Justin, you and Lieutenant Smith go over her findings, compare them to the sample we bring you. Test it before and after it's been liquefied. Raj, take Lieutenant Brown and the rest of the HRI through the second artifact and set up a shift rotation to begin cataloging artifacts."

Martin stopped talking and looked at the crowd that had gathered around him. "But that's for tomorrow. Tonight we have a party to celebrate this great new chapter in discovery." He grabbed a long-stemmed glass from one of the rolling serving carts. "To our new neighbors: the Torvons!"

Everyone that could got a glass and joined the toast.

Chapter Ten

"Mr. Beacham, you may apply the current," Karl finally said after he inspected the setup for the eighth time. It was a simple circuit. Once they had identified the current, voltage, and waveform of the electrical charge needed, Ensign Niels Beacham built a probe that could be connected to their variable charge generator and inserted snuggly into the hole in the artifact. The Ensign was controlling the device from behind a trans-aluminum screen with Martin and Karl safely standing next to him. All other personnel had been evacuated from the landing bay.

They could hear the hum of the generator but nothing else until the ventilation kicked in again. Nothing happened to the capsule.

"Kill the current," Martin said as he rounded their safety screen and approached the artifact. He ran his hand over the inch wide darkened line he had failed to notice in their first inspection and wouldn't be able to see now if Raj hadn't pointed it out to him. He felt no change in the stone. No warming, no cooling, no discoloration. Nothing!

"The settings are the same as we used on that sample Mr. Attah brought in," Karl said as he too rounded the safety barrier.

"It just didn't work." *But why?* Martin thought to himself. *It worked on Ranklin, it worked in the lab, what's different here?* "The electrical circuit," he cried out.

"It's the same circuit we used in the lab." Ensign Beacham defended his team's work.

"No, it isn't," Martin began and yanked the probe from the capsule. "The Torvons don't transfer electrical work the same way we do. They don't use wires, they had fluid conduits back on Ranklin. The wired interface we built isn't interfacing with the fluidic interface they used. We need to apply the electricity directly to the stone." He touched the tip of the probe to the capsule's darkened ring. "Like this."

"You're not," Lieutenant Wilhelm said, taking the probe out of Martin's hand. "That's what we have Ensigns for." He turned and bellowed orders at his subordinate, " Mr. Beacham, Personal Protective Equipment now." Who then went scurrying off to the lockers on the far wall of the landing bay.

Ensign Beacham returned wearing a welding apron, helmet and gloves. Martin pointed to the darken line and explained, "Touch the probe. That should liquefy the stone, hopefully in just the ring. Do not touch anywhere else. If this is a door, we don't want it to become a puddle on the floor."

As Ensign Beacham clamped the probe behind its metal tip into a welding clamp to give himself a better grip, Karl retreated behind the screen to operate the generator. Martin stood off to the side of the young Ensign waiting.

"Dr. Carpenter, please, get behind the screen."

"I need to see what the stone does. I'm hoping it has some mechanism to collect itself and not simply fall to the floor."

"It's too dangerous!"

"And not for young Beacham?"

"At least put this welding helmet on," Karl came around the barrier and handed Martin a full head welding mask. He pulled it over his head, flipped the darkening visor up, leaving the clear visor in the helmet's two by six inch window, and tightened the strap in back. After Karl was satisfied, he handed Martin a pair of work gloves. "And these, too." Only after he inspected Martin's PPE did he retreat back to where the generator waited.

"Hold the probe away from the capsule until it's charged. Lieutenant Wilhelm, charge up the probe."

Beacham touched the tip of the probe to a tall, metal tool chest to verify the probe had current running through it. He carefully brought his half-inch-wide tip against the inch-wide ring.

Martin saw the stone of the ring retreat from the probe. "Keep moving the probe as the ring retreats. Follow it. But don't touch any of the other stone." As the Ensign moved the probe around the circle marked by the ring, the stone that had been liquefied did not reform. It went somewhere that Martin couldn't see. But not onto the floor of the landing bay.

"Sir, the ring has disappeared on this side of the capsule. Do you want me to keep applying the charge?"

"Hold there for a second. Let me have a look." Martin walked to the far side of the capsule and saw a reddish stone running for about five feet on that side of the ring. "Skip that section and start again just above it until you meet back up with where you started."

As he liquefied the last segment of the ring, the stone it had surrounded moved outward slightly. "Lieutenant, sir, kill the power." Ensign Beacham got a small spark as he first tried to set the probe on the metal tool box, but none when he tried it a second time.

Martin touched the edge of the ring and when he didn't feel it was hot began pulling on it. The large round stone, just over six feet in diameter, pulled outward with a little resistance at first, then easier as he pulled it further, from the rest of the cylinder about a foot before swinging over to the side.

"A door," Martin exclaimed as he pulled the welding helmet off his head. "It's a bleedin' door." Karl was around the safety screen and at Martin's shoulder before the hard plastic helmet hit the floor. "Someone get me a camera."

The interior of the door yielded to the pressure Martin's hand had exerted on it to finish pushing it open. Yet it was the long bench on the left side of the rounded wall, with the eight dangling straps hanging from the wall behind it and the console in the middle of the right wall, with shorter benches on either side of it, that held Martin's gaze. "Instrumentation, we've finally found advanced Torvonian equipment," Martin breathed out.

Movement to his right made Martin throw out his arm to block the young ensign, who was being drawn into the cylinder. "Not yet," Martin said without taking his eyes away from interior. "Where's that camera?"

"Patience, son. Your friend went off to get one." Karl came around Martin's other side. "I have to admit, I wasn't expecting it to be in such good condition. It looks like I could fix her up and have her flying by afternoon break."

"That," Martin pointed to the console. "That's the first time we've found any advanced Torvon equipment. On Ranklin, everything was almost a millennium older. Think of what we can learn from... I need to get in there and have a look around. RAJ."

"Coming, Dr. Carpenter." Raj leapt through the open hatch and ran up to the pod.

Martin grabbed hold of Raj and pushed him at the open pod, knowing that his friend's experience would tell him what needed to be recorded before anything was disturbed. And Martin so wanted to disturb things.

After several shots from the outside, Raj pulled a controller off the camera and activated the drone controls. Using an anti-gravitational lifting platform, Raj floated the camera into the pod for additional recordings.

"Oops." The camera dipped a bit as it crossed the threshold of the pod's entrance, but Raj quickly had it back at a proper altitude. "The pod must have similar gravity to that thing outside. I've got it under control now, though." He slowly flew the camera across the pod, letting the automatic settings record images as it drifted. "It looks like the soft materials are still intact. Is that a cushion cover on those benches?" He held the controller over so Martin could view the monitor on it.

"We'll find out as soon as you get the preliminary survey done."

"Why don't we go and get some coffee while the boy finishes his survey, Dr. Carpenter?" Karl touched Martin's left shoulder and tried to guide him around to head out of the bay for a break. "There's nothing any of us can do right now. And it's time for Niels' break."

"I'm fi..."

Karl's scowl cut off the rest of his remark. "They make a wonderful brew in the rec center just down the hall."

"It's going to be another twenty minutes, Dr. Carpenter."

When Raj takes that tone, I'm in the way, Martin said internally. "If you don't need me?"

"Go, I can send Lieutenant Wilhelm if I need you." Raj turned to face Martin but never took his eyes off the monitor showing the progress of the camera. "Go!"

* * *

"Two mid-day Lattes," Niels told the room steward as they selected a table and sat across from each other. "Just enough caffeine to keep you going but not enough to bounce you off the walls. And they taste good, too."

"Been in the service long?"

"Long enough to know when the Lieutenant wants me to distract someone for a period of time." He paused as the steward delivered a large steaming cup in front of each of them. "Is there anything we should know about these, what did you call them, Torcons?"

"Torvons. We don't know a lot about them either. Back on Ranklin we found an abandoned, thousand-year-old colony. Raj thinks he's pieced together a small vocabulary. It's worked on some of the written artifacts we've found but we can't know for sure unless we can find some living Torvons."

"That's how you knew about using electricity on that stone hatch?"

"We've been calling it electrostone and they used a similar chemical compound to what we have here, to build the structures in their colony."

"So what do you think we have?" He pulled the lid off his cup and took a sip before chugging a larger swallow.

"All we can speculate on is that the thing in the landing bay looks like an escape pod. And that it is probably from the semi-sphere you have parked next to the ship. I'm hoping LeRena's team can find some clues in it, today. Something we can use to piece together what happened, and hopefully, find a way to locate the Torvons. Think about it; another intelligent species in our local section of the universe."

"You worked with Wassarans, haven't you? What are they like?"

"They're a lot like we are, only taller and with enhanced sensory perceptions. Wizen CeSonta Cowloom was the one who

52

first recognized the recording we found on Ranklin as music. And you've got a chance to meet them. LeRena brought a few of them with her aboard the *Venture*, they're about fifty percent of the population back on Ranklin." He took a look at his watch. "Raj should be done by now, and I really want to see the tech the Torvons designed." He stood up, pushed his chair back into place, and headed out of the rec center.

* * *

"Toggle switches," Martin exclaimed as he got up to the central console. "They used old fashion switches to control things."

"Martin, they're labeled," Raj ran his fingers over the indentations to make sure they actually said what he was seeing. "I think these three control the three engines in back of the pod."

"I think we can call them that, seeing the interior of this contraption." Karl stepped in and sat on the bench to the right of the console. "Padded seats too. That feels good on my back." He leaned against the padded wall and began reaching for the seat belt. Then stopped himself.

"Here's the power switch for the console," Raj kept reading off the labels. "Here's a series of dials labeled "Fuel Feed" then numbers one through three."

"Is one of these controls marked lights?" Ensign Beacham asked as he went to examine the rear wall. "I think I see panels back here."

Raj reached across Martin and examined the switches on the left side of the console. "This one maybe?"

"Are you sure?" Martin looked at the button Raj was pointing at.

"If I've deciphered their language correctly."

"Okay, but everyone out first. I trust you, but I won't risk anyone besides myself."

After the other three were a few feet away from the pod, Martin covered his face with his right arm and pressed the button with his left.

Illumination flooded the inside of the pod. As his eyes adjusted, Martin could see light tubes like the ones in the earlier dig, only thinner and more efficient.

53

"I guess it's safe to come back," he announced. "Nothing exploded."

With that pronouncement, the light tube above the eight-person bench popped and began draining its liquid over the cushions below.

"Quick, grab something to collect that stuff." Martin was still brushing bits of whatever the Torvons used for glass off himself. Niels leapt back into the pod carrying his coffee cup from the rec center. He held it up to the dripping fluid, trying to collect as much as he could. Raj had grabbed a sample bag and was scrapping the thick gel-like-fluid off the cushions with a screw driver he found on a bench outside. Martin pushed the button again and it popped back to its original position. The lights in the pod faded out.

"Karl, can you repair that tube to keep it from leaking further?" Martin asked.

"I'll get someone right on it." He stepped out of the pod before hollering across the bay, "Henderson, grab some sealing tape and get over here on the double."

Chapter Eleven

Michael tugged on the safety line connected to his wife and, with the help of Ensign Charles Ping, pulled her up to the top level of the unknown Torvon structure. Her hair would have bent against the ceiling, if she had been wearing it in her normal top braided fashion. But that would not have fit into the pressure suit helmet, so Ensign Maria Lopez had her comb it down and knotted behind her head. The swirls of hair color was almost hypnotic as she walked away from you.

"Cowloom, you're next," Michael called down and began pulling on the line attached to LeRena's back. It took a little effort to pull the Wassaran geologist initially, then the line went slack as Cowloom drifted to the ceiling of the level below. As he pulled himself around the edge of the ceiling up to the top level, LeRena grabbed his hand to help Michael finish the job.

Within ten minutes, they had their half of the party safely standing in a long corridor that ran the length of the semi-sphere. The main feature of the corridor was a box-like trench that ran its entire length. It was open at the back end, where the semi-sphere opened into space.

Michael knelt down to get a better look. Inside were a series of plates, each about five inches in width and twenty in height, that looked like rock mixed with metal. He gingerly touched one to see if there might be a residual charge somehow, then placed his hand around one and tried prying it loose. "I think I can get this baby out."

"Michael, hold on. I want to check with Martin first." She took her computer tablet from one of the pouches on the pressure suit. "Martin, Martin, can you hear me?"

"The *Resolute's* computer can find him better if you use his full name, Mrs. Harrod," Ensign Lopez offered.

"Thanks, Maria." Then she touched the transmit icon again and said, "Dr. Martin Carpenter, I have a question for you. Do you have a minute?"

"How's the survey going, LeRena?" His face appeared on the screen of the tablet.

"We're on the top level of the structure now and Michael wanted to pry loose something to bring in. Let me show you." She turned the tablet around and brought it within inches of the panel Michael had just removed his hand from.

"Back off a little bit, I need some context to this thing."

As she pulled her camera back, she tilted it down the line of the trench. "They appear to line the entire run of this box. And Michael thinks they're a composite of Torvon stone and some metallic compound."

"Then I agree. Bring one of them in for analysis. I've got to get back to this escape pod, oh, that is most definitely what it is. See you guys at dinner when we compare notes. Carpenter, out. Did I do that right?"

"You have to press the button again, sir." She heard over the unbroken connection before she lost Martin's image.

"Almost got it," Michael said as he wiggled the panel from side to side, moving it slowly outward until it finally popped from its setting. And a gush of fluid spurted from where it had been. "Quick, I need something to plug these holes." He dropped the plate to the bottom of the box and stuck his gloved fingers into the two holes that had been behind it.

Ensign Ping dropped to his knees next to Martin. "Here's some repair putty." He was rubbing a small amount of gray putty between his hands, readying it for use. "Pull your top finger away, and I'll seal the hole."

Michael lifted the index finger of his right hand out of the hole, which started spraying fluid again, and Charles jammed the putty in the hole like it was a plug. He wiped the top of it and pulled another ball of it from his belt pouch and began readying it. "It will harden momentarily. We all carry this stuff; even the smallest hull breach will kill you if not repaired in time." He quickly had the next piece ready and closed the hole as Michael removed the index finger of his left hand.

Michael picked the plate up and placed it into a sample bag LeRena had ready for him. "That's the last time we're pulling something out of its mounting on this thing!" She handed the bag back to her husband and called Martin again. "If you find anything mounted in that pod down there, don't go pulling it out. The Torvons had their fluid electric system installed here and it's still filled."

"We've had the same problem down here. One of the light tubes exploded shortly after initializing, but we've got it sealed off. Can you get a sample of your fluid?"

"We'll be scraping it off the floor, but we'll try. I'll pass the word on to Katron's team."

"So are we in the doghouse with our dear Dr. Carpenter?" Michael was rubbing the last of the fluid off his gloved hands and onto his pressure suit.

"He wants a sample of that stuff you're so cavalierly rubbing into your pants." She pulled out a sample vial. "Here grab a sample of the stuff you spilled. Martin wants to compare it to the stuff he spilled." She tossed the plastic vial to him. "Human boys!" and walked off across the corridor to see what was in the middle.

* * *

Wizen GuTim Katron's team was still exploring the level directly above the lowest one when he got the warning from LeRena. There had been several rooms on this level that had open doors. Most of these rooms were virtually empty; only the heaviest of items remained, and those had been shifted towards the center of their room. They had found a couple with their door closed, and in them, they had found workbenches slightly shorter than even his human team members liked. But after photographing the previous one, Katron instructed his team to bag and tag everything not nailed down, sending Ensign Abaza to get several containers and a cart to carry them on. After LeRena's warning, he was glad that was all they had collected.

While his three other *Resolute* crew members boxed and loaded those items, Katron and HuPadi Glorran (who hadn't received his Wizen degree yet) proceeded to the last room on this outer corridor of the structure.

"When is Dr. Carpenter going to admit it?" Glorran said. "This thing is a Torvon ship."

"It's pretty odd to design a ship with no back end. And those back edges are way too straight and clean to have been blast damaged." Katron slid the last door into its frame and stopped himself from just walking in.

"Get the camera. We have to record this one before we walk in." He was staring at what looked to be a small office with a long bench mounted against the outside wall, several monitors hanging above them, and a bank of terminal-like devices below each of them. There were also three chairs laying against the back wall like they had been thrown there in haste. "Send it in. Record everything. I have to get Martin up here to see this."

* * *

Martin stuck his head inside the door to look at the wall against the corridor before deeming it safe to contaminate the find. A monitor, over double the size of the two-by-three-foot screens of those on the control table, was the only thing on it. "Send those floating lights in here," he commanded. "And don't touch any of the switches. That pod in the landing bay still had residual power. I don't want to blow up anything else."

Glorran and Katron let their archeologist colleague enter first. Martin walked up to the console table, then looked over to the chairs on the far side of the room. About five feet away. He walked over and started to reach down to pick one up. "You got these recorded, right? With reference indices?"

"I remember how thorough you like things from the last dig, Martin." Glorran held up the camera he had dangling from the strap around his neck.

"Good." He picked up the chair, brought it over to the console, set it up and sat down. In a slightly lower position than he was used to working at. Then he quickly rose, flung the chair out of his way and back towards the wall. With the gravity being lighter than he was used to, the chair flew with enough force to bounce back

58

almost to the center of the room. About two feet closer than where it had been when they had found it.

"I'd hate for you guys to have to work from those positions," Martin said to the frozen Wassaran scientists.

"A little warning next time," Katron demanded.

"Oh, sorry. I got caught up in an idea. Whoever had been using this room must have needed to leave it in a hurry." He turned and walked over to the back wall. "Cabinets? Glorran, bring that camera over here. I want to look in this cabinet."

About a dozen boxes, twenty-four by eighteen inches each, were mounted onto the wall at different heights with almost no space between them. They were constructed of some form of stone/steel alloy and had no locks on any of them. Martin and Glorran got in position, Martin would pull the cabinet door open to the left, based on the hinges they could see on that side of them, and Glorran would be on his right, recording their contents.

Nothing spilled from the cabinet as it was opened. Inside were three shelves, each one containing what looked like parts for something. Martin looked over to the console setup and back to Glorran. "I think we had better leave everything here. We'll record the rest of this site, then have Connie's maintenance staff have a look at this stuff."

He walked back over to the console and climbed under it to have a look at the protrusions under it. "There," he called out. When Katron climbed under also, he pointed to a small round discoloration. "That's the same as the hatch seal on the pod. We can open this thing like we did it."

The UEF crewmembers walked in. "Everything's back aboard the *Resolute*. We stored them in the conference room, like the other team, for sorting."

"Lady and gentlemen, give Glorran a hand recording the contents of these cabinets. Let's you and I have a look downstairs, Katron."

*　*　*

The upper half of the semi-sphere was, without the force field, open to space, but the lower half was wedged against the asteroid.

Martin and Katron had to climb down using the stone ladder against what everyone was guessing was a lift station.

When they got to the bottom, or almost there, they stepped off onto the platform that must have moved up and down on the rails mounted to the inside scaffolding of the device. They crossed the four-by-six-foot platform and stepped into a cavernous room, a very wide corridor that stretched as far as their personal lights could see.

Behind the elevator was a trench like he had seen from LeRena's pictures. Martin called a couple of floating lights down and sent them as far down the trench as he could. The human and Wassaran tried to keep up with the floating globes until they faded from view. Then they began to grow in intensity again. They had been stopped by a rocky wall. The trench looked like it kept going into the asteroid.

He directed the lights over to the center of the wide corridor they were in and began walking across. Every other level had a connection between the two lifts on either side of the front, he assumed this one had a connection also. He crossed several lines of discoloration on the floor and made recordings of them with his computer tablet. But what he really wanted to know, was there another trench on the far side of this level?

"LeRena," fortunately Wassaran names were so different that the *Resolute's* central computer knew who Martin was trying to contact.

"Go ahead, Martin."

"Have you been able to cross over to the other side of your level?" When he got to the central wall, he and Katron stopped and turned to head to the forward part of the semi-sphere. Katron guided the lights ahead of them.

"When we didn't see anything else up here, we dropped back to survey the second level. we'd skipped it on the way up. Michael just had to see what was on top."

"When you get a chance, I need to know if there's another trench up there." They came to markings on the wall that looked like a triple wide door. "And check the floor, we're finding lines of discolored stone, like we did on the pod. I need to know if they are up there, also. Martin, out!"

"These guys are flush with the wall and have no door handle." Martin ran his hand over an actual split between the two sections of wall, with a split between the two sections he assumed to be a door. "Can you find any way to get this open?"

"I think I have a pry bar in one of these pouches." Katron began rummaging through the dozens of pouches mounted to the belt he'd strapped around his pressure suit.

Behind him, Martin could hear footfalls approaching. "They must have finished upstairs." Glorran and the *Resolute* crew members were crossing to where the light globes hung above them.

"Here it is." The bar was only a foot long, extendable to two feet. Katron tried to wedge the edge of it into the gap between the two doors. But the gap was too slight to accept the working edge of the pry bar. When he tried to pound it between them, he lost his balance and fell against the door. His shoulder hit it hard and the door went in slightly. When he regained his balance and stood away from it, it sprang back, settling about an inch further in than its companion. And making the gap wider.

Katron tried again. He got the edge between the two doors but they wouldn't move.

"Ensign, send a couple of men down here to give Wizen WeToma a hand." Martin went over and began pushing on the bar as Katron pulled.

The UEF personnel double-timed it over to them and took over the prying. The door slowly moved, finally gapped and eventually opened to allow the lights and finally Martin to enter. The corridor on the other side was exactly like the one they were in.

Chapter Twelve

The original plan had been to discuss what everyone discovered today over dinner, but they'd filled the conference room where they'd planned to eat with the stuff they'd spent all day collecting. Lieutenant Wilhelm suggested they grab a quick bite in the crew mess hall and spend the evening sorting through their finds.

Captain Young had other ideas, she wanted to squeeze in a briefing, and so she invited them to dine in the Officer's dining room. With almost twenty people involved, counting herself and Sergey, it would be a full room. But her stewards could handle it, she wanted to be there when the puzzle was pieced together.

"If that were a military ship, I would suspect those four trench boxes of yours to be some kind of torpedo tubes." Connie pushed away the remaining entree on her plate and leaned back in her chair. *I'm going to have to remind the cook about Dr. William's restrictions on my portion size*, she noted mentally. "They're spaced properly for the purpose. But you said they go right into the outer wall? No openings to discharge their contents through?"

"None that we can find," Martin reported as he took a swallow of lemon water to wash down the last of his veal. "That was delicious, you have a good chef onboard. Nothing like the frozen entrees the *Venture* carries. But like I was saying, I couldn't even find a discoloration line, to mark where a hatch may have been."

She looked behind her for the steward and pointed to Michael's wine glass, which had a bare residual left in it. "What about those plates lining the sides of them?"

Justin, having arrived late and sat at the end of the table, set down his fork. "That's why I was late, I was finishing up my analysis of the plate Michael sent over. It's definitely electrostone and metal, blended together into some kind of alloy. If I hadn't spent all that time working with the Torvon materials back on

Ranklin, I'd have said it was impossible. Cowloom, have you seen them doing something like this?"

Wizen CeSonta was still picking at his salad, having waved off the main course. He didn't want to start liking food again, it had taken him too long to drop his weight back to where his human doctor felt he would be healthy. "Everything we found in that initial dig was simple electrostone. Simple, there's a laugh for you, we still can't figure out the formula they used to blend the stuff. No, this would have to be a step up in Torvon engineering."

"Just before coming here, I ran one last test. After sucking the remaining fluid out of the plate, I pushed an electrode into each of the holes. As far as they would go. When I applied an electrical current through it, the same settings Martin used with the capsule, it became magnetized. Strong enough to pull the tools I set over a foot away to itself. Reversing the leads, reversed the magnetization vector, my magnetized screwdriver flew across the room. The dang thing's a reversible electromagnet."

"What for?" Connie shooed away her plate when the steward asked if she wanted it collected. "You can serve dessert as soon as Mr Davis finishes," she whispered to him.

Michael turned his attention from Justin back to the head of the table. "If we could ever figure out how to make this stuff and blend in metal as an alloy, we could make some really formidable buildings back on Ranklin. Magnets, okay, knowing that they are magnets, and electromagnets at that, and based on their linear placement, I'd have to say those things are some kind of mass driver, an electromagnetic transport system."

"Am I the only one curious as to why we have a **semi**-sphere?" Sergey Lunkin sat at the first seat down the table from Connie at its head. "I'm no expert on space ship design, but shouldn't there have been a back end to this thing?"

As Connie reached over to squeeze Sergey's hand, *The dear, he's asked the question I'd been wanting them to address*, tablets appeared in the hands of the rest of the diners. Some pushed their plates out of the way so they could set them on the table. For the next few minutes, silence descended on the dining room. The wait staff came in with trays of dessert and turned around again when they saw the occupied main table.

"All the images of the back edge of the structure show an extremely clean, straight edge. Nothing to indicate it was ever connected to something else." LeRena was the first to raise her head from her tablet.

"I can't even find the discoloration pockets like we have around the escape pod's hatch after we opened it," added Raj.

"But you're right, Sergey." Martin concluded. "We've been dancing around this issue since we got here. If it isn't a space vessel, what's it doing in space? With its permanent gravity, it couldn't have been an environmental dome on some astronomical body, like a moon, that simply drifted away. So how did the Torvons keep an atmosphere inside that thing and what was it for?

"Also there's the issue of the escape pods, that thing in the landing bay is definitely a short range space vehicle of some sort, my vote is for an escape capsule. And there are ten empty tubes in the larger structure, each big enough to house it."

Michael handed his tablet to his wife and waited for her to review the image on it. "I blew up the edge of the structure by a factor of 100." He looked over at LeRena and saw her face explode with understanding. Once he saw the others adjusting their tablets, "At that magnification, the edge is no longer the clean lines we've come to expect from Torvon construction techniques. It's jagged, with small beads of material on the inner edge, too small to see with our unaided eyes."

"That looks like...."

"But we never found a way to cut the Torvan electrostone."

"Nor seen any evidence that they cut it."

"Every piece we found was molded into place."

"Gentlemen," Connie interrupted everyone. "I think we're missing the back half of a ship? I think the next question becomes where do we begin our search for it?" Then she called over her shoulder, "Mackins, you can bring dessert in now."

Chapter Thirteen

"Dr. Laudrum, please come to the bridge," Mary Davis announced throughout the ship.

She and Ron McNamara, the other research assistant brought along, were pulling twenty-four hour shifts as the *Yuri* dove into the Vanera solar system hunting for a Ranklinite find. The last time Ron had slipped and tried calling them Torvons, Laudrum had cocked his hand to slap the young man. Then said "Never call them by Pashine's foul name again, do you understand?", as he caught his right hand with his left and massaged it back to his chest. "I will find their true name, or assign it to them. Not some upstart lab assistant."

She spun the chair around that was mounted to the left of the pilot's seat. Staring at the back of his head, "Ron can you get us closer to that gas giant while we're waiting on his highness?"

"You had the mic off this time, right?" he said over his shoulder. Meanwhile, he tapped the track ball and centered the course screen on the planet Mary had wanted to inspect, then let the navigational computer adjust the ship's course to get them there.

"Not again," she swung back to the sensor suite that Bart Higgins had installed in this small space craft. She let out a deep sigh, "He didn't hear me this time."

"I wonder how much longer he's going to punish us for that last slip. I could use a few hours sleep," he yawned over his shoulder.

Mary caught his yawn and responded as the door to the cockpit opened and Dr. Reginald Laudrum marched in wearing his pajamas. "This had better be important. I just got my head down, after listening to those three buffoons for the last several hours."

"Yes, sir, I've picked up the Ranklinite signal you've been having us scan for."

The older man leaned on the back of Mary's chair, she hated feeling his hot breath on the back of her neck, and stared at the sensor screen. "That appears to be the gas giant about half a billion miles from here. Ron, change course at once."

"Yes, sir." Both Mary and Ron had learned it wasn't a good idea to let Laudrum know they'd already anticipated him. *Best let him think it's his idea*, Ron had said after the second enraged lecture Laudrum had given them for using their own initiative. At university, they had stayed under his tutorship because he churned out the best reviewed papers by the Archeology community. Papers they had yet to get their names on, even though he kept promising "on the next one".

"It looks like we can be in orbit around the planet in a few days, Professor."

"Good! Concentrate on that one. Mary, log any further traces you find and don't bother me for the next eight hours. I need some sleep." He turned and walked back towards his cabin.

"Well, of all the..." Mary began as the cockpit door closed.

"It looks like you'd better head down to the galley and grab us a couple more coffees. I'll let you know if the detector goes off while you're gone."

As she was getting up from her chair, "We can't keep going on coffee. When's that old fossil going to relent?"

"Not for at least another eight hours," Ron said as Mary turned the handle on the door. "Just how much coffee will it take to make it another eight hours, now there's a paper for you."

* * *

The galley was about half way down the central corridor that ran from the cockpit of the *Yuri* to its maintenance section. What bothered Mary most about its placement was that the three 'financiers' had chosen the three cabins across from it. They'd been forced to relocate their analysis labs to the back end of the ship, the last cabins before the maintenance room. Where Mary told Dr. Laudrum she could feel the engines messing with some of her tests. She still didn't understand why her advisor let those guys do whatever they wanted.

She opened the top of the coffee maker and inspected how baked the last brew was. It smelled really burned, not even watering it down was going to make it taste civil. She took the pot and dumped the contents down the drain so it could be recycled and filled it up again with clean water. When she reattached the pot, the coffee maker pulled water from the storage chamber she'd just filled. Mary got the last filter bag of grounds from the cabinet and started a new batch of coffee.

"I'd better replace the coffee bags while I wait for the fresh coffee," she said to herself. The store room was across the corridor from their analysis room, so she went down to get another box of a hundred filters. Thinking about how much coffee they had already gone through and how much of it was Ron and her consumption, she didn't hear the door until it closed again.

"Well, little Miss Proper is having to fetch and carry again." Ivan Belinsky had entered the room and walked between the shelves of supplies to block Mary's return with the coffee. "Good, strong woman, too. Hefting that little box around like you are. Need a good strong man, I'll bet. Put the box down and let's have some fun. Everyone is asleep, we won't disturb anyone."

Mary stood there holding the box of coffee filters between them. "Please, I've got to get back to the cockpit."

"No one will know. Or care." He walked up to her and grabbed the box out of her hand and threw it behind him. Then he grabbed Mary by the shoulders and pushed her to the floor. She hit her head against a box of reconstitutable meals which she barely noticed as the Russian knelt down on top of her and pulled down the zipper of her jump suit. Then he pulled the suit's shoulders down over her arms, hampering her movements.

When she twisted to make this difficult for him, he slapped her across her jaw. "We can do this the hard way or the easy way. You'll enjoy the easy way, not so the hard one. I, on the other hand, will enjoy either way." He backhanded her. She ceased her struggles but didn't enjoy Belinsky's easy way.

* * *

Ten minutes after Belinsky had left the store room, the door opened again. It was Ron this time. She stopped crying and dried

67

her eyes. "Ron, I'm over here." She pulled her clothes back on but was still partially naked when Ron arrived.

"What's this box of... Whoa," he said and turned his back.

"No, look. That Belinsky guy did this to me."

He walked up to Mary and wrapped her in a compassionate hug. "The ship's on auto-pilot. We have to report this to Dr. Laudrum."

"And what can he do, space Belinsky?" She finished dressing, rubbed the last of the tears from her eyes and hardened her resolve. "No, we will keep this to ourselves. When the time is right..."

"Then I'm not letting you be alone anymore. If one of these guys can do this, the others would, too." She could see him trying to evaluate how she was feeling. "That is, if you still trust me?"

"Ron." He had never shown any romantic overtures towards her, but always acted like an honorable, trustable man. She pulled him into another hug. "You're about the only one I trust on this ship. Anymore."

As he picked up the coffee box, she added, "We'd better get back to the bridge before anyone else finds out we've left it." *Belinsky, Dortello, and Andreyev ; your day is coming!*

<h1 style="text-align:center">Chapter Fourteen</h1>

Michael stood on the highest point of the asteroid, knowing the HRI's *Venture* was to his back, and watched as the UEF *Resolute* pulled away. The force field generator they'd left on the asteroid could stay powered up for the better part of a year; the *Resolute* would return from its survey of the Vaneran Oort cloud in less than half that time.

The bulbous front end of the *Resolute* moved out of view first, blocked as it was by the three rectangular segments protruding from its central core. Finally, as the engines on its stern cast their bright flames, he dropped on his pressure suit's helmet and darkened the visor. Their yellow glow, this close to him, would damage his unprotected retinas.

Raj had stayed with the *Resolute*, mainly to keep working with the escape pod and deciphering the records they'd unlocked in her quantum memory core. He'd been really thankful that Karl had been able to get power into the pod and that its memory files were still intact. The *Resolute* IT Officer was able to convert the quaternary system the Torvon's used into the binary one humans still did. But he was mostly to be there in case Connie found any more Torvon artifacts, like the other nine escape pods or the back end of their ship.

As the yellow glare of the *Resolute*'s engines faded in brightness, Michael removed his helmet and attached it to his belt. Then he decided to check on his wife. She had been working inside the front end, at least they assumed it was the front end since it had no drive units attached to it, of the Torvon ship. He jumped down to the main wide-open chamber, they'd decided it had to be some kind of landing bay, even if they still didn't know how the Torvons opened it, and made his way to the elevator on the right side of the semi-sphere.

Another piece of Karl's genius, he had gotten the elevator working. Michael waited after flipping the toggle switch on the front of the cage as the lift platform came up from below. He was going to miss that old man. As a member of her crew, it had been his obligation to go with the *Resolute* on her mission. But his knack for figuring out how things were put together and what was needed to put them right again was nothing short of miraculous, in Michael's opinion. But the *Venture* had her own crew, including several maintenance and repair people, who Michael knew had been working with Karl. *I just hope they've picked up some of the old man's secrets,* Michael thought.

As it stopped on his level, Michael stepped onto the lift platform and closed the bar across the opening. He flipped the toggle switch that someone had slapped a piece of tape labeled "up" on. As the switch returned to its rest position, he backed into the middle of the platform, bracing himself for the ascent. LeRena was two floors up, so when the elevator stopped on the next floor he had to flip the switch again to complete his trip.

He found her inspecting one of the living quarters on this crew level, she was in the fourth cabin on the right side as you walked away from the elevator, an inside cabin. He watched her sitting at the desk that was mounted to the back wall and straighten a set of documents she'd probably removed from its open, second drawer. *No point in startling her.* Once she had them sealed in her document bag, Michael knocked on the door frame and entered.

As she turned to greet him, he closed the distance between them and gave her a kiss on her forehead. Which he usually couldn't do unless she was sitting down like this or bending over. "Find anything interesting?"

"Just a bunch of stone papers. Why did I have to draw a clerk's room? Find me the medical bay or at least a dissectible body, then I'd be in, what do you call it...Valhalla?"

"I think the word you're looking for is heaven. You're thinking of that Viking show we watched before Martin's call came in."

"I wish he had gone with the *Resolute* and left Raj. He'd be able to read these things."

"We had to leave someone with the capsule and Martin wanted to stay here. You know Raj still does whatever Martin tells him to. Can't you just transmit copies over to him and have him work on them?"

"We just keep finding stacks and stacks of these stone sheets." She closed the second drawer, which she'd just emptied, and opened the lowest one. She found more sheets in it so she pulled out the top one and waved it at her husband before giving it the once over. "How did they create stone this thin and flexible? How did they write on it in a way that becomes part of the stone structure? I can't smudge the lettering on this sheet; don't tell Martin, but I've tried." Then she pointed over to a side wall, "And take a look at the wall."

Michael turned and pointed to the wall LeRena had indicated. "Over here." He took the step needed to get close enough to examine the doodles all over it. "How did they draw on them? We've seen everything from doodles to full-scale works of art. Of course," he pulled at his chin, "what we haven't seen is any pictures of what they look like today. Have you noticed the lack of mirrors in this room?"

"Or toilet facilities. We've found two or three restrooms on each of the habitation floors. And a single one on the other levels. It's like the dorms you described from that Marguerite State College you attended, isn't it?"

"Now that you mention it, yeah, it is."

She pushed her chair away from the desk, while it didn't have wheels something reduced the friction it had with the half gravity floor. It moved easily. She continued to sit there and face him. "But no mirrors in there either. How did these people ever apply their makeup?"

"Did they even use makeup?" Michael looked as the grin spread across his wife's face. "Another of your jokes. You haven't assumed they used makeup, have you?"

"They're all probably just naturally gorgeous." She pushed on the chair's armrests and stood up to walk over to Martin. "And these short chairs give my legs cramps. I need to get up every now and again." She licked her thumb and reached past her husband.

Rubbing her wetted finger over the series of line drawings on the wall with no effect. "I wish we could talk to some of these people. It would really help our understanding of them."

"Not to mention, their tech looks to be way beyond ours. If we do run into any living Torvons, I hope they don't swamp our cultures" He turned away from the wall and back to his wife. "I don't think I'm ever going to get used to you wearing your hair like that. Down and swirled. Anyone complain about being hypnotized yet?"

"No. Why? Are you finally bending to my will?"

"Only since the day we met."

She bent down to kiss him. When he came up for air and finally opened his eyes, he regretted distracting his wife in her second 'opportunity of a lifetime'. "What am I doing here?"

"Making amorous advances on your wife?" She looked into his eyes, they were radiating the discomfort he felt in the situation. She took a step back from him, "I thought you liked being with me?"

"I love being with you. But what am I doing on this survey? I'm an architect, I was useful on Ranklin because we were finding buildings. Buildings, I can offer opinions, buildings I know something about. But this is space tech. I don't know what I'm doing. I'm just distracting you and the others."

"You've made some real discoveries on this thing."

"I'm tapped out. I have nothing more I can offer you guys. Other than a pair of hands."

"Nonsense, as we open each new cabin, you're pointing out its possibilities."

"No, Martin and Cowloom have been doing that. I need to do something useful."

"Like?"

"I don't know." He thought about the *Resolute* pulling away from them and the shuttle remaining on the right side of the asteroid.

Maybe?

He had to think for a second, he wasn't sure how she would take the idea. "Connie left us a twelve passenger, interstellar shuttle. If we mount one of Shearing's electostrone detectors on it, I could take some of the lab techs into the system and make a sweep for any other escape pods. If there were survivors, they may've made a colony of it."

"You really want to do something, don't you?"

"I'm wasting resources being here, otherwise."

"We'll have to clear things with Martin first. You know how he is about discoveries."

"Then you'll talk to him tonight during briefings?"

"We'll talk to him."

* * *

Michael didn't have a lot to do, like most days, and had taken a seat in the large circular central room aboard the *Venture* that was located one deck directly below the ship's guidance room, their bridge. The Wassaran members of the *Venture* didn't want to call it a bridge, it made the Venture sound like a military ship. the human members of the Board either agreed or abstained, no one dissented.

He sat at his position around the large circular table, reading the last architectural journal he'd brought with them from home. It had no new ideas he could use on Ranklin, so he thumbed off his reader and closed his eyes for a few minutes. The swoosh of the door opening behind him announced the arrival of the others and brought him out of his almost slumber.

Martin scheduled daily briefings to keep everyone working on the project up on what everyone else found and what they should look for tomorrow. He had everyone working ten-hour days, all at the same time, no second or third shifts. Everyone had ended their work day about a half-hour ago, giving them time to clean up before the meeting.

Martin came in last, pushed his tablet into the computer slot at his station, then reached over to turn the room projection system on. "Everyone ready? Shall we get started?" He dropped back into his chair. Everyone else had already plugged their tablet in. Michael called up a mystery novel he hadn't read.

He spent about a half hour listening to people droning on about the number and color of socks; the variety and function of

73

shirts; functionality of footwear; the line drawings on the walls—
one team actually found an inch-thick stylus that would draw
different colors into the wall depending on the position of the dial
on its back end, that they passed around—the number of cabins
explored, bathrooms cleared, storerooms inventoried; along with
all the equipment they found and didn't know what it was for. After
which, Martin finally called for future ideas.

Michael had just been handed the stylus, twisted the knob on
the back end and feeling the different electric jolts the various
settings produced. He waited for a second for his wife to raise her
hand. Then he stuck it in his shirt pocket like any other pen and
shot his up.

"I see you didn't have any discoveries today, Michael. What's
on your mind?"

Where everyone else had sat during their presentations,
Michael stood to make his pitch. "Martin, I'm a fifth wheel here.
We all know that." He looked around the table and saw a few
heads nodding. "I'm not science trained, the way you guys are. And
you've got everything covered here, everything efficiently covered.
I just keep getting in the way."

"If you need something to do," Martin broke in.

"No, I'm looking for something meaningful to contribute. I'm
not made to spend my whole day cataloging what you guys bring
in. I was never trained on how to collect artifacts properly in the
first place. But I can fly a space ship, I can pilot the shuttle the
Resolute left us. Let me take that shuttle and head in system?
Maybe I can find one of the missing escape pods?"

"It's a large system, at least the size of Sol," Justin said.

"But we have one of Shearing's detectors, if it can find
electrostone structures amongst all these rocks out here, it should
be able to find any that have made planet fall. And see if one of
those pods landed on a habitable planet?" He let the thought hang
there for a moment. "There might be Torvons still alive out there,"
he heard a murmur from the Biology assistants, "or their
descendents."

Martin leaned back in his chair. "That was going to be our next step. Captain Young hasn't had a chance to map out the system."

Michael was about to sit back down, stopped himself and pounced on the idea, "I could do that for her. See if she can send us a list of the parameters she needs measured on each planet and I, along with whoever goes with me, can fill in the details. Then you guys will have a map to search the system with, and maybe even a known site, if I get lucky."

"I'm inclined to let you go. How many others would you need to take with you?"

"No more than five. It's a twelve passenger shuttle but there's no sense in crowding it."

"Okay, any of you department heads have spare assistants you can cut loose?"

Justin had his hand in the air immediately. "Yeah. Me! My assistants can handle all the routine analysis you guys are sending my way. I need something to investigate, I need to get back in the field."

"I only have the one assistant but he can cover everything coming in," Cowloom offered. I'm a Geologist, I'd like the chance to see some rock formations again. Ones different from this asteroid's mono-stone."

After Daisy Lawton released her Paleontology staff, Martin had his crew of five. While Daisy was intrigued with the idea of potentially finding living Torvons, her aching knees were keeping her to the lighter gravity of the *Venture*. Even the one-half gravity on the artifact caused her to medicate up whenever she went over to play in it.

"Well, Captain Harrod, it looks like you'd better get your ship and crew ready to go."

"Thanks, Martin." Michael didn't wait for the end of the meeting but was out the door and heading to see what provisions he'd need to transfer to the shuttle.

Chapter Fifteen

Dr. Laudrum pushed open the door to the cockpit, allowing it to slide shut behind him. Mary was currently at the controls, Ron in front of the engineer's panel, and Bart Higgins in the turned around co-pilot's seat, checking over his connected electrostone detector.

Mary turned enough at the sound of the door to verify it wasn't Belinsky, then when she discovered it was Dr. Laudrum, "I've got us in a synchronous orbit above the object, sir."

"It's coming in strong and steady, Reg," Bart looked up from his machines.

Mary returned her gaze to the various shades of blue swirling around the gas giant they were orbiting around. She was afraid that her mentor would give her another talk if she didn't hold this position.

"How deep is the object into the gas layer?" Mary looked over her shoulder to see Laudrum staring at the sonar system. She locked the *Yuri* on autopilot and turned her chair slightly. "I don't see it on this thing."

"That's because it only has a range of a thousand miles," Ron began. "We haven't determined the distance to the planetary core yet. But it's over our sonar's limit."

"Bart, can't you boost that thing?"

"No. We didn't bring that type of equipment. You didn't mention wanting to dive into a gas giant, which this ship wouldn't be able to withstand the full pressure of."

"I need to know how far away that thing is. We're so close to beating Carpenter."

"Mr. Higgins, can we withstand the pressure for a slight descent?" Mary asked.

"Take her down to the edge of the atmosphere and we'll see. But slowly, and if I think we're over stressing the hull, bring us up fast."

Mary reengaged the engines and programmed a fast orbit of the planet to bring them back to their current position over the object while just skirting the fearsome bluish atmosphere. It took them over two hours to round the planet

"We're looking pretty good," Higgins said as they returned.

"Mr. Higgins," Ron sang out. "I've got the object on both sonar and your detector."

"Looks like the blasted thing is just sitting there, with nothing around it? Does this thing have a central core?"

Laudrum had found the last chair in the cockpit as they began their descent orbit and was sitting down when their three benefactors tried to enter the already-full room. Mary breathed a sigh of relief that the three of them, especially Belinsky, couldn't crowd their way in.

"What is our SitRep, Dr. Laudrum?" Andreyev demanded.

"Our **what**?"

"Give me a Situation Report. What's going on?"

"We've found an artifact," Higgins said from his seat, not looking up from the ship's sensor gauges. "We're trying to see if we can retrieve it without crushing ourselves."

"Of course we can," Andreyev blustered. "The *Yuri* was built to land and take off from the Vladimir mining base on Venus. Just take us down."

"Didn't that base implode?" Ron asked without turning away from his equipment.

"A Pressure Compensator lost power, base became unstable," Belinsky said behind the others.

You never said anything about Pressure Compensators," Higgins said. "Where are they located and how can I inspect them?"

"We tooka them out," Dortello said. "The need for my espresso machine was greater. They were drawin' too mucha power."

"Then we're only getting as close as I say to that object. I did inspect and rate this hull before we lifted off. That's our limit."

"If that thing down there can take the pressure, we can," Andreyev began. "Now take us down."

"Dr. Laudrum?" Mary called from her seat.

"Hold your course, child." Laudrum stood up and placed himself nose to nose with Myles Andreyev. "We have come too far and are too distant from help should something go wrong. I will not take unnecessary risks at this stage of our expedition. Now go back to your cabins and I promise to brief you as soon as we have something firm. Mr. Dortello, get out of my chair." Andreyev had taken a single step into the cockpit when Laudrum stood up, giving Dortello just enough room to slide into the open seat.

They turned to go. As Mary caught Belinsky staring at her, he threw her a kiss.

"Mary, what are you staring at?" Laudrum broke her out of the frozen shock Belinsky's move had sent her into, and she turned back to the pilot's panel. She and Ron had not told anyone about Belinsky's attack. "Take us down another thousand miles."

"But let's go slower this time, Dr. Laudrum. I'd like to keep an eye on the pressure building on the hull as we enter this thing's atmosphere. And Mary, remember that as we get closer to the center of this thing, gravitational pull will get stronger. Don't forget to compensate for it."

"Sure thing, sirs." She headed around the planet again, only at a quarter of her original speed. Despite being closer to the core, it took them a full day to get back around the planet. Laudrum and Higgins took turns in their cabins, while Mary and Ron went through 3 pots of coffee.

* * *

They got within nine hundred miles of the core when Higgins decided the hull had had enough of the planet's pressure and ordered Ron, who was now piloting, to take them all the way out of the planet's atmosphere. "We can discuss what to do without all that pressure," he'd said. "Reg, can you come to the cockpit?"

78

Almost a half hour later, after Ron had pulled them free of the atmosphere, Laudrum made his way into the room. "Okay, what's up?"

"We can get within nine hundred miles of the object. After that, the pressure is too great for this old bucket." Mary, having swung her chair around, saw that Laudrum was going to object, but Higgins cut him off. "I know what those guys said about this being a Venus-rated ship, but they removed the devices that pumped up the hull's pressure-resisting capacity. And at just over six thousand miles into that atmosphere, I judge she'll implode."

"Is there anything we can do?"

Mary heard a faint ping coming through the headset she had set on the sensor suite's console. She grabbed them and listened with her left ear.

A double ping was coming from the electrostone detector. She slid the headphones around until they covered both ears and she was sure about what it was saying. "Sirs, I think we have a second object." She switched the sound output from headphones to speakers and pulled her headphones down around her neck.

After a count of thirty pings, one sounded that was out of sequence. Higgins was about to comment when Laudrum waved him to silence. They counted another thirty pings and it happened again. After another cycle of this, Dr. Laudrum and Bart began calculating the distance and direction to the other ping.

"Break orbit," Laudrum ordered. "Here's your new course." He handed the paper he and Bart had been scribbling on to Ron. "Best speed to that location." He rose from his chair and headed to the door. "Now let's see if I can placate our benefactors until we see what we've found."

Chapter Sixteen

"I'm glad Connie left us one of the newer UEF shuttles," remarked Cowloom as he stood up to go back for another cup of tea. "I've ridden in a couple of the earlier models, and there just wasn't enough headroom." He lifted his hand over his head and moved it a couple of times between the shuttle's ceiling and his thinning hair. It took him a dozen large strides to get back to the coffee cart, whose wheels were currently locked in place, stationed next to the door leading to the rear compartment of the small space craft. Taking the carafe labeled Tea, he filled his plastic cup half full of the green tea he'd brewed an hour ago.

"They're really not any bigger." Justin spun the co-pilot's seat around to make sure he could be heard. "I understand the folks at General Stellar Matrix developed a new polymer protective coating that requires less material to block radiation than the old shuttles."

Michael, who'd been dozing across three of the back seats, trying to nap, slid up the wall into a sitting position. "If they'd enlarged the shuttle cabins any, they'd have had to redesign all their capital ships. These things barely fit through the landing bay doors now."

"I heard they're retrofitting shuttles as fast as they can back on Earth," Justin added. "Just for you guys," he slapped Cowloom on his free arm as the Wassaran returned to his front row seat.

"It's a move to integrate our two fleets," WaSon Molaro, one of the two graduate students Daisy had sent with Michael, said from the pilot's seat. "After what happened on Ranklin with those religious fanatics, everyone agreed to better communication. I understand a program is in place to have Wassarans serve on UEF ships and humans on Wassaran."

"And now, you're finding you didn't build your ships right," ByVon Cemper, Dr. Layton's other student, said as he entered the main area after grabbing a quick nap. "All that retrofitting?" He walked up to the pilot's seat and tapped Molaro on the shoulder. "Time for you to hit the sack, as D would say. I've got this for the next eight hours." When the female Wassaran didn't move fast enough, "Now get, before I have to report you."

Most of the outer planets appeared to be on the far side of the Vaneran sun currently. With nothing to survey, they'd spent the last seven days cruising into the inner system. Their instruments showed three planets in orbit around the sun, still a few billion miles away, before the glare of the star blinded those sensors. Two of them in the 'Goldilocks' zone for life to have formed, the third a little too close to the star for the shuttle to go into orbit around it. The closest planet wasn't the one with the closest orbit. The third planet out was about to go behind Vanera, so they set their course for the middle one of the three. They couldn't even assign numbers yet, they still didn't know how many planets were on the far side of this sun. No one had done a proper survey of the system yet. *Well, no one until us*, Michael said to himself as he closed his eyes again.

* * *

"Still glad you went?" He always played the clip of his wife before beginning his report to the *Venture*, it helped focus his thoughts. This was the twenty-fourth daily briefing/call home that Michael made to his wife. Martin had agreed to let her summarize the reports of the survey, to give Michael and LeRena a little alone time.

"Just one more day. We're about fifteen hours out from what we suspect to be the second planet of this system. But based on Cowloom's use of Newton's planetary motion questions, there should be another inner one we haven't found yet. If there is an innermost planet, it should be transversing Vanera any day now." He took a bite of the sandwich Cowloom had made for their evening meal. There was no point in waiting for his wife's response, she wouldn't get his message for another few hours. At first they could hold an actual conversation, but as the last month stretched out, they had learned to express themselves in bursts of words that the other would have to digest before responding a day later. "So if we call this guy Vanera 3, it's in the Goldilocks zone those astronomy guys keep going on about. It has plenty of water and an atmosphere cleaner than Ranklin's ever was.

"We've gotten a positive ping on Shearing's electrostone meter, but plan on doing several orbits doing sensor scans and mappings of the planet before landing." He reached over and touched the screen displaying the data they had already recorded and attached it in a data burst to his message to his wife. "I just sent you what we know so far. Tomorrow we should have the orbital surveys done and the data dump should be quadruple what you just got."

He looked at the timer he started when he's established contact. "I guess it's time for me to shut up and listen to what you have to say. Oh, Highpockets, I love you."

As the timer started beeping, the incoming message light lit up on the communication's board. "Hello, Honey. Things are winding down here. We've scoured all the rooms in this old tub. All that's left is the cleaning and cataloguing and you'd have to be an actual archeologist to enjoy that. Now I wish I had gone with you.

"We've had word from Captain Young. Things are going faster than she'd anticipated, she expects the outer survey to be done in about another month. Oh, you were right, most of the gas giants from this system are on the far side of Vanera. Four of them in total. There might be some smaller outer bodies but she can't tell until the *Resolute* can dive in-system.

"Raj has gone over a lot of the documents we've found. He's been trying to teach some of the *Resolute's* linguistic staff how to read Torvon, with limited amount of luck. Maybe by the time they get back here, he'll have one or two of them trained. We've been piling up a lot more documents for them to go over.

"Those he's been able to decipher are pointing to this thing having been part of a large warship. But there's nothing about what might have happened to it. Let's hope that ping you're getting on the third planet has an escape pod with an active memory core. It's a long shot after a hundred years, but even finding this thing was a Mary Hail. Did I say that right? I never can get your football terms down.

"Everyone decided once the *Resolute* is back, we're going to bring the *Venture* down to that planet of yours. Think you can find enough to keep you busy for another thirty plus days? Well, gotta go. Love you."

* * *

Molaro guided the shuttle between the dual moons of Vanera 3 in hopes their gravity would help reduce his speed and save a bit of fuel. It was a tricky move, since the moons were gravitationally locked in a dance around each other as the pair of them revolved around the planet. "Tides must be hell to predict," she commented as she shot through the midpoint between them, while they were canted at a forty-five degree angle to the planet. She brought their craft into an equatorial orbit around the planet.

On their first pass, they trained all of their equipment on the single northern hemisphere land mass. It resembled one of the leather saddles Michael had seen in those old Western movies Earth kept sending them in their culture exchanges. Really wide in the center with peninsulas extending off its eastern and southern ends. Their electrostone detector was telling them the object was in the center of that land mass. They had time for the imaging sensors to collect several photos before they were out of range.

As they continued around the planet, they found it had two more continents, both in the southern hemisphere, and hundreds of varying-sized islands dotting the blue ocean beneath the clouds.

"Send the photos of the Torvon site over to the big board," Michael said as he walked towards the back of the main cabin. As he and Cowloom sat in one of the aisle seats, the board came to life with the first of the images they had collected. It quickly cycled on to the next one, seconds later another.

"Stop there," Cowloom shouted at Justin, who was monitoring the main computer. "Back up one." As the last image came back up, Cowloom touched the screen just left of center. "Enlarge that section, double magnification." The image doubled in size and Michael could begin to see a long cylinder laying on open ground.

"Again, this time triple it." The image zoomed in even tighter on the area Cowloom had indicated. Now Michael could clearly

83

see the object. It was another of the Torvon escape pods, laying on the ground. Its thruster cones slightly buried into the dirt.

"It looks like it landed and fell over," Michael offered.

"Justin, pan right and enlarge times ten." As it blew up on the screen, Cowloom reached over to the right edge of the screen and touched a silvery object. "Center on that and enlarge again, double magnification."

"Guys, we're coming up on our next pass," Cemper, who was currently piloting the shuttle, called over his shoulder.

"Justin, burst as many images of that landing site as you can." Cowloom turned to Michael. "I think someone got here before us."

"Then we need to get down there." Michael rose from his chair and walked up to the pilot's area. He reached across to place his hand on Cemper's shoulder. "Dip into the atmosphere, so we can grab an air sample." He turned to Justin, "Get your equipment ready, I'll bring it in as soon as we get it. Cowloom, take over here."

Everybody swapped positions and Michael waited across from the sensor station by the hatch to the sample retrieval tube for the vial of collected gas to drop into place. Once it did and the miniature airlock cycled to internal air, he unlocked the small door, pulled a one inch diameter tube from it and headed for the back of the craft. "We may have to cut our five orbits down to three," he said just before the door closed behind him.

* * *

Justin took the vial, punctured it with the needle of his portable spectrographic analyzer, and dialed in the compounds he was looking for. Prior analysis had shown Earth-like components in the atmosphere. Nitrogen came back as making up seventy-six percent by volume, oxygen was twenty-two percent, carbon dioxide was one percent and the rest trace gases. "You'll probably find a higher concentration of CO_2 as you get closer to the surface. It's the heaviest component. Neon and Argon won't be a problem, but I'm getting one gas not recognized. Let me switch to the Mass Spec on this thing."

It took about fifteen minutes for the machine to spit out a one-inch wide report. "It appears to be an element having a number of protons beyond any we've seen before. Stable atomic structure and," Justin flipped open one of his manuals, "sitting right where the next stable noble gas would be on the Periodic Table. I think we're looking at a Nobel Prize here."

"But is it safe?"

"Most of the Noble Gasses are. We can't tell for sure until we actually breath it."

*   *   *

By the time Michael got back to flight control, they were just passing around to the far side of the planet. "Cowloom, what did you find?"

"There is definitely another ship already on the site. I'm not exactly sure of its configuration. Nothing we have, nor anything I've seen from Earth." He sent a full-size image of the vessel over to the wall monitor. The image was almost straight down the needle-like craft that was pointing straight up, sitting on a trio of fins at its base. "It appears to be about four hundred feet tall and twenty feet in diameter."

"It looks like something from before the Unification of Earth, back when we had nation states. Something I may have seen in old movies but I just can't place it. Can you tell if they've got the pod opened?" Michael dropped into one of the rear chairs to watch the screen.

"Not as far as I can see." Cowloom shifted the image to the latest he had on the pod. It filled the screen, but the end with the hatch was pointed slightly up and looked to be in its sealed position.

"Then let's take this thing down. Cemper, how close can you land us to the Torvon pod?" Michael climbed out of the rear seat and into the co-pilot's chair.

"Right, left or on top?"

"If you land us on top of the pod, you'll be the first one off the shuttle. Head first."

"Michael," Cowloom began.

"The door's on the left, so put us on the right side of the pod." Justin came in from the back and dropped into a passenger seat.

85

Cemper fired a short burst on their forward thrusters and slowed the shuttle enough to begin their descent to the surface. The view of the planet began to fill the view screen until it took up about half of it. He pitched the nose down further and dove into the atmosphere, pulling up slightly when the air thickness began registering on their external sensors. The hull was designed to reflect heat up to fifteen hundred degrees Celsius, so he held the external heat just below that.

"Hopefully it won't get warm in here," Cemper said as he pulled level. "I assumed you gentlemen were in a hurry."

Before they had gotten around to the back side of the planet, Michael dashed off another message to LeRena, letting her—and by extension, everyone else—know what they were attempting.

By the time the temperature on the sensor started dropping, they were almost around the back side of the planet and heading into their own sunrise. They over flew the escape pod, to check the area out, turned around and set down twenty feet away from its right side.

Michael could see two men running towards them from the other ship. He opened the inner and outer doors in rapid succession and jumped out to check over the pod.

"Don't!" He heard a scream coming from the direction of the running men.

Michael got around the front of the pod and ran his hand over the darkened line defining where the pod's sealing stone was still intact. Cowloom and Justin climbed out of the shuttle to join Michael before the running men could arrive.

"They didn't get it open." Michael had no way to reach the top that was tilted away from him and had walked to the other side to check where he could reach. "Everything should still be intact."

"I can't reach the control port," Cowloom said stretching up as far as he could. "I hope this thing didn't land with the hatch joint on the top. We'll never be able to swing it upwards."

"Guys," Justin interrupted. "We've got company."

Chapter Seventeen

"Just who the hell are you guys and what're you doing with **our** find?" The elder of the men strode forcefully up and planted himself an inch from Michael's face. He looked Michael up and down, finally stopping at the pin on his lapel. "Damn, Ranklinites," he said to his companion. Turning back to scan everyone present, "I suppose Dr. Carpenter sent you?"

Michael took an instinctive step back to open some personal space between him and the beige-outfitted individual, quickly looking to see if he was carrying any kind of a weapon. The shorter man, who had stayed a step back, was wearing blue coveralls with all of its pockets full of tools. At least it looked that way from the bits of them that stuck over the tops of those pockets. He didn't appear to have any weapons, either. Michael calmed his breathing down after mentally eliminating that threat.

"Do you know what this is?" Justin drifted over and patted the stone cylinder on its side wall.

"Yes," began the other man. He walked past Michael up to the cylinder where Justin was standing. He didn't look young enough to be a student, but had the bearing of a handy-man; mechanic or engineer. "It's our find, our salvage, our property. We arrived days before you did."

"That's a Torvon escape capsule." Cowloom came up behind the last speaker, pinning him between himself and Justin.

That caused the elder to turn on Cowloom. "Torvon? It's not Torvon, it's a Ranklinite construct. That proves you're working for Dr. Carpenter and his pet student, Pashine. They're the only ones calling them by that name. Well, it doesn't matter. This is our find. We got here first. And like you Ranklins, we have no intention of sharing."

"We're here," Michael said, commanding the attention of the man in front of him, "under the auspices of The United Earth

Alliance." *There was a professor that Martin had talked about, one that had caused Raj problems back on Earth, now who was he?*

"Then you have to follow their laws. We located this unclaimed salvage and have staked a claim to it. You have no right to interfere with us."

Justin started to speak, but Michael waved him off. "He's right, Justin. If they found this first, they have salvage rights. We'll just wait in orbit until they get tired of staring at this rock."

"Good luck with that." The younger man walked back over to stand beside his companion. "We..."

"Ron," the other man quickly stopped him. "They'll find out in due time. Let's get back to the *Yuri* and await their departure." With that, he headed back the way they had come. The other man looked over the shuttle one last time and followed his leader back to their ship.

"Hey, who are you guys?" Cowloom asked as he stepped up behind Michael.

As if he'd been listening, the elder turned just enough to holler back, "Tell the good Dr. Carpenter, that Reginald Laudrum beat him to this find."

That was the name I couldn't remember.

* * *

"Okay, let's finish the system checks and get back into orbit. We can keep an eye on this place from there until the *Resolute* arrives to sort these guys out." Michael dropped into the pilot's seat, waved Cemper into the co-pilot's chair then snapped himself into his harness. He looked over to his co-pilot and added, "Maybe they'll get tired of failing to open the capsule and abandon it? Cowloom, you got the door?"

"On it."

Justin, who hadn't shown any interest in taking the helm during the last month, buckled himself into the navigation station. After a moment, he announced, "I thought I'd left everything on." Michael could hear him flipping switches. "I'm not getting power to anything"

Michael pivoted his seat to look at the darkened screens. "I'd have switched them off without thinking when we left the ship.

Maybe they went into a power saving mode? Try rebooting everything." He turned back to begin his own pre-flight checks. The external sensors, which stayed on unless the entire craft was powered down, weren't reading anything. Lighted displays were blank, dial meters sat on their resting positions, even his course maps sat frozen in their last displayed position.

"I already did. Nothing."

Michael reached under the flight control panel, found the master switch, it felt like it was in the on position. He flipped it back and forth. There was no usual buzzing of the circuits as they powered up. None of the lights came on his displays. All of his indicators remained still. Nothing was happening.

He reached under again and rocked the switch back and forth several times. There was still no power going to the system. He turned to Cemper just as the young Wassaran was turning towards him. "Anything?" Cemper just shook his head.

"Once we get the engines powered up, you should have power again."

"Michael, the door won't close," Cowloom called from the back of the cabin.

"A systemic power failure shouldn't happen on one of the newer UEF shuttles." Michael was out of his chair and heading back to the shuttle's electrical control panel. He unlatched the door and swung it out of the way, placing his hand up to arrest its return swing as he stared into the box. None of the individual circuit's indicators were glowing the tell-tale red of deactivation. The mechanical breaker switch for the entire electrical system was still in its engaged position. He pulled it down into its deenergized position and reinitiated it.

Still nothing happened within the cabin.

"Justin, Cemper, go over all the circuits in this thing and see if we're getting power anywhere. Cowloom, wake Molaro and the two of you check out the fuel cells, see if the problem's there. Let's hope we didn't break a line and lose all our fuel. If anyone has any ideas, I'm all ears."

"What do ears have to do with this?" Cemper said as he got up from his seat. "whuumf."

Justin gave him an elbow to his ribs. "It's a figure of speech." Justin pressed the tabs on either side of the navigation panel and lifted the plastic covering away to exposure the inner circuits for inspection.

"That was uncalled for."

"Dr. Layton must be keeping you guys in a glass bubble," Michael said without taking his eyes away from the electrical panel.

After going into the cabin and getting some testing equipment, Cemper got down on his back and pulled the under panel away from the helm to begin his inspection. "Egon, even the circuit testers just deenergized."

"What?"

"I turned the circuit tester on and it lit up briefly, then everything faded off the screen. Just like its batteries died." Michael could hear him smacking the tester against his palm.

"Just look for any system check lights," Michael called from the panel. "If there're any of them glowing green, you have a good circuit. Red, means you have an interrupt somewhere."

"Nothing, no lights at all."

"Then you're not getting any power. Close it up and check the pilot's station."

With the main breaker switched into its lockout position, Michael took the plastic touch interface off the individual breakers and started pulling the circuit chips to see how many of them had degraded. Each one he pulled and inspected had the same clear yellow tint it was supposed to have, none showing the cloudy red of having been destroyed.

He knelt down on his right knee and opened the repair kit attached to the bottom of the box, pulled out the circuit tester, and powered it up. He watched the lights run through their initialization procedure then fade completely out. He banged the small rectangular box against the palm of his hand, but the unit stayed dead.

"What had Laudrum said? 'They'll find out'. What're we going to find out? What's going on?"

"Mike?"

"Talking to myself." He pivoted on his knee and threw the useless box out the still open door behind him.

"Hey, watch it," Cowloom said as he stepped off the ramp.

"Sorry." He pulled a manual screwdriver from the repair kit and began removing the cover plate to allow him access to the circuit board inside the control box. Every level of inspection of the box, and Michael had an Electrician's certification so he knew what to look for, showed nothing wrong with the circuitry. He put everything back together, dropped his tools back in their box and slammed it shut. Closing his eyes, he took a couple of deep breaths to suppress his building anger. *What is going on here? If we can't find out where our power is going, we'll be trapped on this planet.*

He got up and walked outside to see if anyone had found a problem with their power production.

"Kindly watch where you're throwing things," Cowloom said as Michael came around to the left side of the craft, where the pair had been working.

"Sorry about that. Frustration." Michael walked up to stand on the Wassaran's left , both men watched Molaro inspect the fuel cell readouts. "We're just not finding anything wrong in there."

"I'm glad they have mechanical backup gauges on these things," Molaro said, straightening her back while still kneeling. "None of the electronics are working in here either, yet the tanks read three-quarters full. We have fuel to make electricity, and as far as I can see, we are. It's just not going anywhere."

"Could there be a dampening field down here?"

"You're thinking of electromagnetic radiation, Mike," Cowloom explained. "There's no such thing as an electricity dampening field. You can siphon it, divert it, but not stop it flowing through a completed circuit. " Cowloom reached down and helped Molaro up and then put the inspection covering back in place. "Maybe we landed on something that is shunting all our power somewhere. Come on, Molaro, let's have a look."

Cowloom began a circumnavigation of the small craft. Molaro climbed under the shuttle in the eighteen inch gap left between the bottom of the ship and the ground by the four landing feet. Leaving Michael to climb the hand-hold ladder notched into the side of the shuttle to the top, in case anything was resting on it. Ten minutes later he climbed back down.

"There's nothing up there," he began as Cowloom approached from the front of the shuttle.

"Nor anything sticking to the hull."

Molaro began rolling out from underneath, so the two of them reached down and helped her up. "We didn't land on anything I could find," she said. "But there's this whitish stuff sprinkled all over the ground under there." She looked closer at the ground they were standing on. "Like that stuff," and she pointed to what looked like whitish ant mounds dotting the landscape. "I must have rolled through dozens of those little piles. They're all over under there." She brushed off her jumpsuit and stomped her boots to clear the dirt.

A loud popping sound occurred under her right boot, causing her to stagger back against the hull of the shuttle.

"You okay?"

"I wasn't expecting that. I felt it pushing my foot off whatever I stepped on, but It was more the shock of the sound than any explosion that caused me to stumble into the shuttle." She stood up again and was quiet for a second. "Yeah. I'm fine."

"Justin," Cowloom stepped over to the door and hollered in. "Grab a sampling kit, there's something interesting out here." Then turned back to the other two.

Justin was jumping out of the shuttle a few minutes later, holding a double wide briefcase sized box by its handle. Cemper was not far behind him. "We weren't finding anything in there, anyway." As Justin landed, a pop sounded where his right foot hit the ground. He jumped back from it before recovering from the surprise. "Okay, what was that?"

Suppressing a giggle at the young chemist's expense, Michael explained, "That's what we wanted you to tell us. Grab a sample of this white stuff and see what you can find out about it. Just don't hit it too hard."

"It's going to take me a while, with none of my instruments running. I'll have to do a lot of wet work on this stuff." He bent down on one knee, opened his case, took out a small plastic vial and a plastic spatula. He filled the vial easily and closed up his case after putting everything away. "I think I'll set things up out here. Not a lot of light in the shuttle's work area. Cemper, want to give me a hand with this?"

As the two of them disappeared back into the shuttle, Michael looked around their landing site. They had landed on a sandy plain, sparsely covered with a low growing grass. there were more spots bare of the vegetation than actually covered by it. From what they had seen from orbit, there was no water to be found for several miles in any direction. *This is not going to be a fun camping trip.*

"And we'd better figure out some shelter while he does. Why couldn't that pod have picked a decent forest to crash in, something with building material readily available? Okay, what's say we get this door back up so the shuttle can provide that shelter?" He bent down and grabbed one edge of the ramp to begin pulling it up. It wouldn't budge. "Can someone give me a hand here?"

Even with the three of them pulling up on the ramp, it wouldn't move. Cowloom dropped down and sat in the sandy soil. "It's the hydraulics." He took a couple more deep breaths. "The ramp's fighting us." He looked at the arms that raised and lowered it from the side of the shuttle. Inch wide steel tubes holding it in place. "Maybe if we drain the system."

"You guys work on that," the female Wassaran student said. "I think the first thing we need to do is get an inventory of what we have to work with. So I'll be inside for some time." She marched up the ramp and turned towards the rear compartment.

"And speaking of supplies, if the fuel cells are still producing power for nothing, we'd better shut them off." Michael helped Cowloom back to his feet. They went over and closed the valves on the feed lines to the shuttle's fuel cells. "If we ever find a way out of this, we're going to have to remember to turn these back on."

"Let's see if we can find a container to drain the hydraulic lines into," Cowloom began. "I hate to waste anything we have at this point."

Chapter Eighteen

"Do you see that?" Belinsky said, holding the binoculars up to his eyes. "They've got one of those Wassaran babes with them." Standing in the *Yuri's* cockpit, the highest point on the now vertical ship, Belinsky mentally removed the brown-with-an-orange-whirl patterned jeans and tunic from the young Wassaran girl strutting back around the UEF shuttle. "She wants me."

* * *

"She must have enjoyed our little, how do they say it, *rendezvous*," Belinsky had told his two compatriots several days ago within the protected confines of their cabin about his private visit with Laudrum's student. "She has said no word to that Professor and his holier-than—, well, too damn holy for my comfort, fixit man."

The screech on the floor as Andreyev spun Belinsky's chair around made Dortello, who was sitting on the bed, grab for his ears. Andreyev bent over the seated Belinsky, got inches from his face and parsed his words out. "Don't you ever do something that stupid again."

"It is my right."

Andreyev cut him off with a slap across his face. "The Operation paid for this trip. Theirs is any right. We need these intelli— smart guys. I will not have you endangering this mission just to satisfy your lusts before we can achieve our objective. Once we have the secrets of that cylinder, you can kill them, for all I care. But until then, control yourself. Am I clear?"

* * *

Belinsky rubbed his cheek at the memory from over a week ago. "Well, she is not part of Mr. Reg-e-nold's little crew." He continued staring out the window, watching the Wassaran babe pass behind the military shuttle. "I will take her for a ride."

"How, my friend, are you going to do that?" Dortello finished climbing the ladder to the top level of the ship and stepped onto its deck. "That ship is as grounded as we are." With the *Yuri* in a vertical position, what were once separating walls were now floors. And the protrusions in the corridors, that Belinsky kept complaining about every time he banged his elbow into one, formed the rungs of the ladder to allow the crew to go between them.

Belinsky dropped the binoculars, allowing them to dangle from their strap, stepped away from the view port and dropped into the pilot's seat. "So what plan has our fearless leader cooked up for today?"

"That's what I came up here to tell you. He wants us downstairs. It's time for another tribute meal from the locals." Dortello reached back to the ladder, "If we hurry, we might just miss his wrath."

"I do not like dealing with those rodents." Belinsky got up from his seat and joined Dortello descending the main corridor to the bottom of the *Yuri*. In the planet's lighter gravity, he attached his safety line from his belt to the corridor wall and dropped to just above the other man's head.

"Hey, watch where you're landing."

Belinsky grabbed the ladder again, stepping into the rung Dortello had just removed his hand from and pressed the release on the magnet. Nothing happened.

"That trick won't work if you don't have any power," Dortello laughed back at Belinsky. "Now you'll just have to climb back up and detach the thing."

"The hell with that." Belinsky reached down to his belt and unclipped the safety line from where it connected to him. "We're planetside, I only need the damn thing in nickle-gravity."

"Null gravity, you idiot." Enrico leaned his head back to howl up as he continued climbing down. "Zero-gee, free fall."

"I said that."

"No, you said... Oh, forget it." Dortello returned his gaze to the ladder's rungs, shook his head, and continued his climb. Only faster, this time.

"Good, it is a race to the bottom. You are on." The Russian pushed himself away from the ladder and fell from bulkhead to bulkhead until he reached the engine room door. Then grabbed a basket they had constructed to carry firewood from the nearby forest and exited the ship through the open door. Climbed down the ladder etched into the hull's wall until it hung between the bottom of the ship and the ground below, then he grabbed the side rails and slid the rest of the way down to the planet's surface.

Just as their science guys were returning.

"Where do you think you're going?" Laudrum stopped in front of Belinsky and placed his palm against the shorter man's chest.

"You will remove that hand if you want to keep it." Belinsky reached into his lower pocket and rapidly pulled out his knife. He held it in front of Laudrum's face and pressed the release, springing the blade into place with a "Snick."

The hand dropped from his chest and the old man took several steps back from Belinsky. "How did you get that aboard?"

"Personal items."

"But the UE ports screen for weapons."

"Virolic is non-metallic," Dortello said as he emerged from the *Yuri*. "Our people developed it to pass through your weapons detectors. Put that away," he continued as he stepped onto the planet's surface. "These are our friends." He walked over and patted Laudrum on his cheek. "They can't do us any harm."

He turned to Higgins and tried the same thing. Bart swiped his hand away. "Just what are you two up to?"

"Why, off to do a little shopping. Mr. Andreyev is hungry."

Laudrum looked away from the knife and focused on the Italian. "We have plenty of food in the galley."

"We want something different," Belinsky said.

"It's going to run out if we don't start foraging. And who better to do that than our new friends, the local natives?" He turned and began heading towards the forest about a quarter mile away. "Come, Mr. Belinsky, we have a job to do."

Belinsky pointed the tip of his knife at the two men in turn, "You two had better start treating us with more respect." Then he folded his knife shut, replaced it in his pocket and turned to follow Dortello. "You'll never leave this rock if you don't."

* * *

The sparse grassland they travelled on their way to the animal village they had discovered the other day, quickly changed over to old-growth trees. If they hadn't seen a couple of the vermin leering at their spacecraft and followed them back, they would never have known these creatures existed. Belinsky had no interest in them, but Dortello had offered little protest when Andreyev had ordered them after the creatures. "If Laudrum gets wind of them, he'll want to study them. If they have any food, take it."

It was not much of a trail the two men travelled, many of the trees still had limbs just the right height to make Dortello duck under them, and Belinsky snap them off. "They were dead anyway," he remarked after Dortello turned following the first loud crack. "Mr. Andreyev will probably order a fire built anyway."

Dortello stopped and turned to his companion. "But not this trip. We need all the food we can carry coming back. The wood can wait."

Belinsky, who had planted the inch thick end of the branch on the ground and leaned on it when the other man had stopped, now tossed it on the trail behind them. "Then you can come back for it when Andreyev wants his fire."

They kept going forward with Dortello ducking and Belinsky snapping off branches for about another hundred yards. Then Dortello grabbed the next branch he would have ducked under and snapped it off before Belinsky could. Belinsky saw the branch about to be tossed back at him, then flung to the side of the trail instead. *Even he would not have survived my wrath had he struck me.*

A fifty-yard clearing soon came into view. Unlike where they had landed, there was little to no grass growing in the sand that covered its floor. The two men weren't making any effort to walk quietly, as they looked into the clearing with its half dozen lean-to shacks; central, single-piece, stone fire pit with earthen looking tripod and cauldron over it; and single stone building at the far end. All they found of the inhabitants was the scurrying of the inhabitants' tails burrowing under the sand. As they stepped into the village, there was no sign anything lived here other than the fire still burning under the pot hanging over it.

Dortello brushed the debris off his clothes that marching through the woods had accumulated. "I guess they just want us to help ourselves." He straightened up and walked over to the stone shed.

"They should be here to greet us." Belinsky walked towards the central fire pit, making an effort to step wherever he thought he had seen one of the natives slipping underground. "You need to greet us. Show your respect to your superiors," he shouted as he raised his arms and slowly spun in a circle next to the pit.

Looking into the cauldron, a blackish soup was simmering. He was about to stick his finger into it for a taste when a bubble exploded just under it. "Yow, hot!" He jerked his hand back and looked around for the spoon, or ladle, pulled the stone object off its hook to sample the concoction.

"Dortello," he called over to the shed. "You should try this."

"Get over here and help me load up. I want to get moving. I don't like the smell of these creatures," he called from inside the shed.

A moment later, Belinsky dropped the basket he had constructed from green twigs they had collected, between a pile of white roots and black ones. When cut open, both had a greenish core and tasted of mushrooms when boiled. Dortello shrugged on his basket's straps and squatted down with his load of light and dark red roots, to finish filling Belinsky's basket. He wrapped his arms around Belinsky's filled container and stood back up with it. Belinsky struggled into the straps as it was held for him and the two men exited the hut, having confiscated about half the supplies in it.

As they were leaving, Belinsky saw the sand wiggle a bit. He stepped over to the spot and reached into the sand. He felt a tail whipping away from his hand and grabbed hold. He lifted the three foot long furry being out of the ground and held it up until he could look it in its upside-down eyes. It tried to bring the claws on its upper arms around to scratch Belinsky, who just held it further away from him. The creature used its clawless middle hands to grab its legs and try pulling itself up to claw at Belinsky's arm. He bounced the creature a couple of times to get it to settle down. "You are running out of food, little guy. If there is not enough when we come back again, we may have to start cooking you guys."

The creatures eyes widened. Belinsky could see its black, horizontal, oval pupils through the strands of hair trying to cover it. It pulled back the skin on its inch long muzzle and exposed an array of flat teeth. He gave it another bounce. "Settle down!"

"Belinsky , can we get going?" Dortello called from the forest's edge.

"If we must." He swung the creature back and tossed it towards the stone shed. "Make sure there is more food next time."

"You know those things don't understand a word you're saying," Dortello said as the two men stepped back into the forest."

"It may not understand the words I speak," Belinsky marched ahead of his companion, "but he understands what I mean. I hope you can get over their smell if we have to roast them." Belinsky heard Dortello stop, then a few seconds later, hurry to catch up.

Chapter Nineteen

Justin ran the test for the third time. He added two drops of clear reagent into the test tube and applied a glass stopper before inverting it several times. Then he rapidly shook it until he was comfortable he had everything mixed thoroughly and chemicals had time to react. He stuck his arm out from under the canopy to let the sunlight pass through his test solution. The liquid was still clear inside.

He placed the tube back in its holder and picked up the gallon sample jug, twisted off its cap and poured about eight ounces into a clean beaker. He poured the entire contents of it down his mouth.

"No!" Molaro, who had collected the sample of water from a nearby stream, swatted at the cup Justin was holding, but missed it entirely as he had already lowered the empty container.

"Could use some ice." He ran his left sleeve across his mouth to collect the last few drops that had refused to be swallowed. "Otherwise, you've found a perfectly acceptable source of drinking water. I just contaminated the test with my thumb, the first time."

She crossed to the other side of his improvised workbench and faced him straight on. "That was a chemical beaker. Dr. Layton says we should never use lab equipment for ingestive purposes."

Justin set the beaker on the same back corner spot he had originally taken it from. "Dr. Layton isn't a Chemist. It's critical I know from moment to moment the cleanliness of every piece of equipment that I'm using. Besides, look in the white circle on the side of it. I have a J making it as the one I can drink out of. I thought about using C for coffee but there are too many times when I actually have three or more samples to label. J's safely down the alphabet."

She crossed her arms and huffed at him.

"If you promise not to tell anyone, the jar marked S is the sugar I use in my coffee." He watched a slight smile crack through her stern look. "And thanks for finding this canopy. Without environmental control, I'd be roasting inside that shuttle working on this."

Mixed in with the survival supplies Molaro had found in a back shuttle compartment had been a twenty by twenty reflective tarp. It had been designed to drape over the shuttle to keep it from overheating in an emergency like they were now in. But with the hatchets also stored there and the forest about two miles north of them, they had constructed poles to convert it into additional living space. Outdoor, catch the limited breeze, living space. Unlike the shuttle that quickly became unbearable during the day.

After emptying a few of the equipment crates, Justin had constructed a working lab between the shuttle and the Torvon escape pod, just behind the still lowered ramp. Michael had changed his mind about draining the hydraulic fluid and closing the hatch after the heat of the day began warming up the interior of the shuttle. They'd even tore the mattresses from the bunks and were camping under the canopy to keep cool at night. It took Justin a few nights to get used to the glow coming from under the shuttle every night, but after the second day, he got used to it.

"So who has Michael assigned to water detail, now that we know it's safe?"

"As soon as Cemper and Cowloom get the MRE storage bin pulled out and on the sled we built the other day, Cemper and I are off."

"You might want to consider adding some wheels to that sled. Those bins should be able to store around forty gallons of water. At eight pounds per gallon, that's," he froze for a minute, "that's over three hundred and twenty pounds. And that's even taking into account how much the bin weights. Maybe that's why Mike is having you Wassarrans do it, he and I couldn't pull that much weight, how far is it? About three miles?"

"It should be no different than the Dead Man Pull we have in the annual Fitness Games."

"You ever been back to Wassara to see them?"

"No, I tried watching one two years ago but got bored after the first set of competitions. Maybe they had some meaning years ago, but I can't see any now."

"I feel the same way about paddleball. I love to play it, but watching someone else bores me." He picked up the water jug and went over to the campfire they had built the night before and filled the metal tin they had found in the supplies. He set it to heating in the fire and squatted down to wait for it.

"Coffee?" she asked squatting across from him to avoid the stream of smoke following the western breeze.

"It's not the greatest, but instant is better than nothing. It's in the container marked IC back on my workbench."

The liquid in the fire began to slowly pop bubbles. Justin took the metal bar that rested with the other tools around the fire and lifted the tin out by the holes someone had punched into it. He carried it back to his workbench and, with a hand towel, filled his beaker with the almost boiling water. "Want a cup?" he asked Molaro. When she shook her head, he set the tin on the make-shift table next to his bench.

By the time his coffee had cooled down enough to drink, Cowloom came banging down the ramp carrying the storage bin. Cemper trailed, holding the back end. Molaro jumped off the empty box she had been sitting on and pulled the sled over to ramp. The two men set the bin between the two thick branches that defined the sides of the sled, Cemper losing his grip as he tried to switch from holding it under the bin to the lip. It fell three inches to the shed as he jerked his hand away to keep his fingers from being smashed.

"Careful, young man," Cowloom said as he set his end down gently. "We can't afford to break anything."

"At least not until we can find a replacement," Justin added. He took a swig of his coffee and set it back in its proper place before walking over to see how they were doing. "I'm still working on that explosive dust. I don't have time to concoct glue to fix these things."

"We promise not to crack it," Cemper said as he walked around to the front end of the sled and lifted the right hand pole. "Coming, Molaro?"

Minutes later, they were leaving marks through the loose soil where grass wasn't growing. Justin left the cover of the canopy to peer into the microscope he had set up to use sunlight after removing its light assembly.

Cowloom walked up behind him. "Still no luck?"

"If I had access to my instrumentation, I could break this stuff down into its constituent parts, know what elements go about making it up. All I have been able to tell from my wet chem tests is that it's some kind of protein."

"Mind if I have a look?"

"Be my guest." Justin got off the box he was sitting on, offering it to Cowloom.

The Wassaran had to spread the two lenses further apart to accommodate his eyes. "You've ruled out nitrates, phosphates and all the other stuff we normally make explosives out of?" He turned the focus adjustor several times.

"Like I said, nothing."

"Too bad we don't have any electrical power to see if it reacts to that." He pulled away from the microscope and looked over to Justin. "It almost looks like some kind of microorganism, either dormant or dead."

"Maybe we do?" Justin patted the seated Wassaran on the back. "Maybe we do! Where do we keep the spare batteries? The purely chemical ones, not the rechargeable ones." He turned and returned to the shuttle's entrance ramp.

"What good will they do?"

Justin stopped at the bottom of the ramp and turned back to Cowloom. "Until you connect a wire between the leads, they're just inert pockets of chemicals. We might be able to get just enough electricity out of them to run your test."

Cowloom knocked over the box he was sitting on to follow Justin to the storage locker in the back of the shuttle.

* * *

Justin dropped the six flashlight batteries he'd found into a plastic beaker to keep them from rolling off his microscope table. He pulled the first one out and reached over to Cowloom, who was now sitting on his own box on the right side of the table. "You've got the ends of the red wire stripped?"

Cowloom set down the black wire he was finishing and collected a red one. "All ready."

"Give me about three inches of the electrical tape also." He watched as the Wassaran pulled a strip off the black roll and reach for a ruler. "About that long. We don't have to be accurate." With the pocket knife they'd found, he cut the piece off. "Now three more, about the same length." Justin took the first piece and wrapped it lightly around one of the exposed ends. He picked up the black wire and the second piece of tape, repeating the process. The next two pieces he used to secure the other end of the wires to the long cylindrical battery. "Now give me a piece about twice as long."

He secured the battery to the right side of the microscope, so it wouldn't obstruct sunlight from getting to the mirrors funneling its light to the slide the scope was viewing. He stripped the tape off the free end of the black wire and handed it to Cowloom. "Hold this. I don't want it touching anything that might complete our little circuit."

He pulled the red wire around to the left side of the slide holder, removed its tape and applied it to the sample on the slide. With his eyes focused on the amorphous structures under his lens, he reached over to Cowloom. "Remove the tape and place the wire in my hand, stripped end up."

When he felt the wire touching his hand, Justin brought it over and touched it to the other end of the glass slide. When nothing happened, "Nothing yet. Glass is a good insulator. I'm going to bring the two ends closer until they touch and see where, what happens."

Slowly he slid the black wire across the slide, through the mass of stuff they were studying, until the two wires touched. They sparked for a few seconds.

The mass on the slide quivered during the time the battery circuit was sparking, then settled down quickly after the sparking stopped. The amount of material on the slide began to grow until by the time Justin had pulled the two dead wires away from it, the mass was spilling over the sides of the slide.

"Cowloom, take a look at this!" He got up from his box to allow the Wassaran to look through the microscope, dropping the spent wire to the table as he did so.

"What am I looking for?" Cowloom sat down, placed his eyes on the lens and adjusted the focus. "Did you have that much stuff on the slide earlier? And some of it's still changing colors, like it's dying."

"It all looked the same color to me. I'm glad we have your Wassaran eyes along." As Cowloom took his gaze away from the microscope, Justin continued, "Now we know where all our power has gone."

"It's little comfort if we can't get it back. We're still trapped on this rock."

"Along with any rescue mission they send for us." He stood to full height and looked around. "Where's Michael?"

Chapter Twenty

Despite having to stop almost a dozen times to remove obstacles to their sled they hadn't noticed when they had first cut the trail to the stream, Cemper and Molaro had made good time pulling the empty water bin down to be filled. They lifted the filled container out of the water and set it back on their tree-branch sled. Almost immediately, three of the cross branches snapped under the weight. The lowest three, causing the end of the sled to pull apart slightly. It was enough that the side poles spread away from the bin and dropped it to the wet dirt of the river bank.

"Looks like we'd better replace those," Cemper said as he dropped his pulling pole and went to the back of the sled. "You grab the front there and we'll get it off this thing so we can make repairs."

"I thought I heard something crack went we bounced over that last tree root," Molaro said as they set the water-filled container to the side of the sled. "You untie the broken rungs and I'll see about getting stronger replacements."

"Go two inch thick this time?"

"More like three and from green wood. That container is every bit the three hundred plus pounds Dr. Davis said it was going to be." She left Cemper beginning to undo the useless electrical wires they had used to lash their carrier together and walked up the short bank back into the forest.

She walked a couple of yards away from the trail they had built and jumped up to catch a low hanging limb on one of the one hundred foot trees. It snapped off cleanly. "It'll make firewood but won't do for the sled." She tossed it over towards their trail.

She found a tree nearby with branches about nine feet high, about a foot over her head. She grabbed hold of it and allowed herself to hang from one of the branches. It held. She took out the hatchet and removed it from the tree. After an effort of twenty minutes, she grabbed the six inch thick end to pull it back to where Cemper was waiting.

Something caught her attention before she could pull the long branch though the forest and distracted her. She looked back towards where they had left the shuttle, and while she could not see through the forest to it, there was something moving behind some of the trees, watching her.

She dropped the branch to go have a look. In the debris surrounding the wide tree she thought a creature had been watching her from, she could see several animal tracks. Some glowing with more infrared heat than others, indicating where the creature stood still and where it had made its escape. But the tracks and heat signatures disappeared after a few feet. "No one mentioned seeing any animal life before, especially something curious enough to keep watch on me."

She collected the branch and worked her way through the trees, until she broke free of them on the stream embankment. Cemper was about a hundred yards down the river, laying on his back simply staring at the sun.

"Hey, you're back." He opened his eyes and turned to rest on his elbow as she set the ten foot long branch next to the sled. "What took you so long? It'll be dark by the time we get back." He reached up his hand for her to grab.

The hatchet plopped into the wet soil as she dropped it next to him. "Get the sled repaired. I think we've company. I'm going back to check." Before he could reach for the hatchet, she had turned and was striding back to where she had last seen the creature.

* * *

All the warmth from where it had walked had faded away by the time she had gotten back, but a new set of tracks appeared inches from where the original ones had left off. She looked overhead to see if she had missed a branch it might have jumped to earlier but there was nothing above her for at least forty feet. Not anything to the sides, it could have jumped on.

The new tracks were devoid of infrared heat, so they too had been made some time ago. "These were not here before," she said under her breath, knowing she would have to keep her noise down if she wanted to track this thing. "The undergrowth is still wet and the tracks are clear enough that even a human could discern them."

Stepping on either side of the tracks, she kept a careful eye out for twigs, piles of dried leaves or anything else that would make a sound if she stepped on them. But the damp floor smothered most of her footfalls.

After a couple dozen steps, spaced about a yard apart as Molaro was keeping her stride short, the tracks she were following became fainter and two other pairs of tracks appeared. Then all six of them went under the brush growth of a break in the canopy cover. Without her hatchet, Molaro had to push aside the brush to keep sight of the creatures' tracks. And gently, after the first bush where she had made what she felt was a giveaway clash of noise.

She crossed the clearing, even though she had lost the tracks a couple of times to the drying soil. On the far side the two newer types of tracks disappeared again and the single pair deepened their impression next to another very large tree and had a faint heat trace to them. "It had been standing here for a while, was it looking for something?"

On the far side of the tree, a large infrared glow came from the natural mulch around it. She reached down and dug through the leaves, twigs and loose soil to see what was giving off the heat. She found nothing, it was only on the topmost debris. Everything underneath was at ambient temperature.

"It stopped to rest?" She looked around, found a set of tracks leading further into the forest, this time with a heat signature, and continued her pursuit.

About an hour into her pursuit, she brought herself to a stop. "I left Cemper back there to deal with the water retrieval. Is this one of those wild goose chases Dr. Layton is always talking about?" She stood looking at the tracks for a few moments and watched as the heat signature began to slowly darkened. "Right, if I don't follow this now, I'll lose it. He's a big boy, he can drag it back to the camp by himself." Later, as the overhead sunlight began to fade, she ran the same conversation through her head again, only this time she did it while moving with the tracks.

A very dim light up ahead marked a break in the forest covering. She quietly moved closer to what looked like a small village. There were several lean-tos, a masonry shed and a fire going in a central fire-pit. She could also make out several underground heat signatures littered about the camp. No one was occupying the place.

She stepped free of the trees and looked over one of the lean-tos. It's tallest side was constructed out of a single slab of stone. Two shorter stone monoliths anchored the other side of a roof made of woven branches, covered with mud and leaves. They appeared to ring the perimeter of the clearing, in some places only a foot separated a pair of them.

"Did I just see one of those spots wiggle?" She went over to a couple of the closest ones. They weren't fading like the tracks had. Squatting over one of them, she stared at it for a few minutes. "There's a definite quiver happening here." She looked over at another spot, the clearing lost the rest of its lights and stars began to blink into existence. The darkness made them easier to see and she found they were all moving slightly.

"There's something alive just under the soil." She pulled the energy bar she'd nibbled on when she stopped a couple of hours ago out of her pocket. Dinner was a small sacrifice to see what lurked under this encampment. After placing it about two inches away from the heat signature, she backed into the cover of the trees and waited.

Minutes later, a pair of small hands pushed the soil covering it aside and a six-limbed, three-foot long, two-foot wide, four inches thick creature leapt on top of the bar. As it sat upright, Molaro could see a mouth about two/thirds of the way up its blockish body chewing. Soon several more began to emerge out of the ground.

Molaro looked up. the lowest branch that could support her was two feet above her reach. She could jump it and find a perch to watch from, but not quietly. She found a not-so-damp area to sit and watch the evening activities occurring before her. One of the creatures looked her way as the pile of drying leaves crackled when she found a comfortable position, but the darkness appeared to hide her enough that it went back to cleaning the fallen debris, dropping the twigs and leaves into the fire pit.

One of the taller card-creatures, she couldn't think of a better name for them, stirred the pot that had been heating when she surveyed the village. It lifted one of the cooking items from the pot, picked a piece off it and placed that piece in its mouth. Then it banged the spoon against several spots around the top of the pot. The noise triggered the rest of the village inhabitants to gather around the cook pot, pick up bowls that Molaro hadn't noticed before, and offer them up for filling. After receiving a two inch long tube of something from the pot, they went over to various lean-tos and began eating.

After the last one was served, the cook ladled the rest of the items in the pot onto a platter. It made a noise from its mouth. One of the other creatures set down its meal, came over to help the cook lift the pot off its hook and dump the pot's contents onto the fire. The cook lifted a stone poker off the ground while the other creature took the pot down to the stream just north of the village. The cook stirred the ashes in the fire pit until Molaro could see their glow diminishing.

After the fire's glow had diminished to only infrared heat traces, the other creature returned. This time on all six feet with the pot on its back. *If he'd been able to carry the thing upright down to the river and was now having to carry it prone on its return,* Molaro reasoned, *It must have filled it with water again.*

The cook and the water boy picked up their plates and both went to an unoccupied lean-to, used their middle hands to extract the food from the bowl and began chewing on it. Molaro was so focused on them that she missed the first of the others to emerge from where they had been eating and plunge their bowls into the returned pot. After they had apparently washed them out, each was stacked in the same spot they had collected them from earlier.

After the cook and water boy had finished eating and cleaned their bowls, another pair of card-creatures upended the cleaning pot into the fire and took it back to the stream. The cook again picked up the long poker and stirred the ashes until Molaro could no longer see any heat signature emerging from the stone pit.

After the pot was returned and placed upside down on the rim of the fire-pit, balanced against two of the cooking tripods leg, the creatures sat in a circle next to the fire-pit and began making noises to each other.

Dr. Layton will kill me if I don't get a recording of this, Molaro reached into her pocket, pulled her empty hand back out and dropped it into her lap. Without electricity she didn't have any way to make a recording. She leaned her head against the tree and watched this new sentient species go about their nightly rituals.

As they finally made their way to lean-tos for sleep, it looked about two of them to each lean-to, she lifted herself out of the spot she had been sitting in for the last few hours. Rubbing her legs got the circulation going again and relieved the imaginary needles stabbing them. After a few more minutes waiting, she slowly backed away from the village and headed back where she had left Cemper. *I hope he's not still waiting.*

Chapter Twenty-One

As the Vaneran sun was drifting behind the tops of the trees, Cemper pulled the sled up to the draped canopy and lowered his poles to the ground. "Anyone seen Cowloom?" he called out.

"What'a need?" Cowloom stepped down the ramp emerging from the shuttle.

"I'm guessing help lifting the water tank?" Justin commented from his workbench. "It's too heavy for us mere humans to lift. Besides, I need to get this stuff tested before we lose all light for the night." He grabbed a flask and quickly dipped a water sample before the other two began lifting it. He was prepping the sample for analysis when he noticed someone missing. "Hey, where's Molaro?"

"The sled broke as we got to the stream and she went off to find some replacement timbers to fix it. She thought she saw a forest creature while she was there and left me to get this thing fixed while she went off to investigate it."

Cowloom looked at him with a scowl that even Justin could read.

"Hey, she told me to take care of this." Cowloom's gaze didn't change. "I waited as long as I could. I thought it best for me to get this back before dark."

"Moving this can wait. Once I change into my hiking shoes, you're taking me back to where you left her." Cowloom marched back up the ramp and inside the shuttle.

Justin quickly squirted the reagent he held in a dropper into the test tube with the water Cemper had returned with. It didn't change color, the water was clean, so he racked it and went over to where his clothes bin was sitting next to his bedding mattress.

He had his boots on before Cowloom returned. "Hold on," he said as Cowloom emerged. He took a jar that he had a screw on lid for, added three reagents that would give him a bright blue light for about two hours and screwed the lid down tight. A strong shake got the chemicals reacting to full luminance in moments. "Okay, now we have some light and I won't stumble over my feet trying to keep up with you guys."

"And you're going why?" Cowloom asked.

"To rescue Cemper."

Cowloom looked over at the Wassaran youth and back to Justin. His scowl broke. "I guess I was being a little hard on him. Molaro's a strong girl," now it was Justin's turn to scowl. "Okay, an adult Wassaran."

"And?"

"And will be able to take care of herself until we find her."

"Okay, then let's get going. I can only count on light from this thing for a couple of hours." He held the jar in front of them as he led them off to the trail they had cut.

Cemper quickly pulled up to Justin's left side. "Don't you think I should lead the way, Dr. Davis?"

"Go ahead, but I'm keeping the jar. It's the only one we have with a screw-down lid. And it's okay to call me Justin."

"But Wizen CeSonta..."

"Has calmed down." Cowloom pulled up ahead of Justin. "And I also want you to use my given name. Now get up here and show us where she went."

Justin pulled behind Cowloom just as the trio entered the forest along the trail to the stream they were gathering their water in. The blue glow was not drifting strong enough that Justin found more roots the water bearers had ignored earlier. Justin completely missed the descending bank as they emerged from the trees and stumbled into Cowloom's back. He stopped long enough for Justin to regain his balance before turning and going upstream after Cemper.

"She's leaving good footprints," Cemper called to the others. Justin lowered the jar and found impressions in the wet banks almost an inch deep. Of the three sets ahead of him, one of them had a little water filling the bottom already.

When he looked up, the Wassarans had pulled away from him, so he hurried to catch up. Which wasn't easy as the embankment wanted to hold on to his shoes at every step.

"This way," Cemper pointed back into the forest.

"Why were there only one set of tracks for her?" Justin hadn't noticed any Molaro side tracks heading back from where she had apparently gone into the forest to track down the creature.

"We had three rungs to replace and she drug a very long branch back across her earlier tracks. It's why I have the hatchet." He patted where it was hanging from his belt.

"We had better get moving. This thing probably only has an hour left."

They followed her tracks up to the tree line and beyond, but the tracks were harder to read in the forest floor. Justin had to pass his light off to Cemper, who bent over to hold it close enough to the ground to make out the dying impressions she had made.

"I'm glad you brought that light, Justin," Cowloom said, "I can't find any fauna traces in this growth. Everything's plant temperature."

"Even her tracks?"

"She was wearing shoes."

"Yeah, I guess she wouldn't have left any heat behind. You know what's odd?"

Cemper kept staring at the ground. "What?"

"There's no background glow here in the forest. Nothing like what we've got back where we landed."

"You're right." Still squatting, Cemper straightened up and looked around the forest they were in. Placing the jar under his shirt, "There's no glow at all."

* * *

After about an hour of following her steps, the blue light in the jar began to fade. "This thing is about spent," Cemper stood up and announced. He handed it back to Cowloom to give to Justin.

Justin stared into the jar for moment, then shook it for a minute. "Some of the agents precipitated." Justin handed it back to Cemper. "That should last a few more minutes."

After another half hour and three more shakes, the glow faded for good. "Should we spend the night here?" Justin asked as he placed the jar in the largest sample pocket he had in his trousers.

"Cemper, can you feel her tracks?" Cowloom asked. As his eyes began to adjust to the starlight breaking through the tree cover, Justin saw both Wassarans get down on their knees and run their finger tips over the ground.

"I feel a lot of debris and the crawlies eating it but I can't distinguish her footprints from any of it." Cemper dropped into a seated position as his eyes adjusted to the darkness. "I wish we could adjust to low light as fast as you humans can. All this extra vision we have and you guys can see in the dark faster than we can."

"Hey, did you hear something?" Cowloom patted the others.

"At least your hearing adjusts quick."

"Quiet, something's coming." Cowloom gently urged them back away from the trail Molaro's tracks had been making.

"I hear you guys. Where'ya hiding?" Molaro's voice came from up the trail.

*　*　*

Mary quietly worked her way up to the blind they had built so she and Ron could keep an eye on what the Ranklin expedition was doing with Dr. Laudrum's find. She dropped her hand over his mouth and shook him by his shoulder to wake up back up.

"Shhh," she whispered at him before removing her hand. "I think I saw a party of them returning up their trail to the stream. Give them a few minutes to pass before you head back to the ship and bed."

"This moss makes a wonderful mattress. More comfortable than those nylon straps back on the *Yuri*." He yawned, stretched and rose to a sitting position. Rubbed the back of his head and pulled a twig out of his lengthening hair.

"And if we weren't as far away from them as we are, your snoring would tell them we're here." she swatted him on the top of his head. "Can't you stay awake for a single twelve-hour shift?"

115

"They ain't doing nothing to whatever that thing is over there. Besides, it's too dark to see anything, anyway, since they've damped their fire down."

"Quiet." She looked back down the trail but it was too dark to see anything. "Just wait here until they pass, then make your way back to the ship. Dr. Laudrum and that Andreyev guy are waiting for your report."

Chapter Twenty-Two

"Okay, there's a native species on this planet." It was a little warm this morning, but the inside of the shuttle was still a better place to hold a general meeting until they could get enough chairs made, or boxes emptied. "Have we seen any other animal life forms in the area?" Michael asked from the pilot's seat.

"I went all the way to their village without seeing a rodent, bird or lizard. It's like they have all been driven away. I'd swear those card creatures were eating some kind of root last night." They had arrived back at the shuttle by the time the second moon was crossing the path of its larger companion. Both going west to east but at different angles. The time when they crossed was usually about half way through the planet's night. Molaro and the rest had gotten only a few hours of sleep.

Michael dropped his head into his hands for a moment, pushed back his hair and continued. "I know you scientists would just love to run off and study this new species, but we've only now licked our water problem. We still need to supplement our food rations. And if there is no game for us to catch, we won't have a clue as to what is safe to eat or just plain poisonous."

"Maybe we should invest a little time in watching these guys." Cowloom looked over to Michael from the middle row seat he was sitting in. "We don't know if they're hostile."

"They kept scurrying away and burying themselves underground anytime they noticed me. They're more scared of us then we have to fear from them."

"What about disease vectors," Michael hammered away.

Justin held up his hand and began, "Study them or not, if their biochemistry is close enough to transmit diseases, it's not going to matter how close we get. We'll get exposed eventually. If we can examing one of them, we can at least look at their microbes to see if they look like anything we're familiar with."

"We've got a food crisis," Michael got up from the chair and began pacing the middle aisle, "and you guys want to write science papers."

"We could see what they're eating?" Cemper sat on the other side of Cowloom. Michael had also given him a lecture about leaving Molaro behind.

After which Molaro had told Michael that she was a big girl and was able to take care of herself. Since she was almost as tall as his wife, Michael, looking up at her, could almost hear the words in LeRena's voice.

As he was now in the back of the main shuttle compartment, Michael dropped into one of the rear seats and thought about Cemper's idea. The only way they could know if something was safe to eat was to eat it. If they could narrow down the list of items they should try, that just might keep them alive through those trials. "Okay, that's the first good idea this morning. I'll take Molaro out to the village today and see what they're eating. Cowloom, you go with her tomorrow, then take Justin there the day after, finally I'll make another trip this time with Cemper, and hopefully by day five, we'll be able to start trying the local cuisine. Molaro, can you be ready in ten minutes?"

"I'm ready now."

"Then let me get some binoculars, and we'll head out. Justin, any suggestions on sample collection?"

"Ideally, a sample of whatever they are eating, complemented by a sample of their scat. They'll keep me busy while Cowloom gets his turn watching the village. Otherwise, use your judgment; Molaro, ask yourself what would interest Daisy?"

"We'll try. Okay, Molaro, which way do we go?"

"I think the village would be in that direction," she pointed at the rocket of Dr. Laudrum's team.

"So let's go the way you did yesterday. No point in Laudrum staking a claim on them."

They took a couple steps towards the forest before Michael stopped. He walked back over to Cowloom. "We need to start thinking of a way to warn any rescue effort not to land here. See what you guys can figure out while we're gone."

"Too bad we can't just hook up a battery of flood lights," he said as Justin got within earshot.

* * *

Michael sat uncomfortably in the tree, it felt like any minute now he would slip off the limb and plummet the ten feet to his death. Every time a breeze blew through the tree, he began a shallow yelp. He could see most of the village from where he sat, if he focused on it instead of his perch, but his fear was more attention-consuming than the card creatures.

Molaro lay prone on a branch just above him and watched the natives going through their daily activities, trying to find out if any of them were collecting their food stuffs. Suddenly a slightly louder yelp came from below and the creatures froze in their activity and turned towards the tree they were using. Molaro leaned over the branch and brought her finger to her lips.

Michael yanked his hands over his mouth, it caused him to feel like he was slipping again. He grabbed at the sides of the yard-wide branch that had rough enough bark to keep him from actually moving unless he really forced it. His fingers drove into the spaces between the ridges of the bark and sent his fingernails deep into the cork cambium. *I'm hanging by a thread here and I remember that name. I've been hanging around those scientists too long.*

He began to relax his grip as Molaro made her way down to his perch. He anticipated the branch buckling under their combined weight and dug his nails deeper. It didn't even move as she placed her feet on it.

"Enough," she whispered an inch from his nose. "I'm roping you against the trunk." she took the rope she had brought from the pack she had left above. She stepped over to another branch that was only inches above the one Michael was sitting on and pulled it around the trunk. "You're not going to fall." She wrapped four loops around Michael and the trunk before tying it off. "If you still don't feel safe, you'll have to watch from the ground." She grabbed hold of the branch six feet above him that she had been using for a perch and pulled herself up.

Michael whispered, "Thanks," as she disappeared off his perch. He tugged at the ropes a few times until he finally got the

119

feeling they weren't going to break, unravel, come untied or decompose. *Like they had done to me and Martin back when we first found the Torvon city sewer.* He leaned forward against the ropes with a growing confidence now and raised his binoculars up.

Just as he got the focus adjusted, all the creatures dropped to the ground and began digging with their top hands. They quickly slid into the long holes they had constructed and vanished from sight. "You see anything?" he whispered up to Molaro.

"You make any noise I couldn't hear? That's how I found the village yesterday. They sleep in the lean-tos, they must be hiding... Wait, someone's coming in from the right. Is that Dr. Laudrum?"

Michael studied the two men breaking through the forest cover. "No." They made their way across the compound and into the storage shed. After a few minutes, they emerged with the woven baskets they had on their backs filled with what looked like tubers. "Could those be what you saw the natives eating last night?"

"They're the right shape."

The broader of the two men went over to the fire pit and spat into it. He said something to the other one but Michael couldn't hear it clearly enough to understand what was said. As they reached the edge of the forest, he turned and shouted into the village. "If you don't find us something better to eat, we're just going to have to see what you taste like." Then he turned and followed his companion.

After about ten minutes, the natives began emerging from their concealment. Some of them shook themselves off, others brushed away the clinging dirt, still others paired off and took turns cleaning each other. Before long they were back to the activities they had been doing before.

"What the hell is Laudrum doing to those creatures?" Michael began working to undo the knots Molaro had used to secure him in the tree. "Molaro, get me out of this."

She dropped down to his perch and undid his bindings. Then the two of them climbed out of the tree. Michael's anger at how Laudrum's expedition was exploiting the natives was tempered by the growl from his stomach. He quelled that with one of the ration bars he had brought along. "Our first priority is food," he said between swallowing his second bite and stuffing the rest of the whole grain bar in his mouth.

"Last night they cooked and ate some type of tuber, at least it looked like a root product. If we could find where they are harvesting the stuff from?"

"As long it's not from a field they planted," Michael parsed out his words while chewing the last of his lunch, "We're not stealing from these people." He took the water bottle off his belt and washed down the last of the grain flakes clinging inside his mouth.

* * *

They worked their way around to the open egress from the native village and waited for a team of card-creatures to emerge pulling a wheeled cart behind them. Michael caught himself before he could react to the fact that these primitives had developed the wheel, he looked up at Molaro crouched next to him behind the cover of the trees and placed a finger to his lips. He motioned for them to follow.

The stream Molaro had collected water from the day before, ran next to the village, about two hundred yards away. The place the creatures crossed was out of view from the village but down a short embankment from where the two Ranklins were watching. The cart bounced like it was going over a series of stones just under the water, emerging on the far side with only its wheels wet. They climbed the gentle slope on the other side and would have disappeared from view if Molaro hadn't scrambled up a nearby tree.

"The forest on the other side is a lot thinner than here," she called down just loud enough for Michael to hear her. "They look like a different variety of tree, leafy but narrow leaves, almost shaped like one of those spear-heads you people used to use in your wars. Not like the pear, five-bladed, and round leaves of the trees here."

"Are they still going east?" Michael reached for the lowest branch to climb to a vantage point where he could see what was going on but the branch broke off when he tried pulling himself up.

"Ouch." He rubbed his hand where the serrated edge of that branch tried to bite into his palm.

"You okay?"

He looked at his palm as he kept massaging it, some of the skin was broken but not enough to cause any bleeding. "I'm fine. Are they still moving?"

"They're setting the cart down now. It looks like each of them are pulling shovels out of the cart." She sat back against the trunk of the tree and pulled her binoculars up from where they dangled inside her shirt. "Those guys can dig with all four hands. It looks like they're digging up one of the tree's roots. They're starting next to the tree trunk. They've got it exposed, switching to some kind of hand axe and are putting pieces of it into the cart. I think we've found our tuber."

"We're going to have to wait until they leave before we can see."

Their wait wasn't a long one. In a quarter hour, the natives had dug up enough roots to fill their cart to the point where it took two of the three of them to pull it back, where only one had been needed to get it to the site. The third one carried the tools they had used until they got down to the stream. It then put the tools on top of the harvested tubers and pushed as the others pulled the cart across, then up the bank and back to the village.

As soon as they were out of sight, Molaro dropped to the ground and the two of them crossed over to where the aliens had been working. They quickly found a line of freshly turned soil coming from two separate trees. Michael exposed a spot inches from the trunk of one of the trees to see the cut section of the tree root already sprouting new tendrils out of the cut off section.

"No wonder they can use the tree roots for food. The trees replace them fast enough to keep from dying," Molaro said over Michael's shoulder.

Michael looked up at the trees around him. "And there must be hundreds of these trees in this grove. Climb up and collect a few of the leaves for identification purposes. I'm going to see if I can't 'harvest' a root from that tree over there." He pointed to one several yards away, as that was the distance between each of the trees.

Even with Molaro coming back to help him once she had collected her leaves, because they only had the single hatchet between them, it took them almost an hour to cut and pull the root out of the ground. They didn't have time to chop it into smaller pieces. Michael was still kicking the dirt back into the trench when Molaro, after dragging the twenty foot root almost to the forest's tree line, saw the natives cresting the embankment.

"Michael, now!"

He ran his foot against the loose soil, forcing it into the hole by the tree trunk and took off for where Molaro was hiding.

The creature pulling the cart stopped at the top of the embankment and jerked his head in the direction they were hiding. Its two friends came up around the cart and appeared to chat with the first one. Then they went over to one of the trees away from where the Ranklins were hiding and began work.

They waited until the creatures had again filled their cart and left. After the splashing from the stream crossing ceased, Michael began chopping the root in half. It was still flexible enough that they could loop it back on itself, once for the thicker piece Molaro carried and twice for the one Michael had. They made their way downstream before crossing, then they followed the stream back to the path they had created to collect water.

Chapter Twenty-Three

"This is what the card-creatures eat?" Cowloom lifted one of the six-inch long tubers from the plastic bin they had been put in after the root Michael and Molaro brought back to camp was trimmed down. Another of the storage lockers had been emptied and removed from the back of the shuttle to store them. He took a small bite out of the whitish substance inside the brown skin of the root. After a couple of chews, he spit it out. "Bitter, too dang bitter."

"They did boil them, the night I was watching," Molaro added.

"We've got water, we can make a cook fire, but we don't have a pot fire resistant enough for boiling," Justin began. "None of my beakers are large enough even to hold one of those chunks."

"What were the natives using?"

"They had a stone cauldron hanging from a stone tripod over their stone fire pit."

"I haven't seen a lot of stones around here," Michael observed. "We couldn't even find enough to build a fire pit of our own. Just a trench to keep our campfire from spreading."

"And then we have to douse it every night."

"Where did they get a rock big enough to chisel into a cooking pot?"

"Or the tools to chip it?"

"How long were those tripod legs?"

"Maybe we can bake them instead," Justin offered. "If we pull all the mirrors from the shuttle, we just might be able to construct a solar oven. Maybe we can bake these like a potato?"

They managed to find six mirrors varying in size from a couple of inches to a foot square and brought them to Justin's work area.

"We really can't use any of the plastic bins we could pull from the shuttle for this," Justin explained. "Nor can we tape these guys together. If we generate the heat we need to bake these tubers, we'll melt either of them. We need to construct an oven pit." He grabbed the two-foot long shovel they found in the emergency supplies and walked behind the shuttle. He sank the blade into the soil and began digging. In minutes he had a hole deep enough to hold the four hand mirrors people had found and wide enough for one of the two square mirrors to be set in the bottom. "I need to prop this last one up so it can reflect sunlight into our pit. Is there anything in the shuttle we can use as a strut? It needs to be metal."

Michael took the shovel from Justin and drove it into the ground. "Maybe we can use this temporarily?"

"Yeah, we might. It'll need to be a little deeper though."

Michael stepped on the top of the shovel blade and wiggled it from side to side, pushing it deeper into the soil. It just about had the ten-inch tall blade buried when he ran into something and the blade wouldn't go any deeper. "That's odd." Michael pulled the blade away from the pit loosening the soil the shovel was buried in. He brushed the loosen dirt out of the hole he was creating to reveal a smooth, level stone. He grabbed the shovel and began clearing the dirt from it to see how large it was.

After several minutes of this, aided by Justin moving dirt away with one of the metal mirrors he had recovered from the shuttle, Michael gave up digging. He stood up and looked into the others' faces. As a thought began to creep into his mind, he could see their eyes widen also. "The Torvons!"

"It would explain how those creatures could construct a cauldron and fire proof tripod," Cowloom added.

"I got the impression the fire pit was ringed by a single circle of stone, not assembled pieces," Molaro added.

"Like the Torvons would create." Michael brushed the sweat off his forehead before it could start stinging his eyes.

"So what did they bury here?" Cemper asked.

Michael handed the shovel to Cemper, walked over to their water trough, collected one of the hanging metal cups and scooped himself a drink. Pouring about half of it over his head after quenching his thirst.

"It couldn't be another city," Justin said. He dug his shoe into the loose soil and began kicking dirt out of the way in a straight line away from their attempted solar oven.

"But maybe a campsite," Cowloom speculated, "while they waited for rescue."

"We have to find the entrance." Michael grabbed the shovel away from Cemper and started digging a trench going away from the direction Justin was and towards the Torvon escape pod. "Step one, find the edges."

Everyone grabbed whatever tool they could find to begin turning the soil looking for the dimensions of whatever was buried beneath them.

* * *

"Will you look at that, Bart?" Dr. Laudrum used the expedition's binoculars to watch his competition, making sure they didn't interfere with his find. "It seems they have already started their descent into madness." He handed the glasses over to the engineer.

Bart stared at the four men playing in the dirt at the far camp. He lowered the binoculars and turned to Laudrum. "Maybe they're so hungry, they think they can eat dirt."

"We can thank our sponsors that we don't have that problem. They found a way for us to live off the planet. At least until we can figure a way to repower the *Yuri*."

Bart handed the glasses back. "Maybe we should offer a meal now and then?"

"I do believe that would be the neighborly thing to do, Mr. Higgins."

"Not on your life," Andreyev said as he climbed up on the top deck of their grounded space ship. "You wanted those guys off this planet before we tried breaking into that object. Well, if they starve, they're gone. Then you can call back your servants, and we can get back to work."

"Those are my students," Laudrum turned and glared at the Russian, "not servants."

"Just where did you get that cook pot you're using?" Bart quickly asked. "It's neither aluminum nor steel."

Andreyev dropped into the remounted pilot's seat and made a few notes before heading back to the ladder going down. "Some questions are better not asked."

Chapter Twenty-Four

They worked in shifts the rest of the afternoon and most of the next morning, but they finally found a depression in the solid slab, on the opposite side of where they had started digging. Cemper passed the shovel off to Justin, who was standing next to him to take the next turn, and began brushing the dirt away from the small hole with his hand. Neither he nor Molaro had thought to bring any brushes with them.

"Dr. Layton will be furious with us when she hears," he said to himself.

"You need something?" Justin knelt down and asked.

"There!" Cemper announced as when he pressed the depression in about an inch, it gave way to an inset handle. He lifted the ring mounted inside it and pulled. The ground under him shifted slightly. He got up and moved in a circle until he wasn't fighting his own weight. The handle came up an inch, revealing a circular edge that was moving also, but still mostly buried. "Justin, clear away dirt from on top of this thing. Can someone give me a hand pulling this thing up?"

Cowloom grabbed the handle also, while Michael and Molaro started scrapping the dirt off the top of the thing. Slowly, as more of the weight was pulled off it, the stone plug lifted enough to form a gap between it and whatever was below.

After about an hour of work, they swung the plug just past vertical where it would hold its position. With the sun directly over head, they all circled around the yard-wide opening down to the stone floor twenty feet below them.

"Molaro, get the wire. I remember the first time we dropped down one of these holes." Michael lifted his head to call after the retreating figure. "Grab a couple of those synthetic mats also."

"To land on?" Cowloom asked.

"There's a ladder mounted to the side wall here." Cemper pointed across from where he was kneeling, directly under where the handle had been.

"The wire's a backup." Michael stood up and looked around. "We need something to be an anchor, or the four of you are going to have to hold on to the end. Oh, and to answer your question, Cowloom. I remembered why there's no vegetation around this area. The Torvons had a really effective defoliant back on Ranklin, it rotted the natural fiber rope Martin and I were using when we recovered my brother-in-law's kids. The mats are going to protect the wires."

"I can't test the air down there," Justin said. "There's no way to know if it's breathable or not." He used his hand to pull some of the air from inside the hole in the ground up to his nose. "I don't smell anything. But if this thing has been sealed for a hundred years, maybe we should give it some time to recirculate. At least a half hour."

"Killjoy," Cemper said under his breath.

"In the meantime, let's get that solar oven built so we can see if those roots are edible." They all stood to leave just as Molaro came running back with the wire and mats. "Molaro, you still got the binoculars?"

She patted her pocket and nodded. "Yes, sir, right here." She took them out and began handing them to Michael.

"You keep them." He placed a restraining hand on her offer. "I want you to keep a lookout on Dr. Laudrum's group over there, in case they decide this is their discovery, also. We'll be back in thirty minutes," he looked over to Justin. Who nodded. "A half hour, to give that thing a chance to air out."

The rest of them walked over to the southern side of the shuttle and began digging another hole just west of the boundary edge of the underground structure. It took them about twenty minutes to assemble the mirrors and position several six-inch sections of roots in the baking area. It was starting to get warm inside as Cemper dropped the last one in.

"We've got to be careful when tasting these things," Justin began. "No just grabbing one and taking a bite, Cowloom. They could be edible to the native population and poisonous to us."

"Molaro and I saw members of Laudrum's team steal a couple of baskets full. They must be eating them."

"Michael, we have no idea what they are doing with them. For all we know they could be using them for fire wood. No, the consequences are too great. We're going to have to taste test them before we can consider them foodstuffs."

Michael pulled the pocket watch LaRena had bought for him on their last trip to Earth and checked the time while winding it back up. All their other time pieces required electricity and no longer functioned. Cemper kept wondering when they were going to have to resort to the stick in the ground technique Dr. Layton had shown them.

"How long do you think we should cook those things for?"

"I'm no chef, but I'd probably give them a couple of hours, then poke them to see how soft they are."

"Well, we're past the thirty minute mark. Shall we go see what's below us?" He snapped the lid closed and returned the watch to his pants pocket.

Molaro was lying prone on the ground, when they got back, with her binoculars laying next to her. She was drawing circles within circles connected to circles with her finger in the loosened soil above the stone chamber. "No movement," she rolled over as the party approached. "They've been outside a couple of times, doing something around that fire they have. But I couldn't see what." Cemper reached down and helped her to her feet. She dropped the glasses back in her pocket and brushed the dirt off her shirt and pants. "Think it's safe?"

"That's what we're here to find out," Michael said.

"If the air inside hasn't defused by now, we'd need a blower system to clear the place," Justin announced. "And since I'm the lightest one here," he picked up the wire, uncoiled it and began tying it around his waist, "I'll be the one going down."

"Hold on one minute," Michael put his hand on the knot Justin was making. "I'm in charge. It's my responsibility. I go."

"But I know what to smell for. Do you know various toxic odors? Do you know the signs of excess CO_2? Without my atmospheric testing equipment, this becomes MY responsibility. I go."

Cemper watched as Michael hesitated for a second before pulling his hand away from the wire. "Okay, but be careful."

"I'll keep talking all the way down. If I stop, pull me up. Keep the line straight, no slack, but not taut. If I call for extraction, pull me up. If something happens up here, pull on the line three times and slowly pull me up, I'll try self rescue at that point."

"Self-rescue?" Cemper asked.

"I'll be climbing out myself." He pulled the knot tight and raised the loop until the rope was running around his chest and under his armpits. "Well, I'm ready." He stepped over to the opening while the others formed a line with the 'rope' wrapped around each of them in turn.

With the safety line held tight, Justin stepped onto the first rung of the ladder with his left foot, holding onto the wire for balance. "One." Then Cemper saw his right foot disappear below ground. "Two." Justin himself began to slowly descend into the hole.

"Four." As he got waist deep, bright lights began to flood up to the surface and the sounds of laboring blowers could be heard. A couple of areas they had already uncovered lifted up, yet the sound from below said there were a few more.

Cemper, who has in the lead position, turned and looked at Cowloom. It was Michael who made the decision. "Cemper, we can hold him. See what you can do before we burn something out down there."

"Give me some slack," Justin said. "I need to get down there and see what's going on."

Cemper grabbed the shovel and located the closest covered vent. He had it cleared and open in under five minutes. Then he moved on to the others. Within a matter of minutes he had freed half a dozen other vents, relieving the strain he could hear on the motors.

"Motors?" He said the word aloud and let the implications of that wash over him. "They have power! How do they have power?"

By the time he got back to the entrance, Cowloom was beginning his descent, Michael having already gone below. With only his head still above ground, Cowloom said, "You two wait here. In case something happens to us, you need to be able to get help."

"From where?"

He thought about it for a second before responding, "Just keep watch on us." Then he descended below the opening.

Chapter Twenty-Five

By the time Cowloom stepped off the wall-mounted ladder, Michael was sitting in one of the chairs around a central table in the open area, sorting through the items left there. Next to it was a long couch with a shorter table in front of it. He took in the rest of the room. Justin was examining the far work area and there were three beds mounted against the far left wall.

With their need for consumables, if they planned on surviving until help arrived, Cowloom walked across the single room shelter to join Justin. Mounted on the wall was a ledge that ran just over half of its length, with a series of shelves above that. A double basin was at the end of the ledge. Cowloom found a hole in the one at waist level, when he bent over to check the one on the floor, he found it could be easily pulled out. He glanced under the ledge while he was still squatting down and found yet another series of shelves. This time with various sizes of pots. Cowloom pulled one of the larger pots off the shelf and stood up to put it on the counter.

"This should boil our roots nicely." He set the foot-and-a-half-wide cauldron gently on the ledge, it was so light he worried about breaking it.

"You're assuming my oven doesn't work." Justin swatted him on the back of his hand with the ladle he was holding.

"Ow. Hey. What the—?" Cowloom yanked back his hand and began massaging it.

"Will you look at the—? It didn't break. Michael, did we even find stone items this thin back on Ranklin?" He tossed the ladle across the room to where Michael was sitting. "Sorry, Cowloom, but I needed a guinea pig."

Michael caught it in both hands without getting out of the chair, turned it over a couple of times and smacked it against the tabletop. Neither the table nor the ladle even chipped.

"How would you like it if I tested this pot on your head?" Cowloom picked up the pot with his right hand and threatened Justin.

"I think I've already proven how strong this stuff is. Any more down there?" Justin bent over to have a look under the ledge. Cowloom squatted down again. On the two rows of shelves there were over a dozen cauldrons and many more handled cooking pans. The cauldrons ranged in size from slightly larger than the one Cowloom selected to one that could fit in his palm. Each with a loop handle that could be raised and lowered. "They've got a good selection down here. Boiling might be better anyway. Boil off any toxins the roots might contain."

"I don't see any place for a cook fire down here? Do you think they went topside to do their cooking?" Cowloom stood up and leaned against the ledge with his back to it.

"That'd get old real fast," Michael interjected, tossing the ladle back to Justin as he straightened up. He rose from the chair and walked over to the beds. He rapped his knuckles against a spot where the fabric remains were rotted away. "Stone. Not as hard as the table over there and softer than the seat of the chair." He brushed the bed clean and laid down on it. "Could be softer, but I think our mattresses will make this thing useable."

"You thinkin' of moving in down here?" Cowloom came over to examine another of the beds.

"It's better shelter than the shuttle. And it's got power." Michael sat bolt upright on the bed. "It's got **power**. Why does it have power?"

They both looked over to their resident chemist. "Don't look at me. I'm still trying to figure out how the critters eating our power are doing it."

"The Torvons didn't transmit electrical power the way we do," Cowloom speculated. "Maybe those pipes of theirs protect them from the microbes."

"Or maybe they have a chemical treatment..." The lights began to dim before Michael could finish his thought. "They were using solar power on Ranklin," he said as he snapped his fingers.

"Any collectors would be covered by now."

"And we probably used up whatever was remaining in the batteries."

Michael was off the bed as the room finally fell into darkness. The only light came from the opening he was headed for. "Which means we have to find their solar array and clean it off or no more power."

Chapter Twenty-Six

They found the solar array bordering the outside of the shelter, under a few inches of dirt. Molaro was clearing the panels paralleling the tree line when she saw a momentary glimpse of what she thought was one of the Vaneran natives. As soon as she lifted her head to check on her peripheral sighting, the creature disappeared behind one of the larger trees. It was a good hundred yards from where she'd been working, she wasn't sure what she had seen.

She got off her knees and looked to see where everyone else was. No one was close enough for her to quietly call, she'd have to look on her own. She turned and walked over to where she thought it was hiding, several trees into the woods.

It wasn't there. At first she thought she had the wrong tree, but when she forced herself to look into her infrared range, she could see the heat signature of where it had been standing behind it. Looking up, there was no sign of it having climbed the tree. Which it would have needed sharp claws for, since the lowest branch was just out of Molaro's reach. And she could find no marks on the tree trunk.

A single trail ran from the tree or to it. The fading heat tracks weren't clear enough to indicate direction. But since there was only one, she assumed the creature had doubled back on itself when it left.

She was torn between the idea of following the creature and trying to communicate with it or returning to clean up the Torvon solar cells. But not for long. The trail would literally be cold if she stopped to get someone else. As quietly as she could, she followed the tracks as they headed towards the stream, almost perfectly paralleling their trail to her left.

As she got to the embankment bordering the stream, she began hearing a high-pitched whining coming from in front of her. She sprinted the last few feet and broke from the trees to see the creature being swept downstream. Being a narrower stretch of the river than that by the native village, it was faster and deeper. Too deep for the creature to stand up.

Running as fast as she could through the drying mud, Molaro finally got ahead of the creature and waded up to her chest in the flowing water. She grabbed at the flailing creature, caught it by one of its middle limbs, pulled it against her chest and wrapped both her arms around its furry body.

It tried to break her hold as she emerged from the water and climbed the bank to get to a dry enough spot of check it over. When she could finally set it down, it spat a little water from its mouth and ran for the nearest tree. It swung behind it and turned to watch Molaro lay down on the bank and roll into a position where the sun bathed every inch of her front side.

She took a minute to catch her breath. "That's cold water." She sat back up, pulled her shirt over her head and tried wringing the excess water out of it before sliding it back on. Then she turned to look at the creature. She took one of the ration bars out of her pants pocket, a still dry one, peeled down the wrapper and took a bite. Then she held it towards where the creature was hiding. "Hungry?"

It stuck its right side out from behind the tree, just enough to get an eyeball around to watch Molaro. When it made no further motion, she took another bite, pulled off the remaining wrapper, and tossed the rest of the bar towards the creature. Just enough to get it to land a couple of feet from her. Then she folded her arms in front of herself. "It's yours if you want it."

The creature didn't run away. Molaro patiently waited for it to make its move. After a few minutes, she licked the ration bar wrapper to activate its degradation cycle and tossed the ball she had made of it into the water. It was falling apart before it was carried ten yards downstream.

Still the creature watched her with a single eye.

Molaro stretched out and propped her head up on her left arm, keeping an eye on the creature. It stood there, unmoving, for another quarter hour. Then it inched its way out from behind the tree and looked at the food Molaro had offered it, rather than

Molaro herself. Several minutes later, it dropped on all sixes and ran over to pounce on the bar. Then it scampered back to the tree line. It took up its position behind the tree again with a single eye showing.

Molaro just laid there, offering no offensive move towards the creature.

After another quarter hour, she pulled another ration bar out of her pants pocket, this one's wrapper was a bit soggy. But it wouldn't dissolve until she applied the enzymes in her saliva to it. She unwrapped the bar, it was still protected from the water. Took a bite and offered it to the alien. As she held out the bare bar, she licked the wrapper and disposed of it in the stream.

The creature came out from behind the tree and walked upright slowly to where Molaro held it out. It reached for the bar with its upper hands, leaning into it so it could stand as far away as possible. Molaro made no motions to frighten it. Finally it made a grab for the bar, almost touching her hand, but snatching it and stuffing it immediately in its mouth. It backed away a few steps but not back to the tree.

She sat back up. This caused the creature to back up another step but it still didn't bolt for the forest. As she waited, it came a step forward again.

She had one bar left, she reached into her pocket again. This time she set the bar, still wrapped, in the same spot she had set the first one. Folding her arms, she sat there.

The creature looked from the bar and up to her several times before venturing to where the bar laid and picking it up. It passed the thing from one hand to another until all four hands had examined its texture. It looked over to Molaro again, then stuck out a brownish tongue and licked the bar fully on one side.

Without immersion in water, it was going to take the wrapper several minutes to dissolve. The creature began rubbing the side it had licked until the wrapper began to flake away. then it grabbed one of the loose pieces and pulled the degrading plastic away from the ration bar. After it had the bar completely free of its encasing plastic, it popped the entire three-inch bar in its mouth and began chewing. It looked down at the slowly dissolving wrapper in its hand, balled it up, walked over to the stream and tossed it. It was too light to make it from the distance Molaro had thrown it, so it had to try again.

When it looked over to Molaro, she applauded. It tried to mimic her smile but the sides of its mouth wouldn't rise up. It was a flat expression. But it did bang its hands together.

After a half hour of various hand gestures to convince the creature she wasn't going to hurt it, the sound of Cemper hollering for her came from the woods. "Molaro!"

The creature dove for the ground at the sound, dug a slight hole just wider than itself and virtually leapt under the surface. Molaro could tell from its heat signature that it was barely an inch below the surface.

"Molaro!" Cemper emerged from the forest several yards behind her, she had been sitting facing away from their trail. "Molaro, there you are. Didn't you hear me calling?"

She shushed him and pointed to the spot where the native was buried. "I think they're sentient. But I'm going to need more time."

"It'll be dark in a few hours." He began to walk over to her but she held out her hand asking him to stop.

"I'll be okay."

"We're moving into the shelter. Your mattress is already down there but I get the couch."

"That's okay; it was too short for me anyway. Now go, let me see if I made a friend." She thought about it as Cemper was turning. "You got any ration bars with you? They seem to like them." She pointed to the reddish glow just next to her.

He reached into his pocket, pulled two of them out as he began walking over to her. "I'll be glad to give these up. Cowloom volunteered to try the boiled tubers before I left. Justin said they're toxic unless you boil the toxin out. Baking won't do it." She held up her hand again. Cemper stopped.

She cupped her hands. "Just toss them." Cemper tossed the bars the five feet that separated them. She caught the first but the second landed inches from where the creature was buried. It wiggled at the disturbance, but quickly become quiescent again.

"Thanks. Now head back to camp. I'll try to get back before dark." He turned and began walking away. After he entered the forest again, Molaro turned back to the creature.

It was sitting on the bank, holding the plastic wrapper in one hand and nibbling on the bar she'd left on the ground that it held in the other.

Dropping the remaining bar in her shirt pocket, she sat down now inches from the creature. It looked up at her as she did, but made no move to run away. "Friends," she said to it. Then pointed to herself, repeated the word. After which she pointed to the creature and said "Friends" again.

After repeating this several times she pointed at the creature without repeating the word. The creature made a two part sound Molaro couldn't understand. She reached out her palm open-handed and the creature just stared at it for a moment. Then it mimicked her gesture. Slowly she extended her hand and touched the open palm of the creature's right middle hand. It jerked its hand back.

When Molaro didn't make any further motion, just holding her hand where she had touched the alien, it extended its hand again, placing it on top of the back of Molaro's. Slowly she turned her hand around and touched the creature palm to palm. She held it there a moment, then lightly closed her much larger hand around the alien one. This time, the creature did not pull away. This time, it placed its other middle hand under Molaro's hand, and its left upper hand on top of it. It reached out with its right upper hand and stroked Molaro's arm. After a couple of minutes of this, it released her hand, walked closer to Molaro and wrapped all its arms around her chest.

Molaro reached to pat it on its head, but stopped before making contact. *That's not its head, so where do I offer comfort?* She tried stroking behind where its eyes were, quickly finding out that it would only tolerate her motions in one direction. Its fur became harsh and stiff if she stroked it in reverse.

She went to stand up; it was time she was getting back to camp. She pointed to the trail and offered her right hand to it. The creature, who barely came up to her waist, wrapped its upper hand around her index finger and followed her back up the embankment.

* * *

Vanera was low on the horizon as they returned to the Ranklin campsite, but as soon as the alien saw the light coming from the ground, it chattered something at Molaro, dropped her hand and ran over to the hole and peered down. It backed off a moment later and ran back to Molaro as Justin stuck his head out of the shelter's opening.

"What have we got here?" he said, climbing the rest of the way out. They had driven a pair of struts from the shuttle into the ground between the shelter and its solar cells to make climbing in and out easier.

Molaro scooped up the creature and continued on to the shelter. "One of this planet's natives, I think."

Justin walked over to them, but stopped as the creature squirmed in Molaro's arms as he got too close. "That'd be my guess. It bears no resemblance to the mummies we found back on Ranklin. I doubt it'd be a descendant of anyone from the escape pod."

She had stopped walking also, to keep from dropping the squirming alien. "It was drawn to the shelter when we came into the clearing." It settled down, and after a minute, reached out with one hand, keeping the other three tightly wrapped around Molaro, holding its palm skyward to Justin. "Just touch its palm with yours. We kinda established that as a welcome gesture."

When Justin reciprocated, Molaro could feel the creature relax. Shortly it tried to climb down. Molaro lowered it to the ground and as soon as it disengaged with her, it was hugging Justin's leg. Then it went back to the opening and tried climbing down. Due to the spacing of the ladder's rungs, it took some time for the creature to climb to the bottom. It looked around and climbed back up twice as fast as it had descended.

"Who all's down there?" Molaro asked.

"We sent Cemper off to collect more fire wood. But Michael and Cowloom. Cowloom's looking for any kind of entertainment system like he'd found on Ranklin. So far he's had no luck."

141

The creature jumped back into Molaro's arms when it got back up. "It's okay," she said. "They're my friends. Friends." She went over to the opening, urged the creature to climb onto her back, then climbed down the ladder herself. It tried to climb back onto the ladder as Molaro reached the floor, but she quickly pulled it around and held it like she had after meeting Justin. She stepped aside to allow Justin to come down.

"You've got one of the native creatures," Michael said as he got up from one of the beds and approached. "How did you get it to trust you? It couldn't have been easy, after what we saw Lundrum's men doing to them."

"These are my friends," Molaro said to the creature. It shivered as Michael approached. She let go of it with one hand and extended that hand to Michael. "Palm to palm," she held her palm up, "I taught it that was our friendship gesture."

Michael held up a hand as Cowloom began to walk over to them, then placed his palm on Molaro's. Then he extended his upturned palm to the creature and waited for it to respond. "I'd say we have a new friend. Cowloom, come over and shake hands with... What are you calling him?"

"I hadn't thought of that. And I don't know what sex it is, or even if these people have sexes, or how many."

"Then let's call him, err, it, Vanny. A resident of Vanera 3" He stroked just behind the upper shoulder blades of the creature, only once in the wrong direction.

Chapter Twenty-Seven

"It worked!" Cemper exclaimed under the belly of the grounded shuttle. As he had been laying on his stomach checking the pit he'd dug to apply the wires connecting the small solar array he had found in the back of the shuttle supply locker, the Wassarran rolled out from under the shuttle and grabbed Justin to drag him under to see the experiment he'd set up yesterday.

"Okay, so you've filled your pit with the microbes eating our electricity." Justin propped his head on his right hand and stared at Cemper. "So what?"

Cemper turned on his side and faced Justin. "Michael wanted a way to warn any rescue mission not to land on this planet. Well, this is it!"

"A nightly glowing puddle?"

"Hey, what are you guys doing under there?" Michael bent down on one knee and looked at his two colleagues huddled under the inert space vessel.

Justin was facing towards him, so Cemper rolled over. "Take a look at this."

Michael crawled under the shuttle and looked at the glowing pit. "Okay, so? We have lots of these glowing mounds where the microbes dripped out after draining our power. What about it?"

"Like I said earlier, so what?" Justin rolled over on his back and looked into the panel Cemper had torn off to steal wiring away from their ship to run his test.

"We can funnel these guys," Cemper propped himself up on his left arm until his head was touching the bottom of the shuttle and waved his right hand over the puddle, "into whatever shape we need." Seeing the blank looks on his two friends, "Like twenty meter tall letters."

Justin gave a blank look but Michael's eyes brightened with the beginning of an idea. "Letters as large as the escape pod we pinpointed from orbit. Large enough to warn others away!"

"That's what I was thinking."

"There should be more than enough dead wiring in this useless ship," Justin said as he finally understood what Cemper was getting at.

Michael rolled out the other side. "I sure hope Molaro can get her new friends to help us dig those trenches. We're going to have a lot of dirt to move."

"You guys start laying out the field and I'll begin gutting the ship. I just hope this solar panel can give us enough electricity to feed those little guys." Cemper rolled out right after Justin and went up the ramp into the shuttle cabin.

"If it doesn't," Michael added as he looked to see where Molaro was. "We still have the fuel cell we can tap."

* * *

Mary was fascinated by how the native life forms were taking to the Ranklin expedition. They had joined the human and Wassaran members that had been marooned on the Vanera 3, as she had heard the older members call the planet. Not locked up, not lorded over, the way she had seen Dortello and that monster Belinsky do to them, but like playing with the younger Wassarran boy. He was tossing them a ball and they would use their back to hit it back to him.

"And who do we have here?"

Mary, who was on her stomach, rolled around to look up at the other Wassarran youngster. So intent had she been on watching that she hadn't paid any attention to forest noises and let herself get caught.

"Dr. Laudrum wanted us to keep an eye on the artifact he found. Make sure you people didn't try to get into it."

"Get on your feet." The Wassarran walked over to the brush Mary and Ron had set up to hide themselves. "I think Michael would like to have a word with you."

"Please, we haven't done anything."

"We?" The Wassarran reached down, took Mary's hand and pulled her to her feet.

Mary let her binoculars dangle from her neck while she brushed the forest debris from her jeans and blue shirt. "Ron McNamara and I have been taking shifts watching the artifact these past few days."

"Who's he and who are you?" The woman put her balled hands on her hips and stood two feet over the top of Mary's head. It took a bit of effort on Mary's part to pull her eyes away from the swirl of hair the other woman had her hair wrapped up in.

"My name is Mary Davis," she began. "Ron and I are Dr. Laudrum's graduate students. He promised us our Doctorates if we helped him beat Dr. Carpenter to a Ranklinite find."

"They're Torvons, not Ranklinites."

"I'll let you argue that with Dr. Laudrum." She pulled up the log she and Ron had been using and sat down. Mainly to break the tension. Mary pointed at the other one, hoping the Wassarran would sit also and give her neck a rest. "We got here first, but when we landed, all our electrical systems started going down, like we'd been hit with an EMP. but nothing was damaged."

"It's a microbe."

"A what?"

"An electricity eating microbe. Don't you guys have a glow at night under your ship? The dead organisms are bioluminescent." The other woman pulled the second log closer and sat down.

"The popping sounds?"

"The dead organisms also appear to be shock sensitive." The woman reached out her hand to Mary. "My name is WaSon Molaro, but you can call me Molaro." After shaking Mary's hand, she continued, "We've met Dr. Laudrum and another man when we landed."

"That would have been Bart Higgins, he's our engineer."

"Anyone else with you?"

"Only the financiers of the trip, Myles Andreyev, Enrico Dortello and Ivan Belinsky. Stay away from Belinsky." Mary shuddered at the thought of her encounter with the Russian.

"How so?"

"On the flight here, he raped me. That trio has some kind of hold over Dr. Laudrum." Mary put her hands up to her face to hide the tears forming. "He couldn't do anything about it."

"Do you need to get away from the guy?" Molaro leaned forward, bringing her eyes level with Mary's. "We found a Torvon shelter, a large comfortable shelter. We could give you, what do you humans call it, sanctuary."

"I couldn't run off and leave Ron, Bart and Dr. Laudrum alone with those men."

Molaro got up from her log. "If you change your mind or just want to keep an eye on us, feel free to come into our encampment. You don't need to hide out here in the trees. Otherwise, we won't try getting into the escape pod without your permission." She extended her hand to Mary and lifted her off the log. "Maybe if we work together, we just might get off this planet." Before Mary could react, Molaro walked forward and into the clearing back to the encampment she had offered to protect Mary in.

"Are all Wassarran's like her?" Mary said to herself. "She just met me, I spied on her and she was willing to shelter me?"

Chapter Twenty-Eight

"This is why we're forced to eat those MREs again?" Andreyev had returned with his two partners, dragging Dr. Laudrum's party with them, to the native village. Inside the villager's storage shed was nothing, empty, all the food stuffs they had been raiding from the creatures had vanished. Even the cauldrons and stone poles to hold them were removed. He was staring directly at Belinsky for an answer.

"There was never a lot of those potato things here, but always enough for them to share with us," Dortello responded instead.

"Steal, you mean." Mary didn't even try to hide her contempt for the man. Belinsky turned to glare at her. Ron quickly put himself between her and Belinsky . Mary knew if Belinsky tried anything, Ron wouldn't hold him back for long, hopefully long enough for the others to stop the brute.

"Belinsky, it is to you I was talking." Andreyev grabbed the shorter man by the shoulder and spun him back. "Where is my food?"

Dortello waited for Belinsky to respond, but he just stood there smoldering. "We haven't seen any of those creatures in some time, Mr. Andreyev," Dortello responded before tensions could erupt.

Too bad, Mary thought, *we could use a little dissention in their ranks right about now.*

"Maybe they've used up this food supply and moved on?" Laudrum speculated.

Why did the Professor have to break the tension? Mary watched as the red drained from Belinsky 's cheeks and Dortello started breathing a bit more regularly.

"We haven't seen the vermin since we first found this village. Oh, they've been here. Up until a few days ago, they'd been replacing what we took." Belinsky walked past his interrogator, reached down at the corner of the shed and picked up the last of the tubers it had been storing. He walked back over and placed it in Andreyev's hand. "Here's your supper."

"Girl, take this." He stretched out his arm to Mary.

She made no move. Ron grabbed it as Andreyev opened his hand to drop it. *Why will no one let these imbeciles blow?* She had been hoping to drive their sponsors to a point where the resultant explosion would force Dr. Landum and Mr. Higgins to see these men for the hoodlums they were.

"Did you guys ever find out where they were harvesting this stuff?" Bart was always looking for the solution to whatever problem you drop in front of him. "We could just start collecting them ourselves."

"Good idea." Andreyev turned on the engineer. "Take your students and get us supper. Belinsky, show them where to dig."

"We don't know, Mr. Andreyev," Dortello jumped in. "We never found where they were getting them from."

Andreyev was again glaring at Belinsky . "You mean you never bothered to look."

"They were never here when we got here," Belinsky said through clenched teeth.

"You mean you scared them off," Mary blurted out. Then she hunched down to accept the blow Belinsky 's hand was raised to deliver.

Andreyev grabbed him by the wrist, arresting the blow. "She may be insolent, but does she speak the truth? Did you drive them away?"

Dortello jumped in again. "I swear, we never saw any of these creatures since the first time we visited their village."

"Then why did they leave?"

"They tried to stop us from collecting our supplies," Belinsky said. "I may have had to kick a few of them aside. To show them who was in charge."

"And you wonder why they hid from you," Mary whispered barely loud enough for Ron to hear.

"Well if you're in charge, you can find the site where our college friends need to dig. Get out there and look." Andreyev shoved Belinsky out of the hut's opening. He stumbled a bit, but never lost his feet.

He turned back to the door as Andreyev emerged. "And where do you propose I look?"

"There was a trail off to the east that looked like it might have had wheel tracks plowed into it."

"Like the engineer says." Andreyev pointed to the only forest opening from the village. "That way."

"You two go with him." Laudrum looked over to Mary and Ron. "Make sure he finds the right stuff."

"NO!" Mary screamed. "Not with him. Never with him."

"Mary, what's wrong?" Bart draped his arm around Mary's shoulders and led her out of the shed and to the western side of the village clearing. Ron followed closely behind. Laudrum stood frozen by her response.

When they got out of earshot, Ron quietly explained. "Belinsky raped her while we were still on our way here."

"In the forest?"

"No, on the *Yuri*," she spat back. "I will **not** be anywhere near that man unless there are people around to restrain him."

Bart had to think for a moment. "That would explain why you were hiding in your cabin the last part of the voyage. And I suppose why you've stuck around Ron or myself all the time. Does Reggie know?"

"Other than me, this is the first she's told anyone."

"They couldn't have done anything anyway. There can't be any justice against the owners of a deep-space expedition while you're still in deep space." She reached down and patted the side of the ankle high boots she was wearing. "But if he tries again, you'll have a murder to deal with."

"Finding food is important. Too important to let this get in the way." He held up his hand as Mary opened her mouth to object. "The three of us will go and search for these roots. Belinsky can stay behind with his comrades. **We'll** find a way to deal with him later."

Mary could feel the weight of Belinsky 's stare as they returned to the native village. She managed to keep both Ron and Bart between them.

"It'd make more sense for me to go with your students, Reg." Bart walked up to Belinsky, turned his back on the man and addressed Dr. Laudrum. "After all, being an engineer, I can work out the best way to harvest and carry what we need." He turned his head slightly and rolled his eyes towards the short Russian.

"Good luck. Remember, just because we haven't seen any wildlife on this planet, doesn't mean these woods are safe." Dr. Laudrum turned and began walking back to the *Yuri*. Mary knew her instructor well enough to know he didn't catch what Mr. Higgins was trying to warn him about. He would have been too focused on figuring out how to get to his artifact.

Chapter Twenty-Nine

"You two go ahead," Bart instructed. "I want to make one more check of the fire circle." As the two youths walked down the six-foot-wide path towards the bordering stream, Bart walked over to the stone circle, knelt down and touched its cold surface. "Just a hint of warmth. It had to have contained a fire not more than a day ago," he said to himself. He looked up and made sure the three financiers were following Reg back to the *Yuri* before he stood up and headed off towards the stream.

The stream itself was a good two hundred yards from the village with a ten foot bank on either side of it. On the far side, above the bank, was a continuation of the forest. The stream itself was almost fifty foot across, but only ankle deep.

Mary and Ron had already crossed when Bart started to step in on his side. Ron called over. "Careful, Mr. Higgins. The riverbed is slippery in spots."

"Find the pebbles imbedded in the bottom. They gave us secure footing," Mary added.

His first step squished into the dirt below the water and took him a moment to keep it from sliding under him. He found several small stones a good stretched step from where he would have placed his left foot, slightly down stream. Stepping there, his foot didn't sink into the silt of the stream. It only took him a few moments to finish crossing the stream, knowing what to look for.

Ron and Mary were slightly downstream, kneeling over a spot on the bank as he stepped back onto dry land and shook the water off his boots.

"Mr. Higgins, this looks like tracks."

He got down on his knees and stared at the faint marks in the dirt. After running his hand over the several sets of visible prints, he lifted his gaze to follow the bank downstream. "It looks like they were going this way for some reason. I think we should follow these tracks and find out why."

As they were getting up, Mary looked over to the stream. "Hey, this looks like a wheel track?" She went closer to the water's edge and pointed to an even fainter mark in the bank. "It's hard to believe their cart weighed less than they did."

Looking at the mark, which wasn't a clean wheel track, and the increased steepness of the embankment at that point, Bart announced, "I think their cart slipped a little right here. But we should get going. If this is the route to their food supply, we could be in luck."

"No telling what that Andreyev will do if we come back empty-handed."

"I know what that monster Belinsky will. If we don't find anything, I'm not going back."

"Now, Mary, let's not do anything rash."

"I'm sure Harrod's people will take us in."

"Hey, up ahead," Ron, who was a couple of steps ahead to the others announced. "There's a clearing in the forest." He ran up the embankment and around the last tree before the large opening.

"I think we'd better see what Ron's found." Then Mary took off at a run. Leaving Bart to try his best in the slightly wet soil of the embankment, where his shoes would stick in the mud for just a split second making his run harder than he was used to on the ship's treadmill.

When the clearing finally came into view, it wasn't absolutely cleared of trees. The trees growing in the soccer-stadium-sized area were spaced over twenty feet apart with nothing growing between them. Running from most of the trees was a furrow of loose dirt but only one for each tree. Bart climbed up to the area, ran his hand into one of the furrows and dug around to see what was inside. He felt nothing until he got within five foot of the tree. There he touched what had to be a fibrous growth, a vine of some type. He pulled it up and out of the furrow it was in and found it was connected to the tree it ran from.

"A root?" Ron came up beside the engineer to see what he was doing.

"Maybe?" Bart looked to where he had found the end of the root and decided that it only occupied half of the furrow running from the tree. He dropped it back into its trench, covered it back up and tried to find whatever was in the other half of the trench.

He found nothing.

He dug around the base of the tree until he came upon another root and exposed it. "Mary, Ron, look at this. Does this look like the roots the natives have been giving us?"

"They haven't been giving them to us," Ron began. "Belinsky and Dortello have been taking it from them."

"Okay, but does this look like the roots we've been eating?"

"Kind of looks like it," Mary responded.

Bart took the hatchet from his belt, pulled the root slightly up and raised his axe to cut it.

"Don't take that one," came a voice from further up the plateau. "If you take more than one at a time, it could hurt the tree." Cemper came walking up to the trio now looking in the direction he had come from.

Bart pulled his hand out from under the root and slid his hatchet back into his belt loop. "And you would know this how?"

"Cemper," Mary exclaimed. "Is Molaro with you?"

"No, he has to put up with me today," said a human following several steps behind the faster Wassarran. "My name is Justin Davis, by the way." He offered his hand to the standing graduate students, while Cemper reached down to offer Bart help getting back up.

Bart shook the offered hand as he got to his feet, then dropped it to brush the dirt from his hands and knees. "So what can you tell us about these roots?"

"They contain a neurotoxin unless you boil them thoroughly. Not strong enough to do you permanent harm, unless you're as small as a Vaneran, but you'll be sick for several days. You can harvest one root from a tree without causing it any damage, but the Vanerans don't want us taking a second one until the root has had a chance to grow back. But we have enough trees in this section of forest to last forever, if we follow that rule. The roots are pretty fast growing, it takes just over a month to regrow what we take."

"It also appears to be the only thing the Vanerans eat," Cemper added.

"Vanerans?" Bart asked.

"The natives of this planet. Vanera 3, so we've been calling them Vanerans." Cemper pulled a wooden whistle from his pocket. From the looks of its construction, Bart concluded the Wassarran had to have carved it himself.

Cemper blew about four rising notes and creatures began to emerge from the ground.

"We were working on a tree about twenty yards up and next to the forest's tree line, when you arrived. The Vanerans accompanying us hid. They probably thought you were the guys who had been stealing from them," Justin explained as about a dozen creatures crowded around Cemper, hugging his legs. As they looked up, they ran over to Mary and hugged her also.

"They seem to have taken to you, Ms. Davis." Bart was not going to make any sudden moves to scare off the creatures.

"Hey, we have the same last name?" Justin beamed over at Mary. "You aren't from Boston, by any chance?"

"I'm afraid not." She reached down and stroked the slight fur the creatures had.

"Keep your hands near its top. Their mouths are in the center of their bodies," Camper said. "But they do love to be stroked, but only in a single direction. It hurts them, otherwise."

"I'm sorry," Bart began. "I forgot to introduce ourselves. This is Ronald McNamara, Mary Davis is currently being surrounded by the creatures, and I am Bart Higgins." He extended his hand to Justin.

"Well, this is ByVon Cemper. We're almost done here, if you would like to return to our camp with us?"

"No, I think..." Bart began.

Mary Interrupted him, "We would love that."

"Great. Let's get this load packed, and we can all get back in time for lunch."

<h1 style="text-align:center">Chapter Thirty</h1>

"So that's where they've gone," Dortello handed the binoculars over to his boss for him to have a look through the *Yuri's* highest porthole. "The creatures have set up camp around Harrod's people."

"First he tries to steal our goldmine, now he's after our meal ticket." Andreyev handed them over to Belinsky . "But we shall correct his mis-intentions."

Belinsky brought the looking glasses up to his eyes. "I gave those to you to put them away. We must go pay a visit on Mr. Harrod." Andreyev was already over to the ladder climbing down through the ship as Belinsky thought he caught sight of the Wassarran female talking to someone just inside the forest before she walked in herself. He draped the cord of the binoculars over the back of one of the pilot chairs and followed the others out of the *Yuri.*

*　*　*

"We shouldn't need them," Andreyev said as he stepped off the ladder on the third level. "But we've brought them this far." He opened the door to his cabin, walked over to their locked personal trunk, knelt down and unlocked it. "Rico, here's your gun. Belinsky ," he began handing it to the shorter Russian but pulled it back momentarily. "Only if I order you to pull it. Don't bungle the surprise this time." Then he handed over the automatic pistol. Finally he pulled his holstered revolver out of the locker, closed the lid with his gun on top, and relocked it.

Standing back up, he ran it through his belt where it could hang just covered by the light jacket Andreyev was wearing. He added, "No showing them unless we have to." He walked over to the cabin door, watching Belinsky drop his small pistol into his pocket and Dortello slid his into the pouch he had arranged to be

155

sewn into the back of all his trousers. He gestured to the open door. "Shall we proceed?"

* * *

Mary and Molaro were pulling the wheeled cart they had been given by the Vanerans, filled with six-inch sections of roots, back to their encampment when they saw the three men approaching. Mary froze, turned and ran deep into the trees. Far enough so she could still see them approach, but they wouldn't be able to spot her.

Molaro stopped for a moment and watched Mary go into hiding. Then she looked over and saw the men approaching also. By now they had seen her and the cart, so she kept pulling it right up to the nose of the shuttle before dropping the handle bar to the ground.

"Michael, Justin, we have company." Cowloom and Cemper were filling the second cart. Bart and Ron should be working with the Vanerans constructing the warning sign. She quickly glanced over to the trees and found no sign of Mary, even in her infrared visual range.

As the three men approached, the Vanerans that had been in view found a section of ground where they could bury themselves. They were gone by the time everyone reached the spot where Molaro was waiting. The known humans standing next to her and the unknown threesome a few feet in front of her.

"Can I help you gentlemen?" Michael planted the shovel he had been carrying in the ground in front of him.

"We want our work force back," the tallest one, standing between the others, said.

"Work force," Molaro stammered. These had to be the financiers that Mary had warned her about. She could feel her protectionist pressure building inside her. She wasn't old enough to have out grown the hormonal surges that protect young Wassarrans from personal attacks. But she resisted the urges as everyone had been trained to do since the civilization of Wassara. She knew what these men had done to these creatures; keeping herself in check wasn't easy.

"And who would you gentlemen be?" Michael asked, folding his arms in front of his chest.

156

"The owners of that artifact," one of the men pointed to the escape pod. "And the creatures you stole from us."

The human on the other side of the tall man added, "Now give them back to us." Molaro noticed he was reaching for a pants pocket on his right side. Whatever was in that pocket made it appear slightly darker in her infrared vision.

"Belinsky ," the tall man rounded on him. "No!" Then he turned back to Michael. "Dr. Laudrum has already informed you to leave our find alone. We have allowed you to stay here since neither of us can move our space vessels. But the creatures were our work force." He looked over to the cart Molaro had brought in. "Collecting the very same roots I see you are having them do for you. Roots which we will accept in the way of an apology as long as you send all the creatures back to work for us." He motioned for his friends to collect the cart.

"No, you don't." Molaro blocked the two men from picking up the cart handle. Again she saw the smaller man reach for his pocket and the cold thing inside it. "We harvested these roots ourselves. We don't enslave innocent life forms."

"Molaro," Michael quickly injected. "We can spare one load of roots for these men. They obviously haven't eaten for a while." Michael ran his eyes over the obese bellies of the three men. "You know I don't believe you told me your names. What should we call you?"

"In charge," said the tallest one. "Get that cart and let's get going. We still have to cook those damn things."

As the two men brushed Molaro aside, Justin piped up, "Maybe Molaro or I should go with these guys. Just to bring the cart back."

"Good idea." He pulled at his chin for a second before adding, "Molaro, you go with them. I'll have a talk with our guests about going back to work."

"Dortello, Belinsky , let her pull the cart. She brought it back from their harvest with no problem." Then he turned to Michael. "By the morning. I want those aliens back in their village." Then he turned and walked off, motioning the others to follow him.

So that makes the tall one Myles Andreyev, the leader of Laudrum's financiers, Molaro said internally. She picked up the cart handle and turned it to follow the three men back to the *Yuri.* *Odd*, she continued to speculate, *no mention of Mary, Ron or Bart. Do they even care about them?* She lifted the handle and began pulling the cart, following the three men.

Michael walked over to her and placed his hand on the cart's handle. "See if you can find out how Dr. Laudrum's doing. And if you can, see if you can get him away from those men. We can protect him from those men, if he'll let us."

"Are you really going to send the Vanerans back to work for those monsters?"

"Not a chance! We can always hide them in the underground shelter. Now you'd better catch up before they start wondering what we're plotting."

Chapter Thirty-One

"Okay, we're here." Molaro dropped the handle of the cart at the feet of the three men she had followed to their space ship. The door on the side of it opened and she saw Dr. Laudrum begin climbing down the ladder, probably to see what was going on. "Where do you want me to dump these?"

"There's a bin around the side of that fin." Andreyev pointed past the right side of the ladder Dr. Laudrum had just stepped off of. "You can stack them in there."

"What's going on here?" Dr. Laudrum walked up and planted himself in front of Andreyev. "Why have you dragged a member of Harrod's party to our campsite?"

"We's out of food." Dr. Laudrum had to turn to look into the face of Belinsky as he spoke. "She's just supplin' us until they return our workforce in the morning. Get a few of those potato thingees started, like a good girl." He made a grab for her ass as she drug the cart past him.

Without dropping the handle, she shifted her weight to her right foot, swept out her left one and grabbed Belinsky by his wrist before he hit the ground. She gave it a little squeeze.

The Italian reached behind his back and smoothly pulled his hand-sized pistol from his rear pocket and pointed it at Molaro. "Let him go!" With a two-handed grip, he squared the automatic handgun on the Wassarran's chest.

From a yard away, Molaro was convinced he couldn't miss. She released the short Russian's wrist and he stumbled to the ground.

"Damn her." He rubbed his right wrist as he got to his feet, then formed that hand into a fist and pulled back to strike her. He hesitated, looking her up and down, with his hand tracking where he meant to strike, when Andreyev stepped behind him and grabbed his cocked fist.

"She can't really fix supper if you knock her out, Belinsky ."

"She nearly broke my wrist." He pushed his wrist into the other Russian's face.

"From what I've heard about her people, you should consider yourself lucky. When riled, they can snap human bones without a thought." He slapped the wrist out of his face. "Now get back up to the observation deck and keep an eye on the others. And Dortello, put that thing away."

"I really do appreciate this gift," Dr. Laudrum had come around the others and took the other side of the cart's handle. "I can handle this from here."

"I'm to return with the cart, Dr. Laudrum. So the quicker we can get it unloaded, the sooner I'll be out of your hair." She watched Belinsky head towards the ladder, but when she turned her head away and then back, he wasn't climbing it into the *Yuri*. *Where do they keep their observation deck*? she thought to herself. "So if can show me where these go?"

It only took the two of them a few minutes to transfer the hundred six-inch root sections into the plastic bin. "I haven't seen Bart and my students in a couple of days. Have you seen any other humans recently?" he asked her as they were finishing and making sure the others weren't around.

"Mary Davis and Ron McNamara are your students?" As he nodded, she continued, "They're staying with us. They don't seem to like your financial backers. Are you doing okay here?"

"They need me. Whenever we can get into that cylinder, they're going to need my expertise to evaluate the find and prepare it for return to Earth without losing all its value."

"I'm sure Michael would welcome you, if you ever need a bolt hole. Mr. Higgins has told us everything about those three guys."

* * *

About halfway back, just out of unaided human sight, Mary stuck her head out of the trees and called Molaro over. "Belinsky give you any trouble?" she asked when Molaro pulled the cart up to the side of the trees.

"He made a stupid play. But I kept my temper, it would have been so easy to release my protection rage, but he will live to see another day. Did you know they had guns? I thought I saw the short Russian fingering something in his pocket back at camp. But that Italian guy actually pulled one on me."

"Well, the short one's the monster that raped me on the way here."

"And no one did anything about it?" Molaro had heard that human youth didn't have the survival strength surge that her species had learned to control.

"I only told Ron after the incident, but just recently we told Mr. Higgins. That was just before we came to live with you guys." She looked down at the underbrush collecting as she fidgeted with her feet. "What could anyone do while the seven of us were cooped up in that ship?"

"Well, let's..." Something behind Molaro made a noise she knew was too faint for Mary to hear. "Go deeper. Someone's coming." She pushed Mary away from the clearing. She watched as Mary made her way behind a tree several away from where Molaro was waiting.

She spotted Belinsky approaching and stared directly at him. When she saw the recognition in his eyes that she had spotted him, he stopped trying to move quietly. "Ah, you're waiting for me," he said as he brushed the last limb away that obscured his view of her.

She folded her arms across her chest. "What do you want, Belinsky?"

"I know you were interested. All we needed was a little alone time." He stopped within arm's reach of her. Running his tongue over his lips and rubbing his left hand up and down his leg.

"Interested in what?" She stood rock steady in front of the man who was a good three feet shorter than she was, looking down on him. *If only I had ice vision like in the comics*, she thought to herself, *this guy would be a popsicle right now*.

"Playing around." He reached up his left hand to grab her left breast and slide his right hand into his pocket.

She swatted his hand away, hard enough that his foot moved slightly. "Leave now. Try and touch me again... Well, I won't be responsible for what happens to you."

"When I say strip," his hand emerged from his pocket holding a gun about the same size as the one Dortello had held. "Now strip!"

She swatted the gun hand with enough force that the gun flew from Belinsky's hand, he lost his footing and the gun went off.

Mary screamed from behind the tree where she had been hiding, and dropped to her knees.

Molaro could see blood beginning to seep from Mary's shoulder. She rounded back on her attacker. He had dropped to his knees and was scrambling through the forest debris to find his gun. She grabbed him by his throat with her right hand and drove his head into the trunk of the tree directly behind him. She began to get control of herself after she had smashed his head against the tree twice more.

When she let go, he fell to the ground, unmoving, and there were skull fragments and blood dripping from her hand.

As her head cleared of the rage chemicals, she looked over and saw Mary kneeling on the ground, a hand on her shoulder and a look of terror on her face.

"Mary, let me look at that," Molaro said as she dropped to her knees to tend her friend. She pulled the other woman's hand away, the blood wasn't spurting so she placed Mary's hand back over the wound. She tore a couple of cloth strips off her shirt and folded one to place over the wound and tied it in place with the other.

Mary was still staring at Belinsky's body. "Is, is he dead?" she stammered out. Then she shifted her gaze up at Molaro before Molaro could answer. "Did you kill him?"

"I've been trying real hard since entering their campsite to keep my Youth Protective Rage under control. When I saw you were shot, gun or no gun, that guy didn't have a chance. When I finally got things under control, he was already dead."

"Protective Rage?"

"Until about age thirty," Molaro went over to check Belinsky out, "all Wassarrans have a gland that secretes a special series of hormones. The gland is tied to our flight/fight trigger. If we feel the need for protection, it releases chemicals into our bodies to speed up our actions and increase the strength we do things at. Our minds blank out and our bodies get us out of whatever dangerous situation. It's kept the date-rape problem you have on Earth from being a factor in our growing up. Our society has developed so that we usually don't have anything to trigger the reflex these days. But when I thought you'd been hurt, I lost control."

"I don't think I like thinking about it, but I can't bring myself to grieve for the guy." She looked into her friend's face. "Does that make me an insensitive person?"

"This was the first time I've ever experienced the Rage," Molaro said as she got off her knees. She reached down a few feet away from Belinsky's body and picked up his gun, buried under the forest debris but still hot enough from the discharge for her to see in the infrared spectrum. "Both of us are going to have to come to grips with this over the next few days."

"So what do we so until then?'

"Load this guy's body into the cart and tell everyone what happened." She slid the gun into her pocket and walked over to help Mary up. "Things are going to be interesting from here on."

Chapter Thirty-Two

"LeRena Harrod, please report to the communication center." The PA above her head blared out the announcement as she was writing up the tag for the fifty-seventh stick-like object from the Torvonian craft. So deep was she thinking about her husband and the rest of his team that she almost ran the pen through the 'Where found:' section of the tag she had already completed.

She got up from her chair, started walking to the hatch, adding, "I guess you're on your own for a while, Daisy."

"I hope it's Michael," the elderly paleontologist said as LeRena was leaving the room.

Their research ship was round and the control centers were in the center of that circle, the research labs and quarters in the outer hub. LeRena had to go three feet down the corridor separating the two areas before coming to a hatch that would take her into the central hub.

Straight in front of her was the hallway that led to the ship's control room. But she hadn't been summoned there, so we followed the outer edge of the control room, passed the sensor alcove and the navigational alcove until she got to what they were calling the communications room, even though it was just an alcove also.

"Here I am, Solidad." She walked into the room and up to its seated occupant. "I sure hope it's word from Michael," she added as she saw Martin turning to greet her.

"No," the radioman said. "But Captain Young wants to talk with you about him." After the invasion by the Wassarran navy, RoTano Solidad had resigned from the Wassarran navy and stayed on Ranklin. With his electronics specialization, he was immediately hired by the Harmony Research Center, and volunteered to go on this mission to keep the equipment he installed over the last year intact. "Unless a scientist has actually built something, they abuse the hell out of it," he kept telling people back on Ranklin when they would ask him why he was going along.

"She's here now." Solidad said into his mouth piece as he handed a small earpiece up to LeRena.

"...survey and heading back to your position," the Captain of the *Resolute* was saying as she got her earpiece in. "We can either be back at your location before the day is out or head directly into the system, looking for your team as we begin our planetary mapping phase."

"I'd really like to go along," LeRena replied, "but I don't want to slow your search down. It's been almost two months since we've heard from them."

"Con..., Captain Young, do you have a shuttle you could spare to pick Mrs. Harrod up while you proceed into the system?" LeRena looked over to see the concern Martin's face expressed. "Just a thought," he added after closing his mike.

"I think that can be arranged. We're not using our interstellar drive, our shuttles can catch up with us. We'll have one over to you in," there was a pause, "three hours. Can you be ready by then?"

"Yes, Connie. Thank you"

Chapter Thirty-Three

Cowloom and Michael were wiring up the ten-foot loop of the final "D" in their "DO NOT LAND" trench. Currently it read "DO NOT LAN" but after they powered the system down and tied in the last letter, they were hoping it would be enough of a warning in case someone tried to come to their rescue.

Michael bent over the trench and wound together the last wire. "That's it, power the system down and let's get this tied in."

Cowloom walked over to the solar cell generator and depressed the virtual shut-off button, then pulled the connector out of the panels as a final lock-out safety procedure. "Ready on this end," he called over to Michael.

Michael rolled over the five feet to get to the line running into their last letter, wired the two lines together and wrapped it with tape. They wanted bare wires in the letter trenches, not between them. He stood up and away from the electrical wires. "Done. Fire it up."

Cowloom reattached the wire to the panel and activated the circuit. There was a spark from the newly installed letter, but it quickly settled down. He scanned the rest of the letters to make sure everything was 'A-okay'.

Something was moving in the first "D" trench. A small hand reached up and grabbed the upper edge. "Michael, over here." Cowloom ran over to the trench and looked down at several Vanerans trying to climb out of the trench. "Kill the power. Some of the Vanerans fell into the trench over here."

Michael was over to the power station in seconds and deactivating the system, but Cowloom wasn't waiting. He reached down and took the hand of the closest alien and began pulling it up. He quickly looked him over to make sure it was okay. He noticed some of its digits were missing on all its limbs. But he didn't stop, he needed to get the rest of them out before they were electrocuted.

Michael arrived and began helping pull the Vanerans out of the trench. But as the two men were working their way down the letter, the Vanarans were hopping back into the trench and laying across the wires.

The Vaneran Cowloom had just pulled out, brushed against his leg as it went back into the ditch. "What?" Cowloom turned to see all the creatures he had rescued were now back in the trench laying on top of the non-active electrical system. He finished pulling the one he currently had a grip on and looked back where it had been. "Michael, the colonies of microbes are gone." He pointed at the empty spot where the creature he was holding had been.

It squirmed, so he set it down, and it immediately climbed back into the trench and over the wires. "There's something going on here," Michael said as he watched what the creatures were doing. "Justin, Cemper, Ba..., anyone else. Come quick," he shouted almost too quickly. He almost gave away the fact that the three members of Laudrum's expedition were hiding amongst them.

As the three humans and single Wassarran came jogging around the Escape pod, Michael waved them over and pointed into the trench. "What's with those guys and electricity?"

"Who are those guys anyway?" Justin stared down into the trench and scratched the top of his head. "The last I saw our friends, all forty of them were inside the Torvon shelter, still hiding from Laudrum's financiers."

"If the ones from the village are down there," Cowloom speculated, "who are those guys? And what happened to their extremities?"

"Uh, guys," Bart turned from the trench to look at the others. "Why have they started looking our way? Do they want something?"

"Michael turn the power back on." As Michael walked over to the solar panels, Cowloom continued, "After we pulled them out, they jumped back in and hugged the power lines."

"Like they enjoy the electricity," Cemper added.

"Like they consume the electricity," Justin amended. "Look around the trench, the white powder we've been associating with the microbes are gone." He turned and looked into the adjoining trench. "Over here, the small mounds we saw under the shuttle are merging into large ones."

"Michael, how are you coming with that electricity?"

"I'll have it on in a moment. There, it should be flowing again."

The creatures in the first trench laid back down and a smile formed in their central trunk where no mouth had been before. Justin turned back to the second trench and the larger mounds were starting to take on the shape of the Vaneran creatures.

"Little help," came a call from the other side of the escape pod.

Michael looked over to where the shout had come from and pointed. "Cemper, see what Molaro wants." He turned back to the problem in the trenches. "So what's going on in there? It looks like we're growing more Vanerans?"

"Hey, you guys, get over here," Cemper yelled back to the warning sign. "We've got a problem."

"Justin, keep an eye on our friends here, while I see what Cemper wants." Cowloom was already walking around the converging Vanerans that were headed for the electrified trench as Michael worked to catch up with him.

They came around the Torvon capsule and found Cemper standing next to one of the Vaneran carts with a body dripping blood inside it. Mary was sitting on one of their box stools and Molaro was returning from the shuttle carrying a medical kit. They sprinted the last several feet and looked down at the remains of one of Dr. Laudrum's crew.

Michael knelt down and looked under the cart at the crater that had been the back of the man's head. "What happened?"

Cowloom dropped the man's wrist that he had grabbed to check for a pulse. "Well, he's dead."

Molaro cut away Mary's shirt from her left shoulder and began applying a gauge bandage to either side of her puncture wounds to slow down the bleeding. She had handed the kit off to Cemper as she applied pressure to both sides. Cemper pulled the skin sealant from the kit and prepped the bottle to spray shut the two holes. He motioned to Molaro when he was ready, and she pulled her hand away from the front wound while he coated the area with twice the recommended amount of adhesive plastic. After he pulled the bottle away, he touched the area to make sure the sealant was drying. Then they repeated the procedure on her back side.

"That man followed me after I dropped off the food you gave those slavers."

"Michael had stood up to look at Mary's condition. He turned to Molaro after her statement. "And so you bashed his brains out?"

Mary, who had been wincing at the activity on her shoulder, looked up at him. "No, that bastard tried to rape Molaro the way he raped me. But even then, she didn't give him what he deserved, she drove him into one of the trees after he pulled this gun," she tossed the weapon Molaro had retrieved at Michael's feet, "and shot me."

Molaro looked Cemper in his eyes. "It was The Rage. I heard the shot, saw Mary bleeding and the next thing I knew, I had this Belinsky guy up against a tree, and he wasn't even squirming."

He closed the distance between them and wrapped his arms around Molaro and stroked her back. After a moment he pushed her away to look her over, he could see tears running from her eyes. "How are you feeling?"

"Tired, guilty, embarrassed!"

He pulled her back into an embrace.

"Could someone please tell me what's going on?" Bart finally caught up with the group, having left Ron to assist Justin.

Cowloom dropped his hand on the engineer's shoulder and pulled him around to look at him. "It's part of our heritage, a part we have almost forgotten about. It's a survival mechanism we are still out growing, but something that has kept personal crime to a minimum on Wassara. If something threatens the life or safety of a young Wassarran, their fight reflex is amplified neurochemically. "

Michael kept looking down at Belinsky 's body. "LeRena said it was something you guys grew out of, and I shouldn't have to worry about it."

"At her age, no. But Molaro is ten years younger than your wife. This is actually the first time I've heard about an incident in my lifetime. Molaro will be alright, given time. But she'll need us to give her that time."

"Meaning we have to deal with this dirt bag's body?" Bart asked.

"Shouldn't we take it back to his friends," Cemper asked, still comforting Molaro.

"I don't think whoever did would survive those two," Bart added.

"Maybe it's time we bring Dr. Laudrum here for a real talk," Cowloom suggested.

"I'd get that body on the other side of the shuttle if I were you. They've been watching this campsite from the upper window of the *Yuri* since you landed."

"You guys do that," Michael said quietly. "I'll go over and invite Dr. Laudrum to join us."

Chapter Thirty-Four

"Dortello, where is that *mudak* Belinsky ?" Andreyev leaned over the ladder leading through their space ship. "I ordered him to stand watch on the other camp," he yelled down as Dortello stuck his head out of their cabin.

"I have no idea," the Italian hollered back. "I suppose you need me up there?"

"And make it quick, before I bust something we need."

As Dortello climbed the two floors up to the flight deck, Andreyev grabbed the binoculars off the chair they were hanging on and stared out the porthole facing the other camp. He could make out everyone moving behind the shuttle. "Out of my damn sight." As he heard Dortello stepping onto the upper deck he added, "Or so they think." He turned and faced his comrade, "Go over to the Harrod campsite, hide in the forest, and see what they are working on." He turned back to the window and added, "They are trying to hide something. Now hurry, report to me as fast as you can run."

He heard the lower hatch slam shut and watched through the forward window as Dortello made his way over to the trees and disappeared from sight. Then he returned to the porthole facing Harrod's camp and noticed the main man himself walking over to the *Yuri*. He pulled his glasses down to look closer to the ship and saw the professor walking out to greet him. "Don't start making friends, Doctor!"

* * *

"Dr. Laudrum," Michael reached out his hand to the leader of the rival party.

When he got to within three feet of Michael, Laudrum stopped and folded his arms in front of him. "What do you want?"

Michael dropped his outstretched arm. "Something has happened I think you should have a look at."

"Have you done something to **my** artifact?" He leaned slightly closer to Michael.

"This has nothing to do with the escape pod."

"Escape Pod? How do you know what it is if you haven't been playing with it?"

"Because the *USS Resolute* discovered one in the debris field surrounding this system months ago. I really must ask you to come back to my camp and look at something."

"I can't right now. All my assistants are off foraging, and I can't leave the *Yuri* unattended."

"Your people are with us. This is very important." He looked up at the top of the V2 style rocket mere yards behind the scientist. He could just make out the upper porthole but not if someone was looking out of it. "But I can't say anything here. Please, come back with me."

"Oh, very well. It will give me a chance to convince Bart, Ron and Mary to come back, if they are really there." He motioned Michael to head out and fell into step next to him as the younger man turned around.

* * *

"What the hell is he up to?" Andreyev commented as he watched the two men walk away. He was going to have to hurry to catch Dortello and find a hiding place to find out.

* * *

"Dr. Laudrum, I think I may have an idea on how to get us off this planet," Michael said about half way back to his shuttle. "But it's going to require your team's help."

"And how do you propose to do that? With no kinetic electricity, we can't even generate a spark to ignite the fuel we have left in our ships."

"Our ships." Michael looked over at the man walking next to him. The ground was flat enough to allow him to take his eyes away from his feet. "But not the Torvan..."

"Ranklinite!"

"Just stay with me here. They used a different power grid than we do and it's not affected by the microbes living on this planet."

"And without invading my find, you know this how?"

As they were getting close to the UEF shuttle, Michael pointed to an area of ground in front of it. "We discovered the campsite the Torvons—okay, Ranklinites—built when they landed here. Their power systems are still working."

"Well, if you can get power, what are you still doing here?"

"If we tried tapping into the power systems of the... stone builders, as soon as the electricity started flowing through our systems the microbes would just consume it. And we can't retro-fit our shuttle to their liquid electrical system. No, we have to use one of their ships. And fortunately we have one.

"Okay, it may only be a short range craft, but I suspect the *Resolute* is up there looking for us now. I'm just hoping they've seen our message about landing and are waiting for us to do something."

As they reached the front end of the shuttle, Laudrum turned to go to the open hatch leading underground. "Sir," Michael caught him by his elbow, "we have more important business over here."

As Laudrum turned to his left, he saw Bart waving to him and pointing down at a body lying on a mattress. A darkening blood stain was under his head. Laudrum reached down and pulled up the blanket. It was Belinsky .

"You've killed one of them!"

Chapter Thirty-Five

"Okay, here's the problem." Michael placed his hands on Laudrum's shoulders and turned him away from the body to look at him. "Molaro did this in self-defense. Your man there was about to rape her."

"He's not MY MAN." Laudrum pushed away from Michael and took a step back. "None of those three belong on an archeological expedition. And who is this Molaro anyway, where is she? Is she one of your Wassarrans? Well, she should know better and respect human weaknesses."

"Like rape!" Bart came around from the other side of the escape pod. "Michael, I think we have a problem."

"That depends on Dr. Laudrum here."

"No, something much bigger. It's the Vanerans."

"So you've given the natives a name?"

"Reg, this is serious. Stop with your naming arrogance." Bart turned around to head back the way he had come. "They're getting bigger."

Michael started to follow him, but turned back to Laudrum for a second. "If you're still looking for your slaves, follow me."

The three men walked around to where the warning sign had been dug and electrified. "Watch out for that wire." Michael pointed to a bare wire sticking out through the dirt. "Cemper, get this covered up. Or insulated, if you can do so safely."

"Sorry, I missed that one. The microbes seem to be eating into the wires all over the place. I hope Dr. Carpenter and the others can see the trenches we dug," he said as he slid an insulative wrap under the exposed wires running to the lower letters. "I don't think we're going to get the glow-in-the-dark effect you were counting on."

As he looked over the series of trenches, Laudrum saw several of the small card-like creatures climbing out of one and into another. "Are they piling on top of each other?"

"We still haven't figured out what the creatures are trying to do, but the microbes that have been eating our electricity form into them once they achieve a critical mass of what-we-had-thought were dead organisms."

Cowloom walked around the "T" and over to Laudrum. "Apparently electricity, lightning in the usual case, triggers the start of their growth cycle. With enough matter, electricity triggers another growth cycle and you get the creatures from the village. The roots we have been sharing with them keep these advanced beings alive until some form of electricity provides them the means of another growth cycle. That's what we have going on here."

"And we don't know where it's leading to, Reg." Bart scanned the rigged circuit and walked over to one that popped a spark and threw a dirt clod off of it. "Cemper, there's another one."

Dr. Laudrum stood straight up but his body went slack and his eyes shut. "No animal life," he said quietly to himself. His eyes sprang open and his voice increased, "We could be witnessing the genesis of fauna on this planet. A whole new way of creating life."

"I know I've never seen anything like them," Cowloom injected. "Damn," he pointed over to the initial D trench.

A six foot cylinder about a yard in diameter was beginning to pull its way over the edge. Laudrum saw only four limbs where he had been expecting the usual six and its eyes and mouth had shifted to the upper third of its body. It rolled on the ground over to the next letter and fell into another creature with about the same proportions just not fully formed yet.

The two of them began to merge.

"I wonder what the end result's going to be?" Bart asked.

"Are we watching a birthing cycle or evolution in progress here?" Laudrum said as he walked around to watch the creatures in the O closer. There were two sets of them merging into each other. "It looks like they're going to tower over you Wassarrans when they're finished," he said as Michael walked up behind him.

"And it's going on in all nine letters." Michael drew his attention to all the other letters they had dug.

* * *

Dortello had found a blind he could hide behind upon reaching Harrod's campsite. He dropped to one knee, pulled a twig out from under that knee and bent forward to see what was going on. Laudrum had already dropped the sheet over whatever they had on their sled before he could get a look at it. But when Bart Higgins came around the cylinder, he dropped back into a seated position. "What the hell is he doing here?"

"It looks like you've found our missing servants." A hand dropped on Dortello's shoulder as he heard Andreyev's voice behind him. The large Russian dropped to his knees beside him behind the blind to watch. "What are they up to?"

"They showed Laudrum something under that sheet, but I got here too late to see what, and then they started gesturing about something on the other side of our cylinder."

"And now they're heading over there. If that sheet is what they came to get Laudrum about, I think we should have a look." Andreyev stood up and looked down at Dortello until he did the same. They quietly slipped around the sides of the branches that had been lashed together and worked their way around the few trees that separated them from the loosened soil of the clearing both spaceships had landed in. With no twigs to make noise as they walked, they jogged the hundred yards to the shuttle and the sled on the side of it.

Dortello grabbed a clean corner of the sheet and lifted it off the body, they could now see the impression of. Belinsky lay, close-eyed, on the sled.

"It's Belinsky ," he whispered up to Andreyev .

"BELINSKY !" Andreyev roared at the top of his lungs.

"So much for secrecy," Dortello said under his breath. He dropped the sheet, grabbed his comrade and tried pulling him back to the closest point of cover.

"They killed Belinsky and you want me to hide?" Andreyev shook off Dortello's hand, not moving an inch. "No, no, my friend. They must pay for this insult."

A male Wassarran, followed by Bart, quickly came around the cylinder. Andreyev pulled out his gun and put a slug in the Wassarran's leg, he screamed as he fell to the ground. Then Andreyev moved it until it was aimed directly at Bart's chest. "Who killed Belinsky ?" he parsed the words out. "Who is the first of you that is going to die?"

Bart froze, threw his hands into the air, looked down at his companion, then back to Andreyev . "He was trying to kill Mary."

"An American child! He was killed over a child!" Andreyev started to move his gun away from Bart. As the engineer started to relax, Dortello brought his around to cover the engineer. After a moment, Andreyev sprang his gun back into position. "That was why. I want to know who. Who killed him?"

Something smashed Andreyev in the side of his head hard enough to drive him into Dortello. Dortello had his finger on the trigger, but his bullet flew harmlessly into the air as the collision forced him to fall to the ground.

"I did, you bastard," said the female Wassarran currently standing on Dortello's gun wrist and picking up Andreyev ' pistol from where it had fallen. "And I suggest you behave, lest I lose control again."

Mary ran around the fallen men and pressed her hands against the male Wassarran's bleeding leg. "Med kit," she hollered.

The rest of the men came running around the stone cylinder with Michael bounding into the open hatch of the shuttle. He was back in an instant with the requested med kit. Mary was already cutting off the damaged pant leg with a knife she had been handed. Michael opened up the kit and handed her a gauge bandage.

"There's no exit wound," she said, still staring at the wounded leg after having run her hand around the back side. "We have to get him stabilized, then find a way to dig it out. Sorry, Cemper, I don't know if human pain-killers work on you guys."

"Thanks, Molaro," a male human said as the Wassarran still standing on Dortello's wrist handed him Andreyev ’ gun. "Cowloom, you grab the other guy's."

From behind Dortello, the human and Wassarran had come around the cylinder. As the Wassarran reached down to extract the pistol Dortello had a death grip on, Molaro applied more pressure on his wrist until his hand spread away from his weapon.

"Now, if you guys would like to get up?" the human training Andreyev ' gun on them said. "We can try and find someplace safe for you."

* * *

After they cabled the two financiers to a tree with some of the excess electrical wire they had extracted from the shuttle, and Mary had given Cemper some intramuscular pain medication that was starting to have some effect, they lifted Cemper onto Justin's workbench that he had rapidly cleared off.

"Okay, who's got the best shot at getting this out?" Michael asked as they stepped away from Cemper on the table.

Everyone just looked at each other. None of their specialties were anywhere close to medicine.

"Okay, we've got to get this thing out," Michael continued. "I'm in charge."

"But at least I've had some biology," Justin finally piped up. "I'll give it a try."

"Now that's irony for you," Cemper laughed from his bed. "I'm the one Dr. Layton had field trained." He broke into a fit of giggling. Molaro and Mary tried to hold him down. "For medic duty, that is."

"Well, add that side-effect to your pain-killers, extreme giddiness," Molaro mentioned over Camper's head while holding his shoulders against the flat of the table.

They collected what tweezers and needle-nosed pliers they could find and took them into the shelter to prepare on the cook surface down there. "Hey, grab a couple of test tube clamps and sterilize them also." Justin asked as he laid out the adhesive closures and spray-on skin that was pre-sterilized in the med kit.

"I'm a little bigger that a test tube, Justie." Molaro pushed her friend back down on the table as he laughed at his joke.

"But hardly as quiet." Justin looked over to watch Cowloom scramble down the ladder. "I hope they hurry, I don't know how long we can keep Cemper from bleeding out."

178

Michael felt this was a good time to pitch his idea to Dr. Laudrum, and get his permission to open the escape pod. He tapped him on his arm and motioned that they move over to the front of the cylinder. "I acknowledge the fact that this is your find, but working together, I think we can all use it to get off this planet."

"Electricity doesn't work down here." Laudrum reached up and ran his hand gently over the nose of the cylinder. "We have fuel. I'll bet you do, too. But without a spark, it's useless."

Michael looked over to see Cowloom and Mary emerging from the underground shelter. "Let me show you something." He walked over to the opening and began climbing down.

At the bottom, he helped Dr. Laudrum get his footing on the Torvon floor, though Laudrum brushed away any assistance.

"Cozy little place you have down here." He looked all around and walked over to the kitchen area and opened one of the cabinets.

"So there's enough light for you to see those pots, then?" Michael swung one of the dining chairs around and sat down, leaning the back of the chair into the table.

"Of course there is. It's daylight."

"Down here?"

Laudrum froze, holding a cup he had fished out of the water basin. He looked around the room, then back at Michael. "Where's the light coming from?"

"Somehow the Torvons have developed the technology to generate light from their stone creations. But only if they're electrified." He walked over to the ladder they had come down on and pressed a button on the wall.

The room went dark.

"Hey," about three people yelled.

"Sorry," Michael said as he pressed the button again to bring the lights back up. " It's even got a timer."

"But how are they getting power to their circuitry? I thought those microbes ate all electrical power."

"They don't conduct electricity like we do. They have a liquid that conducts their power. I'm guessing the microbes just can't digest it. They had access. The native creatures lived down here with the Torvons until they died. It's how they got all the cooking equipment they were using in their village. And since there were no bodies down here when we discovered this, it had to be the Vanerans who'd—hell, I don't know what rituals they have, but they did something with the bodies."

"Okay, you've got power down here. How does that make it possible for us to escape?" Laudrum thought for a moment then looked in the direction of the cylinder. "No."

"Yes."

"If that thing is the vessel they arrived in and it could still be powered up, why didn't they take off again?"

"And go where? They didn't have a ship to go back to."

"That thing is almost half the size of the *Yuri*, they should have been able to return home."

"We found a piece of their stone ship in the asteroid field surrounding this system. Their ships have to be as large as any of the UEF's battle cruisers. No, they had nowhere to go."

"And we do?" Laudrum had returned the cup to the water it had been soaking in and walked over to one of the other dining chairs to sit down.

"Until we landed, I was in regular contact with my wife." He held up a finger to hold Laudrum's response. "The time lag between responses was getting greater, but I'm sure that after this long, she'd be mobilizing a rescue mission to come get us." He lifted a second finger to join it. "So much so that we have been building a warning they can see from orbit: 'Don't Land'."

"So if we can get that thing up to orbit, you think there'll be someone waiting for us."

"And since we'll be using this thing, you'll still have your find."

"But how do you know it's an escape pod?"

"The *Resolute* found one in the asteroid field. It's why they called us out here. Dr. Pashine was learning its controls when we took this shuttle to try and find any other pods or Torvons who had escaped whatever befell their ship."

"You opened it?"

"They have an electric lock on the outside of the front hatch. We used the power frequency we learned worked from our digs on Ranklin and unsealed it. We were then able to seal and unseal it from the control systems it had on the inside."

"But we can't use electricity on this planet. Or can you run a cable from this habitat to the cylinder?"

"Their systems don't use cables. They literally have pipes running the power fluid from one system to another." Michael patted the breast pocket of the shirt he was wearing. He could feel the Torvon writing stylus he had been carrying since he had picked it up in the Torvon ship's nose section. *It might have power*, he said to himself. "I just might have an idea." He pulled the device out and held it for Laudrum to see. "They used this to record messages on sheets of their stone compound. It just might be able to transfer power over to that escape pod."

"How does their stuff keep working after a hundred years?"

"How was it working after over a thousand back on Ranklin? They got good tech!"

"Then let's get that pod opened and get off this rock."

Chapter Thirty-Six

"Okay, hold that closed while I apply these strips." As Michael and Laudrum emerged from the shelter, they heard Justin instructing Molaro. "Now, get your hand away while I seal that wound with this stuff." He held up the can of synthetic skin and started spraying over the closure tape he had just applied to Cemper. The tape would dissolve in a couple of hours, and the synthetic skin patch would pop off a couple of days later.

"How is he?" Michael stayed a few feet behind the surgical area to keep from contaminating it.

"He fell asleep when I pried open the wound." Justin said as he set the skin canister beside Cemper's head. "We got lucky. Those guys were using space-ship loads, unlike what we'd found in Belinsky's gun. The plastic slug wasn't deep and was still intact. It even crimped a bit when I grabbed it with the pliers." Justin motioned with his head to the bloody tools below Cemper's foot. He picked up the slug from the table and spun around to hand it to Michael. "Yeah, we got lucky," he said, dropping it into Michael's hand.

Justin pulled the gloves off his hands, walked over to the fire pit and dropped them in the hot ashes from last night's fire. Molaro cleaned off the table and discarded the soiled medical items there also. The unused tape and synthetic spray she replaced in the med kit before pulling off her less bloody gloves and tossing them in the fire pit also.

"You guys take care of Cemper until he's coherent again and keep an eye on our friends over there." He pointed to Andreyev and Dortello, still tied to the tree. "Doctor, let's go see if we can get your artifact opened."

Justin and Molaro went over to a basin they had set up next to the water trough, dipped their hands into the water and scrubbed them clean. Michael and Laudrum walked to the front of the pod.

"Hey, Bart, Cowloom, could you guys join us over here? We're going to try and open this thing." He ran his hand over the section of the hatch where they had attached the wire back on the shuttle. He found the hole they had used, pulled out the pen and stuck it into the hole.

Nothing happened.

Cowloom reached over and tried pulling. The hatch didn't budge.

"Do you have to activate it?" Bart asked. "There's a button on the top, see what happens when you push it."

Michael reached up to where the pen was sticking in the hatch and pressed the button on top of it.

For a second, they heard something happening inside the cylinder. Michael pressed it again and the sound grew louder, something was happening inside. While it lasted three times as long as the first press, it still died away. A third press got a longer and louder response, but it still did not open.

"Let me try something." Bart walked up to the hatch and pressed the button three times in rapid succession.

The sound became louder and more intense until finally, air hissed out from inside the cylinder, and the hatch opened an inch. Cowloom grabbed the edge and pulled it further until it swung ninety degrees from its mountings.

"After a hundred years," Laudrum said.

"They have good tech," Michael added as he stared into the pod, already beginning to light up.

"Cowloom, we need to know the status of this thing. How much did you learn from Lieutenant Attah?" Michael asked.

"We were both leaning on Raj and his translations, so some." He pulled himself into the pod and walked up to the control panel.

"At least he knows where the controls are," Bart said, following him in. "That's a start."

Michael climbed in after Laudrum did. Laudrum went all the way to the back and looked over the seating arrangement for the pod. He pressed the seat cushions that, despite having to protect the rider from accelerative forces, looked as if they were made of stone.

"Softer than you expected, aren't they?" Michael placed his hand on the back of the pod, staying with the archeologist so they'd be out of the way of the two men working out the controls.

"Stone that gives?"

He sat down on the seat across from Laudrum. "We found the same thing on the one in the *Resolute's* hanger." Then he moved his finger to his lips and pointed at Cowloom and Bart.

"From the little Raj taught me, a few symbols." Cowloom stared down at the panel just below his chest. "This dial," he pointed at one just below a linear crystal track, "is currently pointing to a word I think means "Off". It follows around to several more that I know are numbers but not ones Raj taught me. And that word on the far right, I don't know what it is, but it's not "On"."

Bart pulled his ball cap off his balding head and scratched it for a moment while standing back to get a good view of the board. He replaced it and added, "If that's Off," he pointed to the left side of the dial, "and those are numbers," he ran his finger over those symbols to the final one, "and you're sure that's not On, then my guess would be their concept of "Full"."

"I don't see an indicator underneath. That crystal track," Cowloom point to the one above the dial again, "must acknowledge how much power they're using?"

"That'd be my guess. And since it's currently off and we have lights in here, it's not internal power." Bart moved slightly to his right and looked over all the other switches in front of him. "Know any of these other symbols?"

The Wassarran looked up and down the board. Then he reached out and pointed to one on the far side of the board from the dial. "That one looks like "Go" or "Power Up", I just know it was associated with starting some of the play-back devices we found on Ranklin." He turned his head towards Bart. "Devices that still worked after over a thousand years!"

"There's hope for this thing yet. I wouldn't give the *Yuri* another year, even if we still had electricity." He tilted his head to look at the top of the board. "Those things look like monitor screens?" He reached up to point at the button under each of the four lined together. "Any clue what that says?"

"No, but there's one way to find out." Cowloom looked from Bart over to Michael, both men nodded in agreement. He pressed the button under the rearmost screen. A blue haze filled the screen, then gray, then white lines began to appear until finally a rear view of the pod sketched itself on the screen. "The camera for this thing must be on top, just behind the ring holding the four engines out back. You can make out the back end of the pod and part of one of the engines. The rest are angled just below where we can see them."

Michael motioned Laudrum to have a look, and the two men got up to stand behind Cowloom. "What's the peg next to the button do?" Michael asked.

Cowloom touched it. It moved under his finger. The view from the rear shifted also. Cowloom started moving the peg left and right, the monitor followed his movements. "Joystick," he turned to Bart and said.

"I need to go out and have a look at those engines. See if they have enough thrust to get us off a planet." He started for the entrance.

"They were space worthy a hundred years ago?" Michael queried.

"As an escape craft. From a vehicle already in space. We've got a massive gravity well to overcome." He jumped down from the hatch and walked around the pod.

"See what you guys can make out of this while we're gone," Michael said as he jumped out to follow Bart. He rounded the hatch door and looked over the field of growing Vanerans as he walked to the back of the pod. One of the large creatures began to pull itself from the furthest letter. "The thing's going to be over twelve feet tall," Michael commented to no one. "It's beginning to look like Molaro.

He bent down as he came up to their solar cells and switched off the unit. "No point in running this if we aren't creating a warning beacon."

Before he could get a step away from the device, the creatures in the trenches began to howl in pain. The creature that had pulled itself up fell into several smaller pieces back into the trench.

Ron ran back over to the solar array, getting there as Michael bent back over to switch it back on. "They're dependant on continuous electricity at this point," he said. "It appears once they achieve the state we found them in, they need a continuous charge to keep evolving. Jolts, like they would get from lightning strikes, just aren't enough."

"I know it's free electricity, but it's hard to overcome the training to switch power off whenever you aren't using it. I guess you'd better stay here, in case someone as stupid as me comes along."

"What the hell's that noise?" Bart said as he came back from behind the pod. "Is somebody dying?"

The howling was beginning to die down as power flowed again through their wires. "We just learned why there can't be any of these larger Vanerans around, that's all. Shall we have a look at these engines?" Michael grabbed the engineer around his shoulder and turned him back to the rear of the capsule.

"It's as I thought," he pointed to each of the four bell-shaped nozzles at the base of the pod, two of which were half buried in the ground. "These guys are way too small to generate the thrust needed to get off this planet. They're less than a fifth the size of the ones on the *Yuri*."

"Can we pump more juice through them?"

"Unless your Ranklinites, er, Torvons, were wizards, these nozzles won't hold the flow. This thing was built to work in space. Launched from a ship already out of a gravity well, not escape one itself. At least we've got power again."

"But we can't use that power to get either of our ships into orbit nor can any rescue mission come and get us. Unless we find some way to get to orbit, we're stuck here."

Bart swept his hand over the pod. "We don't even know if this thing has any fuel. Or even what kind of fuel it uses."

"Oh, it's got fuel." Laudrum came walking around the left side of the pod. "Your Wassarran sent me back here to tell you guys that it looks like this thing's tanks are over half full, or just under half. He said he wasn't sure about the calibration of the readout dial."

"So we can fire these engines, but they won't get us to space," Michael said. "And we have two ships that could get to space, but we can't fire their engines."

"Mighty perplexing problem," Bart added.

"What if we used this capsule's power to ignite the *Yuri's* engines? We've still got enough fuel to reach orbit."

"The systems are incompatible," Michael said as he dropped to a sitting position and leaned against one of the capsule's engines. "They used a fluidic system and we use a wire system. Otherwise, I'd have rerouted the solar arrays powering the shelter and used our gravitic drives to get off this planet."

"Bart, didn't they use strap-on rockets in Earth's early space program?"

"Yeah, sometime around the mid-twenty-first century. So?" The engineer stepped back and started walking in a slow circle. "Wait a minute. We could remove the engines and fuel from the Yuri, weld them onto this thing and ignite those engines with the exhaust flames of this one. Wait a minute," he stopped moving. "We've got no welding equipment, no way to strap them on that will hold during a launch."

"I might have the answer to that." Justin came over from his operating theater. "Michael, we found a large supply of the powder the Torvons use to build their stone implements. We could weld things onto the side of the capsule with stone."

"But will the stone stand up to the pressures of launch?"

"It's what this thing's made out of." Justin patted the side of the capsule.

Chapter Thirty-Seven

"I bought this ship. It is mine. You do not have the right to tear it apart." A bound Myles Andreyev stood in front of the *Yuri*. Dortello inched as far away from him as he could but the cord connecting their two sets of wrists to the line running to the female Wassarran would only let him get a yard away.

"You want to stay on this planet, that's fine by me." Michael stepped up to within an inch of Andreyev's nose. "But we don't. And as leader of your expedition, neither does Dr. Laudrum. He's authorized the dismantling of this ship and the use of her engines to boost the Torvon escape pod off this planet. You can help and come along, or remain behind. The choice is yours, but either way, you're our prisoner until we leave."

"What do you want me to do?" Dortello asked.

"Help Mr. Higgins with the rigging to lower the ship on its side." Ron walked over to him and untied his hands, releasing him from Andreyev. "Come with me." The two men walked over to where Bart was engineering a tower to drop the *Yuri* on its side.

They had spent the previous day cannibalizing the UEF shuttle for all the metal framing materials they could find. It wasn't an easy job, Ron had counted seventy-six times that someone had cussed about the fact they didn't have any power tools to work with. But they extracted enough framing material from the hull to build a tower almost as tall as the *Yuri*.

The plan was to attach a series of lines about three-fourths of the way up the *Yuri's* hull, pull it a few inches off the ground, then gently let the nose fall and control it until the ship was sitting on its side. They had arranged for the metal sheeting of the shuttle's hull to form a sled and using the stone wheels they had removed from the Vaneran's carts, bring the *Yuri* back to the shuttle for dismantling. It was a good thing the newly born Vanerans had recognized the humans as their friends—except for Andreyev and

Dortello—and were going to help them pull the ship the mile separating the two camps.

"What's it going to be, Andreyev? Are you going to help or get tied back on that tree?"

"I'll not help the murderers of Belinsky !"

"Molaro, tie the bastard back up."

Ron watched as she led—yanked, really—the Russian over to the nearby line of trees. She pushed him to the ground, wrapped the first loop around the tree across his neck and wound the rest of the line around him and the tree. Then she knotted it on the far side of that tree and started back to Ron.

"Too tight," Andreyev hollered at her as she left. "I can't breathe."

"Then you couldn't complain about it," she called back over her shoulder.

Ron tossed the rope up to Dortello as he waited close to the top of the steel tower. He'd climbed up on the inside of the three tresses lashed together to form the structure and stood with one foot on each of two of them, leaning his chest and arms outside it to catch the rope. He got it on the first try and coiled it around his right arm as he pulled it up.

He tied one end around a metal girder and tossed the other up over the lifting beam going between the top of the tower he was on and the one where Bart was waiting. When the line came back down, he caught it and tossed it over to Bart, who threw it back to him. They did this several more times to get a half dozen circuits around the rocket. Dortello tied it around the line he had thrown over the top beam and dropped the remaining line to the ground.

After they climbed back down, Bart ran the line through a series of pulleys he had carved from forest vegetation and hooked it up to a nearby large tree. Then everyone—except Cemper, who was in a chair they had fashioned and carried to the site—grabbed the end of the line and, along with a couple of the natives, pulled until they got the ship off the ground. It wasn't the couple of inches they had been hoping for, but it was enough to allow the vehicle to swing.

From behind where the rocket would lay, Cemper mimed instructions to a few more twelve-foot tall Vanerans. They pushed the bottom of the *Yuri* up while Bart and his crew lowered the top of the craft onto the improvised sled.

Ron left the lowering crew and ran over to where the *Yuri* was descending to guide the sled so the ship would sit squarely on it. The eight stone wheels they installed took the load easily but the hull metal of the shuttle bent enough under the weight to rest on the ground.

They could move the *Yuri,* but it wasn't as easy as they had planned. It took them the rest of the day and most of the next to get it to where they planned on dismantling it.

* * *

The following morning, Michael climbed out of the shelter just behind the Vaneran they were calling Ginny. They were using female names and pronouns for all the giant Vanerans since they all appeared to have adopted Molaro, a female herself, as their template. He was a little surprised that the Torvons had built the entrance to this shelter wide enough for her and the others to get through, even if it was only by a matter of inches. Even the ceiling inside the shelter was easily high enough to accommodate their full twelve foot height. Though it was getting crowded with nine humans, three Wassarrans and six Vanerans sleeping down there. Still, Michael knew it was better than trying to sleep outside with all the nightlights glowing.

"Michael, get a move on," Justin said from the base of the ladder. "She's out already."

Michael, who had been waiting about three rungs up the ladder, blinked several times, while shaking his head slightly, to pull himself out of his mind and back into the bunker. Ginny had already climbed out. He climbed the rest of the way up, accepting her hand as he stuck his head above ground.

"Help Michael," she said as she pulled him out of the hole and set him off to her right side.

It seemed the day after they'd been born in the electrified trenches, they had a slight grasp of English. What vocabulary they had, Michael guessed, they'd learned from Molaro while she was

190

helping them in their more primitive state. No one even realized they had any ears. They had remembered enough of it that when they'd developed a lung and larynx system, they immediately tried to replicate it. The day they were born had been a mishmash of sounds as they practiced to get the words Molaro had spoken to them.

Each day they were learning new words from whoever they hung out with. Ginny spent most of her time with him, and he spent most of his time with Cowloom inside the pod, trying to learn its systems. Today he planned on working with the crew disassembling the *Yuri,* if for no other reason than to talk with her so she could catch up with her siblings. Something for him to remember when he got back to the twins.

"Pod?" Ginny pointed her left arm towards the escape pod Michael had been working in since they had gotten the *Yuri* down here.

"Not today." He pointed towards where they had parked the *Yuri,* "Today I'll be working with Bart, getting the engines out of their spaceship. I'd love your help."

"I love to help."

Bart had gotten up earlier that anyone else, somehow knowing when it was light out, and was already cutting the last section of the ship's back plate where the engines were mounted. They had found a single oxy-acetylene welding rig in the maintenance section of the ship. There had also been an electro-welder with the equipment. "Useless" was all Bart had said about it when Ron started pulling it free.

Bart took a break and closed off the gas valves as Michael and Ginny approached. He patted the Vaneran helping him on her left arm. "Take five." Linda had been around Bart enough to know when he was taking five, and pushed the plate back into place, since it only had an inch of metal holding it in there.

"I'm going to need everyone out here to control the removal of this thing, shortly." He wiped the sleeve of his thick jacket across his forehead to absorb the sweat dripping from it. The day was too warm for the jacket, but it was the best protection he had from the slag popping away from his cutting. "What can I do for you, Michael?"

"What can I do to help?"

"Round everybody up. Get a couple of lines connected to those bars I attached to the back here. And see if we can get a section of the shuttle's hull to act as a ramp so we can slide this thing out and not damage the engines. Do that while Linda and I get some breakfast."

"Powdered eggs," said the Vaneran wishfully.

"As many as you'd like. I hate the things myself, but it's what we've been having for breakfast since leaving Earth."

"As I hate those roots we have been living on for years. We need new food, better taste."

"We may have to run some edibility tests before we leave here," Michael said. "How long a ramp you want?"

"At least ten foot. More if you can get it. Remember those engines aren't light, probably need double hull sections." He walked up to the removed hatch and hollered in, "How you guys coming with that disconnect?"

"We've been dealing with some pretty stubborn bolts in here. About another hour." Michael couldn't quite identify the voice hollering back, but thought it was Ron.

"Come on, Linda. Looks like we can have a long leisurely breakfast." The two of them walked towards the shelter.

"See if Cemper is up to supervising the effort," Michael called after them. Bart waved his hand above his head in acknowledgement.

Ginny and Michael went in the direction of the stripped shuttle. They swung by the pod to ask Cowloom if he could break in an hour to help, then found Molaro leading two of the Vanerans away from the shuttle with the water cart.

"How we doing on water? Think it can wait until later today?" Molaro stopped as Michael talked, but the Vanerans, who had made the trip before, kept heading for the forest trail.

"Unless you want to take a bath, I think so." She dropped her hand on the passing cart, "Hey, Mandy, Lindsay, hold on a second." As it came to a stop, she returned to Michael. "What'a you need?"

"Bart is about ready to drop the engines out of the *Yuri*. He's going to need a ramp built and help when he finishes the cut. Ron'll have the engines ready on the inside in about an hour. Which means that's how long we have to get a ten-plus foot ramp ready for Bart." Michael was turning to head over to the pile of disassembled shuttle pieces but stopped himself. "Oh, and he needs all hands on deck for the lowering."

"The girls and I can get the ramp pulled together. Why don't you round everyone else up? You're the boss, after all."

"I wish you'd forget that. Want Ginny to help?" A smile broadened on Ginny's face. Michael knew they all liked working with Molaro better than anyone else.

"It would be easier with the four of us. Thanks."

"Ginny, you don't mind, do you?"

"I very much like working with Molaro. Thank you."

Michael found Justin tinkering in his lab again, testing out the Torvon stone powder they had found in the shelter, so he let him know. He rounded the pod and found Mary, Laudrum and the last two Vanerans monitoring the trenches.

"Hey, guys, we're going to need your help pulling the engines out of the *Yuri* in about an hour. Can I count on the four of you?" Michael felt his neck stretching as he followed the Vanerans standing up from the seated position they were in.

"We'll be there," Laudrum said as he checked his watch. "Eight thirty."

"Anyone seen Dortello this morning?"

"You may have to kick him out of bed," Mary said. "Unless he was following the other two, he spent all his time in their cabin."

"How did you know that?" Laudrum asked.

"I wanted to know where that Belinsky was at all times. Unless I had my door locked."

"Thanks," Michael turned to leave. "I'll check the shelter. Probably a good idea to see that Andreyev is securely restrained while I'm at it."

Chapter Thirty-Eight

Bart checked the four posts. Each was made from a piece of the Yuri's hull supports. Steel girders measuring six inches thick, four at their widest and twenty-four feet long, were buried until only four feet of them were above ground. Then they were anchored with a collar of Torvon stone Justin had cemented them in with. He couldn't move any of them. Using one of the pulley wheels from the UEF shuttle had in its spare parts bin, Justin had made an earthen mold and cast twelve copies of it from the Torvon stone compound. Bart used these to construct four sets of triple pulleys, one for each post. The two pulleys forward of the engines were connected to each side of the lower control bar Bart had tried welding in place. They weren't great welds, since he didn't have any welding rods and had to rely on melting the two pieces of steel together. Ginny and Michael on one with Rachael and Justin on the other. The upper bar was attached to the two pulleys behind the engine assembly. Since they would be pulling the engines out, the other four Venerans were assigned to them. Molaro with her two, and Mary supervising Peg and Linda on the other. Ron, Cowloom and Dortello were inside, waiting for word from Bart when they should try pushing the freed plate away from the spacecraft.

Bart turned the cylinders of gas on and ignited the nozzle with a burning twig. He dropped the twig to the sandy soil and ground it out. With the knobs on the cutting nozzle, he adjusted the flow to get the intensity of flame he wanted and applied it to the last inch he had left before it was free.

The bottom plate of the *Yuri* groaned as it strained to break free of the last ounces of steel holding it to the ship. Until it finally snapped and thudded together as the two cut bottom edges smacked into each other.

Bart shut off the torch and jumped away from where he'd been working. Placed the nozzle over the two tanks and closed their valves. Then he pulled a large wrench out of his tool belt and rapped on the side of the space ship. "Take her down," he shouted loud enough for the guys in the engine room to hear, knowing if they did, everybody did.

It took several minutes, broken into three extreme efforts followed by a short rest, to get the ten-inch section of the ship to move unto the ramp. As it dropped the few inches, the ramp bowed slightly under the weight of the steel ring but held. Three more tries got the equipment far enough down the ramp that gravity assisted them and the pulling became easier on those trying to get it moving and started resisting those trying to keep if from careening down. Those in the engine room had stopped pushing and instead were guiding the engines and tanks out of the hole in the back of the ship so they wouldn't collide with the sides of the hull and be damaged.

They got about three-quarters of the way down the ramp when Bart heard a metallic snapping sound and saw the left side of the upper bar begin to bend.

"Halt," Bart hollered before the right side could break free. Everyone froze in place, keeping tension on their lines. "Michael, you and Justin tie off your ends. We're going to have to re-rig this thing."

After a couple of minutes, Justin announced, "Secure."

Bart waited. "Michael, you tied down?"

"Oh. sorry. Yeah, we've got it secured, also."

Bart walked up to where Michael's line was tied off. He tugged at it and said, "On a project like this, if we don't stay in communication, someone's gonna get hurt."

"Sorry, I'm usually on the planning end."

Bart went back and undid the line that connected to the loose bar. Then he ran it behind the plate housing the engines. After that, he undid the other one and connected the two lines behind the plate, threading them through the maze of engine connections.

As the last of the fuel tanks were clear of the ship's hull, he turned to the men still inside the engine room. "Ron, you guys keep an eye on that connection. Anything starts to give, you sing out."

He jumped back off the ramp. "Okay, let's try this again. Michael, Justin, take up the tension."

"Ready," they both called back.

Molaro, Mary, begin pulling. Slowly pulling."

The engines began sliding down the ramp again. It took another ten minutes until they had the entire assembly on the ramp. "Okay, hold up. Michael, Justin, tie off again."

"Secured," they said almost in unison.

He was behind the plate disconnected from the rigging he had done earlier, freeing the two lines. "Molaro, rig this one through that hole in the bottom of the ramp." He tossed her line out from behind the plate. "Use this carbineer so we don't risk cutting the line on the burnt edge." He reached into his pocket, pulled out a steel ring with an openable side and tossed it to Molaro, also. "Mary, here. Do the same." First he threw the line and after he saw she had passed it off to Linda, he tossed her a carbineer also.

They quickly had the system re-rigged and ready for the day's final pull. "Michael, Justin, get ready."

"Ready," they said.

"Mary, Molaro, you ladies ready?" He could see they were physically ready, but he needed to know if they were mentally there, also.

"Ready," said Mary.

"Let's get done," replied the Vaneran standing closest to Molaro. Molaro simply nodded her approval of the sentiment.

It only took a couple of pulls to get the ramp to drop off the back edge of the hull. Ron and Cowloom were ready with a couple of very thin but manageable logs to catch the ramp as it fell. It whumfed to the ground without any damage.

"Keep pulling it back. we need to clear the ship. Ron, you and Cowloom do what you can to keep those logs underneath." He wasn't done with orders. "Michael, Justin, get back here and release your lines. Hook them up to the front of the sled."

"Sled?" Ginny asked.

"Now that it's down, the ramp is no longer a ramp; now it's a sled," Michael told her.

"Keeping up with names hard work."

"But you're getting better at it every day."

After they got everything set, they spent the rest of the afternoon pulling the engines over to the escape pod where Bart could begin extracting the useful pieces and attaching them to the sides of the capsule. They were able to get a few logs under the sled to help, but since their pulley system was in a fixed position, it was all muscle work, no mechanical leverage.

* * *

That night, everyone slept soundly, except for Cowloom. Even wrapping his pillow tightly around his head couldn't suppress the noise of Vanaran snores.

Chapter Thirty-Nine

"I'm just glad we found the switch to release the chair for this panel." Cowloom was strapped into what was obviously the pilot's seat for the escape pod. His legs were being pulled to the back of the craft now that they had lifted the front of the cylinder so that it pointed skyward. "There's no way I could fly this thing if I had to stand against a hull side-wall."

"Just be glad your arms are long enough to reach all the controls. Justin had to stone set that thing so it didn't slide all the way to the back of its track." Cemper was allowed up but restricted to light work. His week of bed rest had been driving him crazy. Needing help walking, these last two weeks, was keeping someone else from getting the ship ready for flight. So he spent as much time as he could planted someplace where he wasn't tying someone up helping him. Always wanting to see what was going on though, today he had managed to convince Ron to let him try climbing the ladder they'd removed from the *Yuri* up into the escape pod and the rope ladder they had inside down to a seat where he could watch Cowloom learning the controls.

His leg still ached, though there was no chance of any more blood loss. The day after they had removed the bullet, Justin had reapplied the spray skin to his leg, but that was the last time he'd needed to. It was his muscles underneath the patch that hadn't completely healed. Every so often his leg gave out under him, if he didn't have someone keeping watch on him. Crutches didn't work, as soon as he adjusted to working with them, his leg would buckle and he wasn't putting enough weight on the wooden pole to keep him from falling down. There were times when the Vaneran, Peggy, just picked him up and carried him where he wanted to go. It was embarrassing at first, but when he saw how delighted she was when he talked to her, he decided she was actually getting the better of the deal.

"Discovered any new switches today?" Cemper asked from the back. He stretched across all the seats in the back row, using backs as a bed to lay out on.

Cowloom released the bar connecting his seat to the control console and turned it to face Cemper. "Not today. And I don't think I want to play with any more of them. I don't have Raj's command of the Torvon language, but I do think I have figured out this thing enough to get us back into orbit. If anyone's waiting to pick us up. You interested in learning the launch sequence?"

"That sounds more interesting than sleeping here all day." He balanced himself on the backs of the seats and took the couple of steps, carefully balancing on their contoured sides, over to the rope ladder and pulled himself up to where Cowloom was sitting. "So how do we light this rocket?"

Cowloom pulled himself back around and locked his seat into position, then attached the rod that acted as a safety in case the chair's swivel pole mechanism failed. "It's my understanding that Bart will have the engines he's attaching to the hull turned on before he climbs on board. Since they have an electronic igniter, they will be flowing fuel until I have the Torvon engines fired up. Once they ignite, we should be able to sit back and ride this thing to orbit. I don't expect we'll be in any condition to try doing anything else.

"So the first thing we have to do after Bart climbs in, is seal the hatch. He'll pull it shut, and activating this switch applies the Torvon current to convert the stone sealant to liquid and back again. Making the hatch as if it was a part of the hull. It doesn't matter the position the switch is left in, flipping it the other way activates the process."

"Seal the door, check." Cemper had his right arm wrapped around two rungs of the ladder above him and his left one holding the rung at his shoulder. His legs driving into a rung for further support. It wouldn't matter if his bad leg lost balance in this position.

"I'm sure there are a lot of procedures we're supposed to go through before firing the engines, but I don't have the expertise with rocket design and the Torvon language to do more than hold down this switch." He pointed to the largest of the tabs on the back panel of the board, right before what looked like a series of gauges. "It immediately springs back into its upper position if you let it go. So you have to hold it down for as long as you want the engines to burn. We assume there is some mechanism for steering this thing, but we haven't figured out what. And since we're going straight up, I really didn't care."

"Hold switch down, check."

"Oh, and before you do any of that, make sure this chair is in launch position." Cowloom undid the bar holding him facing the panel, activated the chair mechanism and turned it so he was facing towards the hatch. He reached down with his left hand and pulled up another bar. "Connect this to the panel the same way you connected the one to face you forward. Bart said this launch will put a lot of stress on our bodies."

"What kind of stress?"

"Pressure. Gravitational pressure. It is not going to be the smooth transition into space we're used to."

<h1 align="center">Chapter Forty</h1>

"Yup." Bart dropped the wrench back into his belt loop and grabbed a rag to wipe his hands off. "Had to study how they launched rockets back when we were first getting into space. Astronauts described it like strapping fireworks onto their back. Very bumpy ride. With no inertial compensators on this thing—or at least if there are, we haven't figured out how to activate them—we're going to be pressed back into our seats by many times the force of gravity."

"Can we survive that?" Cemper stood before the engineer pushing with both hands down on the cane Molaro had made for him. It had her impression of a lenix head carved into the handle. A lenix was a large mammal from Wassarra, much like the terran wolf; it was a pack hunter, and having a lenix head cane was thought to elevate the user's status in their group. "Just something to remind you of home," she'd told him.

Bart tossed the rag in the laundry pile next to where he was working and wrapped his arm around the boy's waist. He wasn't tall enough to reach his shoulders. "I'm done here. Let's find Justin, he's still got to cover these things."

"But can we survive those pressures?"

"Those first astronauts did. We should know about ourselves tomorrow."

Over by the tree line, they found the young chemist pouring a mixture of the stone powder into one of the several dozen ring molds he, Rachael, and Peggy had dug into the earth.

"What brings you guys over here?" Justin greeted the approaching two men. His attention was distracted by the sounds of Andreyev, once more trying to break the line holding him to the tree. "Take it easy, or we'll secure you to that tree so you can't walk around."

Bart walked up to the edge of where Andreyev could stretch his line out to, then turned his back on the Russian. "We've finished the engine refit. We've got one booster on each side of the escape pod for you to protect." He looked over the field of several dozen mold holes. Each mold had an inner diameter of three feet and a wall of six inches, and were filled with the stone solution Justin had prepared from the stone powder in the underground Torvonian shelter. "Anything we can do to help?"

Justin squatted down and applied Michael's pen device to the mold he just filled. He activated it and the mixture in the depression turned from a watery reflective solution to hard white stone. "If you watch closely, you can see the stone forming from the point of contact all around the circle." He looked back up at Bart and Cemper. "That leg still bothering you, Cemper?" He stood up again.

"It's getting better. I've haven't noticed it trying to give out yet this morning."

"Let's not push things. Keep an eye on Andreyev over there. Bart, you can start pulling the rings out of the mold and stacking them over by the dome mold in the center." He walked over to the next mold, a foot away from the one he had just hardened. He squatted over it and processed the slurry the mold contained. "Rachael, can you get this one?"

Bart tried getting a grip on the ring but the stone filled the cavity in the ground so thoroughly that his fingers had no place to go. He finally gave up and dug at the outside edge of the ring until he could slide his fingers under the half-foot thickness of it. With that purchase on the stone structure, he was able to pull it out of the soil. But not without destroying the mold Justin had dug to cast it in.

"Hey, Justin, I hope you didn't need this mold anymore." He pointed at the ground as Justin turned to look from about eight molds away. He lifted the ring on its side and draped it over his left shoulder to carry it where Justin had wanted them.

"Nope. Dirt doesn't have enough stretch to make molds that last for more than a single use. Just set it in the center and leapfrog Rachael and Peggy to yank the next one."

Justin moved from one to the next, solidifying each ring as he went. Half way through the field of molds, he stood up, stretched his back, wiped his brow and called out. "Peggy, could you spread a thin layer of the stuff you were pouring into the molds between each of the rings you guys have pulled out?"

"Stone them together?"

"Something like that, thanks." He moved on to the next mold and kept solidifying them.

Bart moved over to the two dome molds and set the ring down, it had been heavier than he had thought, yet not as massive as he had been expecting. "Maybe we should glue these together over by the ship. This single ring was heavy enough."

Justin walked over to where Bart had dropped his ring and bent down to lift it again. He picked it up a few inches and let it fall back down. Bart could see him running his finger to each of twelve rings before turning back to him. "Good idea. You might want to think about how we're going to lift them into place once they're finished. Cause you're right, each housing is going to be quite heavy."

He turned to Rachael, who was approaching with the bucket of stone solution. "Let's wait on that. You and Peggy need to get these rings over to the pod. Once we get them there, we can stone them together."

"Okie, dokie."

"She's been hanging around Ron too much," Bart said. "I'll grab Linda and start getting some scaffolds built."

"We should be done here in about an hour." Bart heard over his shoulder as he was already headed over to the shelter where Linda was taking a break.

* * *

Michael and Ginny were also in the shelter when Bart arrived and agreed to help him extract the poles they had buried as anchors for removing the engines. Their twenty-four foot lengths were ideal for raising Justin's stone canisters to cover the engines, besides being the longest beams from the ships.

Digging under the stone collars each had been given wasn't a problem but they had to dig a trench away from each post to get the twenty feet they had buried in the ground to tilt out. Both carts had to be used to transport each girder back to the pod. They repeated this three times and left the fourth buried. Bart had plans for a tripod.

Once they were all assembled, Bart decided that twenty feet, the height his tripod was going to stand, wouldn't be high enough to lift Justin's cowl into place. Standing around thinking about the problem, he turned to Michael and asked, "We need something to act as footings for each of the tripods legs. Something about six feet tall. I don't know if we can build dirt mounds and pack them hard enough to hold the weight. Is there anything left in the shuttle we can cannibalize?"

"I see what you mean." Michael slapped the side of one of the steel girders resting against the pod's hull. "We have to get at least how many feet above those tanks?"

"Justin is making each cowl about fourteen feet tall. The top of each tank is ten feet off the ground, meaning we need about six more feet to rig the thing to be lifted."

"There's no way we have enough of the stone powder left to do that." Michael stood looking at the attached engine, raised his eyes to look at the top of the tank. And kept raising his eyes to the top of the pod, another two dozen feet above the tank. "What if we used the top of the pod to run a girder across? If we hung a cowl from each side, balanced, it should stay in place."

"That might work!" Bart announced. Then he looked at the height of the pod. "But how are we going to get one of them up there?"

"We still have those pulleys, don't we?"

"We'll need everyone on the lines, but it might work!" Bart was off to the *Yuri,* where he'd put the four pulleys in one of the maintenance lockers.

* * *

Justin rolled the last of the domes over to where Michael and Bart were burying anchor posts in the ground a few feet from either attached engine, placing it against the stack of rings Peggy and Rachael had made. He leaned against the stack on one side of the ship. "Okay. I give. What are you guys working on now?"

204

Michael planted his shovel into the ground and grabbed a deep breath before answering. "Any stand we make out of the steel beams we have won't be tall enough to lift your stone covers over the engines. We're going to lift one of the beams to the entrance of the pod and use it to lift your creations."

"Sounds like a lot of work." Justin walked over to the pod and looked at the narrowest gap between the tank and the pod. He patted the pod and said, "Why not just build the cover in place? That way, you only need a tripod tall enough to lift an eighteen inch dome, it's the tallest piece of the thing. I can lock each piece to the hull, then attach it to the one it's sitting on."

"No anchors, no lifting a beam thirty feet in the air, no balancing across so it doesn't pull off?" Despite finally breathing normally again, Michael took a deep breath. Then yelled, "Bart," as loud as he could.

* * *

Peggy and Rachael lifted the first of the rings into place, since it was going to be mounted within their reach. When they got it where Bart told them it needed to be placed, Justin applied a patch of stone powder slurry to each side of the ring where it touched the pod. Then he applied the necessary current from Michael's pen device and watched the slurry harden.

"Okay, ladies. One hand at a time, let's let it go and see if it holds." They each pulled a hand away and the ring didn't move. Justin applied another coat of the slurry, hardened it and had them remove their other hand. "Okay, grab the top of the ring and push down as hard as you can." With both the Vanerans' weight on it, the ring didn't move. "Okay, get the next one ready, while I slab slurry on this slab." Justin giggled to himself.

While they were doing that; Bart, Linda and Michael constructed a tripod out of the three beams they had planned on using earlier.

As the afternoon progressed, more of the Vanerans came out to see what was going on. After which, Bart pressed them into service while Michael rounded up everyone else who could work. They managed to finish construction as the sun was drifting down to the tops of the surrounding trees.

They angled the ladder they had removed from the *Yuri* to access the entrance to the pod until it was just above the dome of the right hand engine cover. Ron started having the Vanerans climb up and out onto the cover. He got Peggy, Linda, Ginny, and Lucy sitting on it before it ran out of room for Rachael or Henrietta.

"If each of those ladies is four hundred pounds," Bart began.

"Then each of the engines is really secured." Justin patted the engineer on the back.

"Let's call it a day." Michael looked around at the crowd. "We've done incredible work here today, people. Someone want to go bring Andreyev in?"

"No," came a chorus from almost everyone.

"Cemper, you up to getting him?"

"My leg's getting a lot stronger."

"Well, hang on to your cane. If he gives you any trouble, brain him with it."

"Isn't brain where smart comes from?" Ginny turned to Michael and asked.

Everyone except the Vanerans laughed. "In this case, brain him means to hit him on the head," Cemper said as he started out to where they had Andreyev tied up. "Oh, he'll smart if he tries anything." He slapped the lenix head into his left hand as he walked away.

He came running back minutes later, before Michael had a chance to climb down into the shelter. "He's gone."

Michael looked over to the tree he was supposed to be tied to, but it was getting too dark to see anything that far away. He looked up at Cemper's face for an explanation.

"The ropes are all there. Untied. It looks like someone untied him."

Michael turned and almost jumped down the ladder. He looked around the room before asking, "Where's Dortello?"

The Italian was nowhere to be seen.

"When was the last time someone saw him?"

People muttered a few 'No idea's or just shook their heads.

"What was his assignment today?" After a few seconds of quiet, he added more forcefully, "Did he have an assignment today?"

Dr. Laudrum sat forward on one of the stone easy chairs. "I think we forgot about him in the excitement of finishing the escape pod."

"Both he and Andreyev have gone missing." Michael was pacing the shelter to keep his nervous friends focused on him. "We'll make the final checks in the morning, disconnect that power line from this shelter to the pod, and lift-off by noon. That sound good to everyone? If they come back, they can lift-off with us; if not, well, I need to get all of you home."

He needed something to break the soured mood. "Tonight, let's have a farewell party for our Vaneran friends. Ginny, let's make some powdered eggs."

The Vaneran banged her head on the shelter's ceiling as she jumped off the bed she'd been sitting on and ran for the kitchen. "Do they even feel pain?" Michael asked himself.

Chapter Forty-One

Something banged noisily outside the shuttle, bringing Cowloom back to wakefulness. "I came out here to get away from their damnable snoring," he complained to the nobody else in the shuttle. He shifted the top of the sleeping bag he'd stretched out over the last two mattresses left in the sleeping section of the cannibalized vessel and got to his feet.

He was rubbing the crust out of his eyes as he got to the shuttle hatch to see what had forced him to consciousness. Two figures were over by the entrance of the Torvon shelter, dragging something to it. He was about to call out when his eyes focused on the Russian they'd had tied up until that afternoon.

He pulled himself away from the opening, forcing himself against the wall as tightly as he could. He watched the two men dragging one of the steel supports they'd used earlier that day to form their lifting tripod. It was something heavy enough that even the Vanarans could not move it by themselves. The banging he'd heard was the two of them dropping the beam against the stone top of the underground structure. It was the Italian, Cowloom could never remember his name. Okay, he wasn't really trying, the guy smelled foul and Cowloom did his best to avoid him. It was he who kept losing his grip on the hunk of steel, that caused the other man to let the front end go, causing the steel to crash into the ground, smacking the Torvon stone underneath.

Now that he was awake and could hear the scraping noise and the banging the two of them were causing, Cowloom had to wonder why the people sleeping in the shelter hadn't woken. "If Michael and the rest of them can ignore the Vaneran's snoring, I guess this ain't going to wake them." Cowloom vocalized his thoughts.

The night was dark, neither of Vanera's moons were showing, but the remnants of the energized microbes still dotted the landscape, not as many as on the first night they had been sleeping on the planet. Most had been carefully transferred to the warning pits but there were still enough that Cowloom had to be careful if he tried leaving the shuttle.

"Lift this thing a bit higher, Dortello." The two men lifted the end they had been pulling up, almost over their heads. The Russian shifted his left foot back and said, "Okay, drop it and get out of the way."

They let the beam fall. It crashed across the stone hatch with a noise that Cowloom knew was greater than anything the Vanerans made while sleeping. He looked out and estimated the beam, too heavy for anyone on the planet to lift by themselves, was laying across the hatch. Blocking it from being raised by anyone inside the shelter.

"Now we wait for them to want out," Andreyev—that was his name, Cowloom finally remembered, Myles Andreyev—said to his comrade. They both walked over to where the mattresses and stumps had been left by the fire pit. "We might as well get some sleep while we wait for them to want out."

"And then?"

"First we get our guns back, then have them give us those two *tyolkas* who killed Belinsky and we have our revenge on them. Finally, we will commandeer their ship to have them fly us off this rock and leave the bunch of them stranded here, like they were planning to do to us."

"But will their friends take us and leave?"

"We'll have guns. Those science eggheads won't."

Cowloom quietly crept up to the flight deck of the shuttle, where enough of it had been removed to allow him to look outside and watch as the two conspirators stretched out on mattresses from the shuttle and went to sleep. He looked over to the large wrench laying on the floor under the communication console. "I could knock out one of them," he said very quietly. "But not both. Not quickly enough, not without doing some permanent damage."

He dropped to the floor and sat there to think about his next move. "I can't shift that beam by myself." He lowered his head into his left hand and pulled his eyelids open. "If I tried rigging the pulley up," he raised his head just enough to look through the gap where the control bench had been before they had removed it for the steel hull plate it was attached to. The Italian was just beginning to snore. "The noise would wake them up and I'd be caught also. Then they'd probably kill me." He dropped his head again and thought for several minutes.

He was on the verge of falling back to sleep when the noise of the Italian's snoring increased and jerked him up against the supports still ready to secure the shuttle's control console. He made just enough noise to cause the man to shift his position and continue snoring, this time with decreased volume.

"I need some kind of weapon." Cowloom got up from the floor and went back to the shuttle's hatch. He stepped off the ramp, avoiding the remaining glowing piles of microbes and gently scooped a patch of them up, dirt beneath them and all, before carrying them into the back of the shuttle. They provided him enough light to search for something he could use in the morning. "I have to let them open the hatch."

* * *

Light through the open hatch leading into the shuttle supply locker flooded from the flight deck of the disabled ship. Cowloom gently raised the lids over his eyes and rubbed away the last of the sleep that was holding them shut with his hands. He was startled momentary by the rubber band he held in his right hand until he remembered what he had been doing the night before. Dangling from each end of the band were short metal rods he had also located in the replacement parts bin.

He also remembered he needed to get some kind of position before those other two woke up. He made his way up to where he'd been watching them the night before. Looking out through the holes in the shuttle, the Russian was already awake and standing over the Italian.

"You've slept enough, Dortello." He kicked the other man's legs. "It's time to get up. Laudrum and those traitors should be up by now." Andreyev reached into one of his shirt pockets and pulled something out that he bit the end off of and chewed while the other man climbed to his feet.

210

"Why do you always have to be so rough?" Dortello said, kneeling on the ground on the opposite side of the mattress from Andreyev before pushing himself up into a standing position. "I would rather have slept in the *Yuri* than out in the open."

"Do ya want off this rock or not?" When the Italian nodded, the Russian continued, "Then you have to do as I say!" He reached over and slapped the other man on the cheek. "Like you always do. Now come on. Let's see if these guys are going to be reasonable." He turned and walked over to the shelter's hatch.

Cowloom moved from the front of the shuttle over to the open hatch. The two men took positions on either side of the beam holding the hatch in place. They squatted down and lifted the beam a few inches before dropping it again. The hatch rang hollow while the rest of the shelter just gave up the flat sound Cowloom had heard the night before.

Andreyev squatted down again and as the other man began to, held up his hand to stop him. He reached over to the round hatch, right next to where the beam was crossing it and wrapped on it with his fist. "Hey, anybody down there? Anybody up yet?"

Cowloom could hear a voice reply but it was too muffled for him to hear anything that whoever it was had said.

"Then you had better let me talk to Reggie." Andreyev cupped his hands around his mouth and hollered down. "I've got a few conditions before we let you guys out."

Cowloom pulled back from the opening and slid into a seated position behind the shuttle's hull. He could still hear Andreyev's end of the conversation but unless he wanted to reveal himself or they opened the hatch, he wasn't going to hear the other side.

"Now, if you choose to be reasonable, we can make this noon launch window you've been talking about." Cowloom tilted his head toward the hatch to listen. "I just need you to accede to a couple things. One, we want our guns back, that includes Belinsky 's. After we let you up, I don't want any of you to try being heroes. And with me and Dortello controlling the guns, I'm sure you'll all behave.

"Second, I need those two hellions who killed Belinsky . They will have to be punished, Belinsky has to be avenged. It is our way.

Besides, eliminating them from the launch ensures our extra weight is not a problem. And you will wait below while we deal with those murderesses.

"Third, we will be in charge of the launch. Your ship will recover the Ranklinite pod and secure it for a return to Earth, which is immediately where we will go. And we will dictate landing coordinates once we're in interstellar space. Do you agree to these terms?"

Cowloom looked at the pathetic strip of rubber he held in his hand. "This isn't going to help if they get those guns back." He tossed it forward, bouncing it off the front end of the shuttle's cockpit then pushed himself upright, checked to see if anyone was looking, and slipped back to search for something else.

"You'd better hurry up and decide. You're the ones with the deadline," he could hear Andreyev calling down. Cowloom lifted one of the hydraulic replacement cylinders out of the parts locker and tried wrapping his hand around it. While it was too thick for him to control it single-handed, using both hands he felt he had a solid club. Now if he could just get close enough to use it.

He leaned the piston against the shuttle's hull and peeked out the hatch. Andreyev and company were starting to lift the beam holding the shelter entrance closed. They raised it about a foot and slid one of the tree trunk stools under it. The entrance cover was able to lift up just enough to allow someone to pass the weapons demanded out to them. Once the three pistols were pushed out of the shelter, Andreyev kicked the support out from under the beam and it dropped back on top of the lid.

Cowloom heard a muffled "Ow" come from under the hatch. "I hope that was just someone banging their head," he whispered. He watched the two men check their weapons to make sure they were loaded. Andreyev shoved the extra pistol into his pant pocket, sighted his gun at the shuttle Cowloom was hiding in, and dropped his gun hand to his side. He squatted down and rapped the grip on the top of the shelter's hatch.

"Okay, that's number one. Are you ready to send out the girls?"

After a muffled response, Andreyev turned to his partner. "Okay, let's get this thing off, but you stand on the hatch while we do so. I don't want them springing out on us."

They positioned themselves and lifted the beam up. Then pivoted it over until it was completely off the shelter's lid before dropping it to the ground.

"You're right, Andreyev," said the man on the lid. "They were trying to push up early."

Andreyev dropped to his knee and banged on the hatch. "Behave down there. Or we'll seal you in forever. Send the girls up." He waved the other man off the lid.

As he stepped off, it raised slowly until it rested against the roof of the shelter. Mary proceeded to climb out using the poles before stepping across the opening and waiting for Molaro to climb up.

"Now close the lid again." Andreyev waved his gun at the Wassarran. "You just stand there and look pretty," he added to Mary as she started to help.

Cowloom had to move. Going out the shuttle's main hatch would have revealed his presence. But if he could bend the remaining metal under the pilot's console, it might provide enough space for him to wiggle out. He grabbed the cylinder and went forward.

They'd removed the inner hull to get at the wiring in the flight console. Then they'd removed the I beams holding the exterior plates fixed. While most of the plates were fixed to a beam running along the side of the shuttle, one plate was dangling. It was connected to a single point on the plate to its right. Cowloom was able to push it aside to squeeze through the opening while he heard Andreyev lecturing Molaro and Mary.

He pushed the cylinder out ahead of him. Then shoving the plate aside with his left arm, he reached for the ground with his right one. Pushing against the floor to drive his body out, he got through the opening and fell undignified to the ground. But quietly enough that he never interrupted Andreyev's speech.

Getting to his feet, he picked up the piston and peered around the front end of the shuttle.

The two men had their guns pointed at the two women. "So I hope you have made peace with your desecration of noble Belinsky. For you surely will burn in hell for killing him."

Cowloom had read too many earth novels not to know this was the moment. He charged from around the shuttle and when he got within six feet of Andreyev, began screaming at him.

As the Russian turned to see what was happening, Cowloom took a two-handed swing at his head. The man crumpled to the ground. He turned to the other one to find Mary grabbing his gun out of his hand and Molaro delivering a human roundhouse to his jaw. He, too, crumpled to the ground.

Mary dropped the gun she was holding by its barrel and wrapped Cowloom in as much of a hug as she could reach, just above his waist. Molaro lifted the lid off the shelter and called down, "It's worked. We're safe."

He could hear the people begin to climb out of the shelter. As he did, he pushed Mary back a few inches, turned to Molaro and back to Mary, asking, "What worked?"

Molaro bent down and picked up the gun resting inches from Andreyev's fingers. As Michael emerged from underground, she pointed it at the shuttle and squeezed the trigger. The gun clicked twice as she did, but didn't fire. "Bart took the firing pins out of these things before we handed them up."

"We figured the shock of their guns not firing would give us enough of a distraction to subdue them," Mary added. "But what you did worked even better."

Michael walked up to the group and slapped Cowloom on his lower back. "We thought they had you. It may sound unkind, but I'm glad the Vaneran's snoring bothered you."

"So what are we going to do with these two?" Justin said, giving the unconscious Russian a light kick in his torso.

"As much as I'd love to leave these two on this planet," Laudrum came up behind Michael and dropped his hand on Michael's shoulder. "We can't ethically leave them here. If you have a UEF cruiser nearby, we'll need to turn them over to the authorities."

"I fully agree," Michael said. "Let's get these two into the pod and secured into a couple of the less comfortable seats. We have a launch to prep for."

Chapter Forty-Two

"You've got this." Michael patted Cowloom's shoulder. While the Wassarran was firmly strapped into the Torvon seat in front of the escape pod's control console, Michael was hanging onto one of the loops they'd tied into the rope that stretched down from the open hatch to allow people to raise and lower themselves from the vertical spaceship.

He pulled his foot out of a lower loop, relaxed his grip slightly and with the friction of his shoes, he slowly slid down to the back end of the pod to check on their two prisoners. "They strapped in tight?" he asked as he stood on the back wall looking upside down at the two bound men and the women flanking them.

Michael could see Andreyev's eyes widen as Molaro pushed her right foot into his chest again and tugged the lashings holding him down for the fifth time. At least Michael had seen her repeat this maneuver five times, he had no idea how many more times she had pulled his cinches tighter when he wasn't looking. "I think I'm getting close."

"He still has to breath."

"Yeah, but you didn't say he had to comfortably breath," Mary added as she tried doing the same thing to Dortello.

"Just make sure they're ready. We've got ten minutes until takeoff." He walked back up the pod, pulling himself back up the rope handhold by handhold. Slapping a strapped-in Cemper as he went past.

Justin was coming down the other line. He slid into a seat along the opposite wall from Cemper. Since the chair was mounted on the side wall of the pod and not against the back, Justin had to hold himself in his seat by pressing his right arm into the seat adjacent to his until he was strapped in. Once he latched the restraints, he released his right arm to pull them tight. Michael could see him leaning slightly towards the back of the pod, but only when he was comparing Justin to his seat. Laudrum came down the line right after him. Michael and Justin held him in place while he strapped in.

Michael finished pulling himself up to the pod's hatch, slipped his right foot into a nearby loop and lifted himself over the edge to see how Bart was doing. The engineer waved as Michael's head cleared the opening.

Michael waved back. "Everyone's ready. Bart, start those engines." He looked over to the Vanerans standing just behind Bart and waved at them. "Linda, get your people into the shelter until after this thing is gone." He changed his wave to an urging motion to urge them on.

Linda turned and hurried the Vanerans watching the last of the preparations. Bart went to the far side of the craft and opened the one valve. Michael saw him listening for the hissing of escape gases, or at least that's what Michael assumed he was doing. Then he ran around and opened the other side. When he was convinced the engines were primed, Bart pulled the large loop of the rope hanging along the side of the pod over his head and under his arms. "Ready," he gave a thumbs up and grabbed hold of the rope just above the knot.

Michael pulled his foot from one loop and stepped into the loop on the other end of that line. Then he allowed himself to fall down the inside of the pod, pulling Bart up to the hatch faster than he could have climbed the ladder. Grabbing the edge of the hatch, Bart scrambled into the pod and pulled the lid closed. He dropped down to the seat next to the one Cowloom was in and started buckling himself in.

"Seal the hatch. Michael, you secure?" he called down as he patted the buckle closed, locking his shoulders and legs in place.

As Michael was doing the same thing, he said, "Launch her, Cowloom. Let's go."

Cowloom pressed the button they had decided was the activator for the Torvon engines. They felt the push as the pod's engines fired up. It was a gentle push. Cowloom and Bart easily were able to turn and lock their seats in a forward position, securing them for the thrust they were expecting momentarily.

The thrust was gentle and the Torvon engines were quiet. "Just slightly more intense than a gravitational drive takeoff," Michael found himself saying.

But after several seconds, a loud roar cut off his last words, only slightly muffled since it was outside. Everyone facing forward were slammed back into their seats, the rest strained against the support straps that held them in. "That's got to be the *Yuri* engines," Bart exclaimed. "They lit, they actually lit!"

"You mean you weren't sure?" Cowloom shouted over the roar filling the cabin.

"Of course," Michael could hear the strain in Bart's voice. "I didn't think they'd be this strong. I'm never blasting off without inertial dampeners again."

After an hour-long minute, Michael shouted up, "How much longer do we have?"

"At full discharge, we had ten minutes of fuel in the external tanks," Bart forced the air out of his squashed lungs to shout back, every word getting quieter than the last.

Cowloom forced himself to turn his head to the display on the control console, and looked through the single porthole in the pod. "It looks like we're only a few miles off the ground. Everyone okay back there?"

As the forces pushing him into his seat seemed to increase slightly, Michael began to hear popping sounds throughout the pod. "What's that?"

Justin, who was holding onto his straps, looked over to where Michael was seated. "The microbes. They were pressure sensitive. We've probably passed their threshold of gee-force tolerance. It has to be them popping"

"That means we'll be decontaminated by the time we reach your ship," Ron announced.

"Assuming there's a ship up there when we get in orbit."

"But that drone we found last month?"

"They may not have waited." Michael turned his head forward to address Cowloom. "Do we have any idea how much fuel we'll have in the Pod's engines for maneuvering once we get to orbit?"

"We'd need Raj to figure that one out. I don't know what any of these readouts mean, or even if they are readouts." He was again staring at the control console. "Hey, I see blackness ahead. I think we're going to make it. Bart, how long do we have left on the external engines?"

There was no answer from above.

"Bart. Bart. Bart, are you okay?"

"I gotta sleep," came from the chair above. "Let me sleep." It was a very parsed reply, strained and breathy, barely audible over the cabin noise. But it told Michael that Bart was still alive. And they only had a couple of minutes left until engine shutdown.

Suddenly the pressure lessened. Not completely; they still were being pushed into their seats harder than they were on the planet. "We're outside the atmosphere," Cowloom announced. "We've made it!"

A couple of minutes later, the noise from the external engines died and the pressure against their bodies disappeared. They weren't floating, but they also weren't having to fight for every breath anymore.

It took Michael a moment to realize he was no longer being pushed against his left hand restraint and could sit comfortably against the back of his seat. His feet no longer pulled to the back of the pod but to the floor instead. The pod no longer felt like it was vertical but rather like it was horizontal.

Michael released himself from his seat and walked back to check on their prisoners. Both were unconscious but alive. Michael noticed the med kit in the seat next to Molaro. Then frowned at her slightly when he saw the smile on her face. He turned and walked forward again, knowing that given the opportunity, he'd have drugged the pair of them also.

Justin and Ron were getting up and heading for Cowloom before Michael could pass them. Ron knelt down next to Bart and began checking him over. "He's still got a pulse, weak but steady. And he's starting to sweat."

"Well, let's see if we can find the *Resolute* so we can get him medical help." Michael peered out the porthole into the blackness surrounding them. Trying to force one of those points of light to be the Earth Force ship.

The ship lurched. Michael stumbled back but had his feet spread to keep him upright. Ron was trying to stand up from checking on Bart and fell back to the floor. Justin fell back against the right wall.

"What was that?" Michael turned to look at the wall Justin was pushing himself away from, wishing there had been a viewing port in it.

"Gravity," hissed a response from Bart.

"Are we falling back to Vanera?" Mary called from the back of the pod.

"We're still climbing, as far as I can see," Cowloom said, staring out the pod's window.

Michael pulled himself back to where he could look out the porthole also. "Then why has the rotation of the planet changed?"

"And Bart said something about gravity." Justin had pushed himself away from the wall and helped Ron up so the two of them could check on Bart. "Unfortunately, he's asleep again."

Something banged against the right wall.

Michael lurched over to it and ran his hand over the area he'd heard the sound come from. "No leaks, whatever that was."

"Torvon Pod," began to sound from the walls. "Please shut down your engines. This is the UEF *Resolute*, we have you in Gravitational Retrieval. But your thrust is making it so we cannot bring you into the landing bay. Please shut down your engines."

Michael looked over at Cowloom, who was trying to pull up the launch button he had pressed earlier.

"Give me that," came a new voice from the wall. "Guys, Raj here. If you place your right hand on the button you used to start the engines, there should be a dial about two feet to the left they used to control, er, throttle—okay, is that the right word? Throttle the engines. If you rotate it, the engines will slow down and speed up. But if you depress it, they will stop. Depress the dial."

Cowloom reached across, found the dial and turned it slightly before pressing it down. the pod became quieter than Michael thought possible.

"Mr. Harrod, if you're aboard, this is Lt. Attah. We'll have you aboard in ten minutes, fifteen tops. Dr. Williams is standing by if there are any casualties. Welcome back, sir!"

Chapter Forty-Three

Michael was the first to jump down from the pod. He crossed over the deck to where the medical gurney was waiting. "Dr. Williams," he extended his hand to the UEF officer in a lab coat complete with a caduceus pin on his lapel. "We have one person who may have suffered a heart event on the way up."

The medical staff around the gurney didn't wait for orders but wheeled it up to the hatch of the pod. Ron and Justin had already begun helping Bart, who awoke as the pod entered the *Resolute's* landing bay and stayed conscious after that. "I'll be fine," he was saying as they lowered him to the gurney that was a mere two inches below the lip of the hatch. "I just need a little rest."

"I'll be the judge of that," Dr. Williams said, raising the man's wrist enough to check his pulse. "Get him into the diagnosis bed and run a cardio sequence on him. I'll be down after I look over the others." The three med techs rolled the gurney out towards sick bay.

"Mr. Harrod," Lieutenant Attah walked up to Michael and stood at attention. "I'm glad you made it back." Before Michael could open his mouth to reply, the man dressed in naval blues continued. "But the Captain wants to see you right away. If you'll follow me."

Michael looked back at the pod before following Attah. Andreyev was being lowered to the deck with Dortello standing bound behind Molaro. "Lieutenant, those two need to be escorted to your brig. I'll file charges with Captain Young later."

"Very good, sir. Sergeant N'Cube, see those two to the brig." The lieutenant motioned to the bound man on the deck and the one being lowered to it.

"Yes, sir." the sergeant snapped. "Wilkins, Bell, collect those two. The rest of you form up and show these two our comfortable unwelcome guest quarters."

"Now, Mr. Harrod, if you'll accompany me to the bridge." As they reached the landing bay internal doors, he pressed the intercom button on the wall. "Lieutenant Attah to the bridge."

"Bridge here," came First Offer McSton over the intercom.

"The pod is secure, and we are ready to depart."

Without even an acknowledgement of the message, a klaxon sounded throughout the ship. Michael could see Vanera falling away from the magnetically-sealed landing bay door before the solid door was lowered into flight position. He stepped into the ship corridor and followed Attah to the central elevator and up to the bridge.

* * *

Sergey was waiting on the bridge, but rose from his chair next to the Security Duty Officer, an area located next to the elevator doors to monitor who was accessing the ship's bridge. "Michael, I'm glad to see we got you off the planet before we had to leave." He extended his hand.

"Leave?" Michael shook it automatically. He lowered his eyebrows and looked quizzically at Ranklin's highest security officer.

"Yes, leave, Mr. Harrod." Captain Young turned her command chair around until it was facing the elevator Michael had just exited. "We've been waiting a month up here for you to find your way into orbit. I couldn't figure out why you didn't want us to land until we lost contact with our planetary survey drone. But yesterday morning, ship's time, we got a distress call from your Harmony Science Ship. We just got our shuttles back aboard when we detected your launch. I'm glad you could make it back before we had to come to your other expedition's assistance.

"Mr. Hanley, see to quarters for all those we just collected. It's going to be two days before we can get back out there. Sergey, go along and brief Michael's people on what we know."

* * *

Everyone was assigned a room, given a badge for entry into those rooms and how to find them if they got lost exploring the UEF vessel, as well as limited access so they could explore where they were allowed, and time to freshen up. Michael took an extra long shower, as announced by the water conservation timer he had to override three times. After the two hours everyone was given for all that, Sergey had them meet in the small conference room he had commandeered for the briefing.

Bart was the last one to arrive, wheeled in on a wheel chair by one of the medical techs. Lieutenant Attah sat next to Sergey and everyone else sat around the oval table. Michael went to pull out a chair to allow Bart to stay in his wheel chair, when the lieutenant pushed a button on the wall and one of the chairs dissolved into the floor.

"All the furnishings in here are programmable matter," Attah explained. "It makes configuring the conference rooms easier than actually moving furniture."

"Well, I see you found the escape pod you went looking for," Sergey began the briefing.

"We found it first," announced Dr. Laudrum.

"And it will still be yours once we get back to Earth," Michael added.

"But what happened on the planet?" asked the salvage specialist, Lieutenant Attah.

"When we set down by the artifact—we detected it from orbit and could see it well enough to land along side it—a microbe infected our electrical systems." And Michael went on to relate everything that had happened to their party. Bart filled in the gaps about the Laudrum Expedition after Michael finished.

"If our drone become infected and lost electrical power, that would explain why it crashed."

"At least it let us know you were up here. It took us about a week to figure out your daily transit," Cowloom added. "And that's when we started building the message to quarantine the planet. And that's when we evolved the local life forms." Molaro took over the briefing and spent the next half hour talking about Venerans.

Finally Sergey broke in to brief about the *Resolute's* current mission. "Yesterday, we picked up a distress call from our science vessel. It seems another space ship, an unidentified space ship, was closing on their position. As it came into scanning range, it was identified as being constructed of Torvon stone. We stayed in continuous contact with the *Venture* until this morning. We haven't heard anything from them since," he looked over to Attah.

"At oh eight hundred this morning. If it hadn't looked like you guys were getting ready to launch, we'd have left already. Captain Young is boosting at top speed to get back and find out what's happening. Any questions?"

Everybody's hand jumped into the air.

"Any questions we might have an actual answer for," Sergey amended.

All the hands dropped.

Chapter Forty-Four

"Martin, get all your teams back in the *Venture*." LeRena stared at the deep space sensor screen. The white bleep on the green screen kept coming closer. Granted they had it set on maximum range, but whatever was headed their way was moving fast enough to close the light year gap by the next day. "We have something headed our way and I don't want anyone cut off when it arrives." She keyed the communication circuit without ever taking her eyes away from the sensor screen.

"We've just opened a maintenance locker down here."

"Close it, lock it, do whatever you have to do to secure it, but get your teams back here. I want us ready if we have to move." She tossed the mic to the communications operator. "Contact the *Resolute* and let her know what's happening." Then she turned to the sensor tech. "How soon can we figure out who that is coming our way?"

"They're not broadcasting any ID code and we can't get a visual until they're within three AUs of the system. That'll be fuzzy at best, but if it's a known design, the computer will peg it. If not, we'll have to wait until it's within one AU before we can get a clear image."

"I hate waiting."

"Ma'am, your husband is always telling us that you're the most patient person he's ever met."

"Little does he know." LeRena walked towards the hatch leading to the top floor's central corridor. "Want anything from the commissary?"

"Just a coffee."

"Coffee with two sugars here," added McWilliams, who been talking to the *Resolute* a moment before.

*　*　*

Sitting at the bar eating his breakfast was Aaron when LeRena walked into the commissary located in the central hub of the fifth floor of the *Venture*. He stuck the spoon he'd been holding upright into his bowl and turned. "Morning, LeRena. Anyone got something useful I can do around here?"

It was well past noon, but Aaron had taken to staying in his cabin, after they discovered he couldn't tolerate the environmental suit needed to explore the artifact. Sure, they had an atmosphere contained inside the structure, but LeRena was enforcing the safety measure of having all entrants wear environmental suits in case of failure of the force fields holding the air in. She wasn't going to bend the rule for one man, even if she knew the inactivity was driving him to despair.

"Three coffees and a sugar packet," she said to the attendant. She turned so she could lean her back against the bar and look at the biologist. "We may be having some company."

Aaron picked his spoon out of his oatmeal, leaving a small dab on its tip. "Connie on her way back with the *Resolute*?"

"I wish. No, this is something else. Coming in from outside the system, from somewhere in the opposite direction of Wassara, Ranklin, or Earth. And whatever it is could be here by this time tomorrow." She turned slightly to acknowledge the coffee tray the attendant placed next to her left elbow.

"I'll be sure to stay out of your way." He turned to look into his bowl and worked harder on eating the tan mush.

"Aaron Fuller," she turned him in his swivel chair to face her. "You were one of the founders of the Ranklin colony, you were responsible for the treaty between our two peoples that led to its successful growth these last three decades." She paused for a moment until his eyes drifted up to meet hers. "I wasn't. If this new ship is another alien race, I'm going to need your help with them. So snap out of this melancholy, finish your breakfast and meet me on the bridge in half an hour." She turned, picked up the coffee tray and headed for the door. "And put some nuts in that mush you're eating."

* * *

Martin had gone around to each of the teams surveying the contents left behind on the stone ship and ordered them back to the *Venture*. All except the team working on that locker located inches from where ship's edge contacted the asteroid they'd found it against. When they had opened the floor to ceiling locker, there was a hissing of escaping gas for a moment. Martin knew it had been under ship's pressure ever since the vessel had been separated from the rest of the ship. That made these artifacts all the more valuable; they hadn't been exposed to the vacuum of space.

HuPadi Glorran and William McHenry, two of Raj's students, were busy boxing the clothing from the upper shelves, working their way down. Martin stepped up behind them and looked deep into the middle shelf. Amongst what looked like footwear appeared to be a reader along the same design he'd seen in the Torvon excavations on Ranklin.

"Excuse me." He pushed between the two students and reached in to pull the inch-thick device out of the back of the locker. Far enough back that it looked like it had been tossed in there at the last minute. Pulling it out, his hand brushed against a stone box that was too small to hold any of the shoes present. He pulled it out also.

He looked over to Bill. "You recorded the contents already?"

"First thing, sir. Shelf by shelf."

"Then skip tagging everything, just get it boxed up and get back to the ship. We've got company coming." He was speaking automatically since he was thinking about what he might find on the reader he held in his hand. Wishing Raj was here to translate.

* * *

"Martin, what's going on out there?" LeRena released the button on the armrest of Captain Henry Ferguson's chair. "You were supposed to have all your teams back here by now."

"I'm bringing the last one in now. Can you meet me in the electronics room?"

"What for?"

"We may have found something in that last locker, it may be a record of what happened."

"I'll be there in a few minutes." She turned back to Ferguson walking back to his chair. "I hope that clears the way for any evacuation if we need to, Hank."

He looked down at the sensor panel he'd stayed near. "Looks like the last two are crossing the asteroid now. We should be ready when you call on us."

"Good." She turned to Aaron, who had been standing against the back wall. "Aaron, let's get down to electronics and see what Martin has. He'd better have something really impressive for delaying us." She was in the open elevator holding the door for the biologist.

* * *

"There's no charge in whatever passes for a battery in this thing." The electronics tech, who spun his stool away from his work bench handed the four-by-six-by-one-inch box to a standing Martin as LeRena and Aaron walked into the room.

"Is there any way you can charge it?" Martin turned the box around and around, staring at it.

"They had a touch plate charger back on Ranklin," Aaron said while holding his hand out to Martin. "May I?"

As Martin handed it over, LeRena said, "Is this what you called us down here for? We have other problems to worry about, Martin."

He picked up the other box he'd brought back with him and lifted the lid off it. "These look like memory rods. And there's a hole in that thing they fit in. When I found the device one was already in there, probably the last recording made by its owner. And it was tossed in the locker like he was making a quick exit. It may have a recording of what happened to the stone ship. If we can only find a way to charge it?"

"Here it is." Aaron handed the box to Martin. "That fuzzy patch on the top there. We found if you placed that against a Torvon power conduit, their devices charge up."

"I don't remember that." Martin said, running his finger over the spot.

"You didn't think we slept while you went back to Earth, did you?"

229

LeRena reached over to the box and Martin gave it to her. "We had charged Torvon circuits back on Ranklin because they had solar cells charging them. We don't have those here, do we?" She looked over to the electronics tech.

"Not on the stone ship, ma'am. And we can't connect our power system into it," he replied. "I wouldn't know where to begin.

"So I hold the answer in my hand, but I can't read it?"

"That about sums it up," the tech confirmed.

She set the box on one of the benches next to the box holding the other rods and walked out of the repair shop.

* * *

"Ship's sensors are able to image the approaching craft." LeRena was again on the bridge when the call came up to the Captain. "Transferring sensor imaging to your view screen."

The view of the asteroid and the stone ship disappeared from the front wall of the *Venture's* central hub, blackness filled it momentarily, then a view from deep space filled the screen. The stars in the background were clear but in the center of the screen was a blurry image. "It's still about three AUs out, sir."

Captain Ferguson pressed his intercom button. "Still no ID on the incoming?"

"I'm afraid not, sir. She's running silent."

"Send radio language greetings." He turned to LeRena, "There's no point in trying the Quantum radio. If they're not broadcasting any ID code, they may not have the tech to receive a Quantum signal."

"Hank, I've never questioned you before. You know what you're doing," she replied.

"Captain, we have a radio contact from the *Resolute*."

"Put it through."

"*Venture*, this is *Resolute*. We have collected the landing parties and are in route to your position. Do you feel you can hold out for two more days?"

"They'll be here before you, then."

"If your position becomes untenable, bug out, leave the solar system. We'll find you again."

230

LeRena reached over to press the communication button. "Mrs. Harrod here, is my husband okay?"

"The doctor's checking them all out in sick bay, but he did walk out of the escape pod, ma'am."

"We'd at least like trying to talk with whoever is coming. Can you have Dr. Pashine available?"

"LeRena, this is Captain Young. It's going to depend on timing, we recorded a radio dead zone around the two gas giants. And it looks like we'll be in that area about twenty-four hours from now. I can't stress strongly enough, if you feel in any way threatened by the new comers, get out of there."

"Any chance I can talk with Michael?"

"Dr. Williams will have them for at least another hour. I'll have him call you when he's cleared. *Resolute* out."

"Captain Ferguson, this is astronavigation. We just did some computations on the incoming object. It appears to be three times the size of the *Resolute*." the voice on the other end got excited as a shrill alarm ramped up in decibels. "Hank, that's the stone detector. That's a Torvon ship headed our way."

Ferguson pressed his intercom again. "Acknowledged, Astronavigation." He turned to LeRena, "Still want to stick it out?"

She walked over to the view screen and touched the fuzzy spot of the Torvon ship. "More than ever!"

Chapter Forty-Five

After another hour, the image in the view screen was sharpening into focus. Where a fuzzy circle had been earlier, a semi-sphere resolved itself. LeRena paced in front of the screen, staring at the image.

"Could we already have half of their ship?" she asked without turning to anyone.

"There's no way to tell, ma'am," the astronavigator said over the open intercom. "They're coming in straight on. We have no idea what's behind the front end."

"But another thing," Captain Ferguson said. "One hundred and eighty million miles in an hour, they're currently subluminal. They've been dumping speed since they hit the edge of Vanera's gravity well. How do you want to play this, LeRena?"

"There's no point in sending out standard greeting messages, our cultures use different communication systems. Bring the *Venture* to the top of the asteroid, about a mile above it. I don't want them to think we're trying to hide from them. If we go out to meet them, it might be seen as a hostile move, so we'll wait. I think it's time to see if that contact protocol we wrote up actually works."

"All hands, prepare for first contact. Secure quarters and report to assigned laboratories to secure all research. Department heads report to..." He switched off the intercom and looked over to LeRena. "To where, ma'am?"

She was already headed to the back of the bridge and the elevator. "The conference room. Keep me posted on where the Torvon craft is likely to dock." The doors parted and she walked across the corridor to where the elevator doors parted for her. She pushed the uppermost button to take her to the conference room.

She was whisked up. The doors opened on a large, circular room, the same size as the ship's bridge, only it was mounted on the top of the saucer while the bridge was on the bottom. In the center of the room was a circular table capable of seating twenty people with computer connections for their portable workstations. Each of those connections were wired into the viewing screen mounted to the farthest wall from the elevator. But the most spectacular feature of the room was the dome. The dome was over a dozen transparent panels joined together to give everyone a view of outside the research vessel.

LeRena walked over to the head chair and activated the screen. She pressed intercom button to the bridge. "Captain Ferguson, could you pipe the view of our guest up here to the conference room?"

The blue screen changed to the star field outside, magnified several orders of magnitude, with the Torvon ship centered in the middle. "It changed course when we positioned ourselves above the asteroid. It's coming our way."

The elevator door opened behind LeRena. She turned to see Martin enter the conference room. "Martin, it looks like you'll need to brush up on your Torvon."

"I'm not as fluent in it as Raj." He pulled out a chair across the table from her and plugged his workstation in. He pulled a set of ear pieces out of the side of it and inserted them into his ears. "Too bad he never got that translation app built he talked about."

"Then we'll all be depending on your skills." The elevator opened again and several more department heads and assistant heads filed into the room. Aaron was the last man to arrive, and when he took the last chair, next to LeRena, LeRena began briefing them on what was coming. What they had less than a half hour to get ready for.

She called down to the bridge, "Captain, do we have an ETA on the *Resolute*?"

"This time tomorrow. She's just dropped into that magnetic zone where contact is impossible for the next several hours."

"Thanks." She released the intercom and looked straight at Martin. "That means we'll be on our own for this contact, no military backup. Martin, get cleaned up, you're leading the contact team. Aaron, Katron, and Solidad, I'm counting on your impressions when they arrive. And Dr. Cook, you tag along to keep an eye on any health issues the Torvons might present us with. The rest of you will wait here. Martin, if you can bring them up here."

"Shoon," Martin said as he stood up to leave.

"What?"

"Just practicing the greeting Raj taught me." He walked over to the elevator and waited as the other four assigned to his team entered. "I may have to rely on a lot of hand gestures. I just hope they have a lot of the same concepts we do," he said as the doors closed.

Chapter Forty-Six

The loading bay doors on the floor above the bridge, the lowest floor of the saucer section before it constricted to the dome of the control center, stood open with only an electronic curtain keeping the atmosphere inside the large round room. LeRena hoped the Torvons would make their way to the *Venture* through that magnetic curtain. It was where Martin Carpenter and his team were assembled to greet them.

While the team was going over ideas on how to establish communication with the Torvons, members of the *Venture* crew had assembled an oval table with ten chairs around it, five on each side. Behind the table, Martin had set up the largest conference monitor aboard the *Venture* and displayed a welcome message in Torvon to greet their visitors. Martin sat in the central chair on the far side of the doors with the monitor over his head. Aaron Fuller and WeToma Katron, representing the Biology and Chemistry departments, sat on either side of him with RaTano Solidad and Dr. Cook on the ends.

"The Torvon ship is establishing a parking orbit alongside your hatch," Captain Ferguson said over the intercom.

"Can you guys see the size of the thing?" LeRena said from the upper dome of the saucer, the normal conference room. The Torvon ship had maintained a course straight for the *Venture* until moments ago. When it turned sideways, it was a long cylinder domed in the front and the rear. There were no obvious signs of engines or how the thing was propelled through space. Of course, the same could be said about the *Venture*, since it used a gravitational drive system, but at least you could tell *Venture's* up and down by the landing legs protruding from the saucer.

"That thing's got to be two miles long, at least," GuTim Kazil, their other chemist, said. "It's over three times the size of anything in the Wassarran fleet."

"Definitively bigger than the *Resolute*," a voice Martin didn't recognize said over the intercom.

"Let's hold down the side chatter," Ferguson said over the open intercom channel.

Solidad went over to the magnetically screened door and stared at the parked vessel. He could no longer see what they assumed was the top or bottom of the craft as the main body blocked his view of space. "I think I see something opening over there." He pointed to the center of the stone hull in front of him.

Martin and Katron pushed their chairs back and stood up, keeping the table between them and whatever was happening. The light from the other ship was increasing as the rectangular door on it swung open.

"Something shimmering is coming this way. If that's a force field, we need to try building bridges with our tech," Solidad speculated. "Yup, it's a bridge. Someone's stepping out of their hatch."

"Get back over here," Martin, who was once again seated, ordered. "We need to present a welcoming front, not be hiding like spies." Solidad was back in his chair before the first space-suited figure was half way across the invisible bridge.

As their first visitor stepped onto the solid deck of the *Venture*, he quickly ran to the far right wall. He was followed by another and another until the line of them stretched to the open loading bay door. Then they started filling the other side of the room. The last few spread to either side of the original lines, leaving a gap for the door area that the final one entered and stood in front of the door.

As they took up their positions, they each leveled a small rod at Martin and his team. All except the last one to enter. He pulled his left arm up to his helmet, which had a three inch viewing slot, and tapped his suit's forearm a few times. Then reached up to his neck and turned the helmet to the right before lifting it from his head. He then stepped forward enough to place the helmet on the table in front of himself.

In front of Martin stood a creature with the flat saucer face like the mummies he'd found in Ranklin. Yet it had a very short nose, almost like a simple hood over the three slits he'd seen in the mummies. He didn't see any tails on these shorter creatures, but their space suits were bulky enough to hide any such appendage. The piece of a ship they had found had no accommodations for using their tails like they had seen in the Ranklin site.

Martin rose from his chair and said, "Shoon." Holding his hand across the table at the unhelmeted Torvon.

Every one of the rest of the Torvons took one step forward, pressed a hand to their hips which made each of the rods they were holding glow at their ends. The leader barked a command. Martin, while fluent enough with their written language, didn't understand what was said. Until one of the suited figures' rod stopped glowing for a moment and the monitor behind Martin burst into tiny pieces that fell straight to the deck.

Martin leveled his offered hand and pulled his other one up to the same height. Palms open to show they were empty, he raised both above his head. The Torvon across the table spoke a few words to his men and some more to Martin. None of which he recognized.

The Torvon barked the last of the words again and his men took another step forward.

Aaron slowly got to his feet, raising his own arms above his head. "I don't understand their language, but I'd say he was telling us to stand up." The rest of the sitting members of the contact team rose with hands in the air.

"They're speaking too fast for me to translate. Or their speech patterns have changed since they left their colony on Ranklin." Martin said slightly louder. "Any thoughts on what we should do?"

"Bring them to the bri..." A blast from another of the Torvon's rods destroyed the speaker mounted in the ceiling. All the others kept theirs pointed at Martin's team.

The main Torvon barked another series of commands and teams of two suited figures flanked each member of the Human/Wassarran team. He watched as the Torvon turned his head, looking around the loading bay for something. "Probably the elevator," he said under his breath and pointed to its location. The Torvon looked at the door Martin had pointed to and issued an instruction. When Martin looked puzzled at him, he pointed to the door Martin had indicated and said something to his men flanking Martin. Rods poked Martin in his back, making him understand he was to walk over to the elevator he had pointed out.

Aaron and the others were herded around the table towards the open bay hatch. Martin saw them stepping onto the invisible bridge as the elevator doors opened.

It was a big elevator, a cargo elevator. It would have felt quite spacious if Martin wasn't focused on the six wands pointed at him. The Torvon commander had brought six of his men, each still helmeted, with him. Martin pointed to the control button display. When the Torvon spoke again, Martin decided he wanted him to select the right button for the bridge. He reached over and pressed the bottom button.

It took only a moment for them to descend the single floor. Martin had already turned around, knowing that the door on the opposite side would open. It caught his Torvon guards by surprise as they had to push him towards it to get their rods behind him again. Waiting for them was Captain Ferguson standing at attention. The entire bridge crew were flanking them. They stood at ease. None of them had a weapon to train on the Torvons. As a Science vessel, the *Venture* didn't carry any.

The Torvon soldiers pushed their captives to the floor and walked forward to form a line in front of their prisoners. Their commander walked from behind Martin and took up a position on the right of the line of Torvons. He scanned the bridge, then barked another order staring at the line of bridge crew.

"Martin, what does he want?" Ferguson asked.

"I don't know. I don't know if even Dr. Pashine could translate what they're saying." Martin replied. He dropped his hands to his side, the Torvons had stopped watching him and were spreading out around the bridge. They started removing their helmets, attaching them to the back of their suits and studying the ship's controls.

The elevator door opened again, Martin turned his head and saw more Torvon soldiers entering behind him. "How did they know where the bridge was?" Martin said just loud enough for

Ferguson to hear. Then he had a nasty thought; this wasn't all the remaining Torvon soldiers. He glanced up at the still functioning monitors mounted around the ceiling of the bridge, showing each level of the ship as well as the main laboratories. Torvon troops were spreading out all over the *Venture*. In the loading bay, he saw more troops entering the ship.

The troops ran into the top deck conference room and quickly surrounded LeRena and the remaining science personnel. Martin watched as they began herding them to the elevator.

"It has to be hard to see through those slits." Katron tried to run his hand up to the eye slot in their helmets. His hand was struck aside and the Torvon next to the man, blasted the chair next to Katron into dust.

"Just do what they want," Captain Ferguson said quietly.

"We should have assumed we'd meet these guys eventually," Martin whispered back. "And spent more time learning their language."

Within a half hour, the Torvons had removed everyone from the *Venture* except themselves, Martin and the bridge staff. The new Torvons coming over to the *Venture* weren't suited, but rather wore green trousers that seemed to bulge in back and a white shirt that was seamed in front. One of them brought a cart over and began collecting the helmets being removed by the troops that had stayed there.

Martin watched the monitors while they ransacked the ship. After they broke into the examination room, where Martin had the artifacts currently being investigated, they stopped and waited for their commander to arrive. He rifled through the items, tossing most of them aside until he found the reader and box of memory rods Martin had found hours earlier. He opened a pouch on either side of his waist and deposit one in each of them. He spoke to the soldiers there and left the room as they continued searching.

"Wasn't that the stuff we found in that last locker?" Captain Ferguson turned to ask Martin.

"Damn, you're right. If we could have just charged it," Martin speculated.

They finally found the commander coming from the elevator in the loading bay, walking over to the open hatch, and heading back to its ship "I wish I could determine which sex he is," Martin mumbled watching the events.

"What? You keep referring to all these guys as male," stated Ferguson's female first officer.

"Oh, the Torvons. We know from the mummies we found that they had two sexes. I just don't know what markers to look for inside those suits."

"So what's the plan?" Captain Ferguson asked, still standing feet from the chair he usually sat comfortably in. He was staring at the controls of that chair rather than the monitors. "Do we just wait for the *Resolute*, or find a way to communicate with the Torvons?"

"They're male, Martin. Hip width," the first officer added.

"Martin, you said you can't understand their speech, is your grasp of their written language any better?" HuPadi Glorran, one of Cowloom's assistants, who'd been taking a turn at bridge duty, asked.

"Yeah, maybe slowing things down and seeing them on paper would allow you to translate easier," the first officer offered..

"You may have something there. Raj was the one who figured out how the language sounded. Anybody got some paper and a stylus?" Martin began patting his pockets until he found something to write on and with.

Martin framed a message in his mind using the Torvon words he knew, knew for sure. He didn't want to write "Take me to your wiener" instead of leader by mistake.

"Okay, on the first sheet, I have "No hurt" and the second "Our questioning peace" and on the third, I've got "What do you want".

"You might want to change that second one," Captain Ferguson. "Don't want them thinking that we're questioning the concept of peace."

"How about just the word peace?" Glorran asked.

Martin discarded the second sheet and replaced it with one having the Torvon word for peace written on it. He put the pad back in his pant pocket and the pencil in his shirt pocket, hoping to get the Torvon commander to understand the need to write responses.

Martin walked up to the Captain's chair where the person who'd commanded the Torvon takeover was sitting. As he reached out his hand to get the Torvon's attention, one of his still-suited troops barked at him and pointed his energy rod at Martin.

The commander swiveled the chair around to see what was happening. Seeing Martin holding the white slips, he stood from the chair, issued an order to the trooper, who took a step back, and stood in front of Martin on a dais that almost brought him up to eye level.

Martin offered the first sheet of paper to the Torvon.

He stared at it for a moment. Martin pushed it closer and the Torvon finally took it. He lifted it up and stared at it for a bit longer. Martin then handed him the second one, which he stared at for a second before taking. When Martin handed him the third one, the Torvon took it immediately. After a moment, he began rattling off words Martin couldn't understand.

Martin held up his hand, then staring at the energy rod of the commander's guard, he reached into his pocket and pulled out the pad of paper. With the pencil from his shirt, he wrote the Torvon word for inscribe. Tearing the slip from the pad he handed it to the commander before offering the pad and pencil to him.

The Torvon looked from the note to the pad, smiled as he began to understand Martin's request, or at least Martin hoped he was. He took the pad and pencil and wrote on it. As Martin read the note the commander handed back to him, he mentality pumped his fist. The creature had written words he could understand: "You read Torvon?"

Chapter Forty-Seven

"No, we still haven't heard anything from the *Venture*, Michael." Connie sat in the *Resolute's* Captain's chair looking up at the distraught architect. "That monster of a ship on the far side of the asteroid could be jamming our signals." They'd even tried hailing the long cigar of a ship, but with no results. "But we're still trying."

Michael stepped away from the chair and began pacing behind it. They were within a half hour of rendezvousing with the *Venture* and they couldn't get any kind of answer from them. He stopped directly behind Connie. "You don't think they've been killed?"

"Our visual scans from when we were in that communications dead zone, showed they moved off the asteroid before making contact with the new craft. Since then, they have returned to the asteroid. Someone's in her who knows how to operate her. Your friends are there."

As they pulled into the system's outermost asteroid field, the larger ship began to pull away from the asteroid the artifact ship segment was clinging to. Michael couldn't tell which end of the ship was which, they both had the same rounded shapes. But he quickly decided the end coming towards them now must be the front.

"Hold position," Connie ordered her helm. She turned to Lieutenant Shelby at the security station. "Get three shuttles out there and rendezvous with the *Venture*. Find out what's going on over there. But I want you here in case our friends out there try something." As Shelby began speaking into his security network, Connie made more plans. "Dr. Pashine, please report to the bridge. Lieutenant Attah, locate Dr. Laudrum, Wizen CeSonta and the rest of the *Venture* representatives and escort them to my conference room. All department heads, assemble in the conference room."

It wasn't more than a couple of minutes before Raj was walking onto the bridge. "How can I help?"

Connie turned her chair at his words. "We need you to record a friendship message in case that ship's Torvon. Mr. Leonard, see to the recording."

A young officer waved Raj over to his station.

Connie began getting up from her chair. "Mr. McStron, please escort Mr. Harrad to the conference room. See if you guys can come up with some ideas about how I can deal with this ship."

"Aye, aye, sir." He rose from one of the science stations on the bridge, saluted Connie and turned to Michael. "If you'll follow me, sir."

* * *

The view screen came to life in the conference room as Commander McStron fed the images from the bridge monitors into it. They'd backed off the image using a probe until the entire mystery ship was in view; it had the bow of the *Resolute* in the shot, it had to back up so far. The ship had also come to a complete stop and the two vessels appeared nose to nose.

Off on the left side of the screen, the three shuttlecrafts could be seen heading over to the *Venture*. The lead one over half way there.

"It looks like the big ship's leaving them alone," Justin commented as he leaned back in his chair.

"Sergeant N'Cube," Lieutenant Shelby's voice came over the ship's intercom. "Take your shuttle and land on the asteroid. Proceed through the hatch near the top of the saucer."

"Acknowledged, sir." The shuttle behind the lead one veered to the right and headed to the asteroid.

"Gotta love those security officers. Setting up a pincer movement in case of trouble." McStron turned away from the monitor and looked over his assembled geniuses. "We need ideas."

"If that's a Torvon ship," Michael began, "there's no way we can talk to them short of knocking on their door. Something we discovered about the escape pod, the communications equipment is not compatible with ours."

"We'd have given you a call if it had been," Justin finished the thought.

"But the equipment on the *Venture* is," McStron said. "Why aren't they talking to us?"

"I'm afraid that's for your teams to find out." Dr. Laudrum was up, pouring himself a cup of coffee.

"We never found a lot of weapons, at least what we think of as weapons, in either the Ranklin dig or down on the planet." Michael crossed his hands on the table and leaned toward the *Resolute's* First Officer. "I think we can assume the Torvons are a peaceful people."

"But you did find a type of rail gun on that section out there."

"It could be that," Cowloom leaned back into his chair. "It could also be their propulsion system. Even a nut cracker. The point is, we just don't know. I never saw anything they would have used for protection in that shelter of theirs, and it was well stocked."

"So, what, just sit here and wait?"

"This thing got any lights in its front end?" Ron McNamara said from under the view screen. "We could try blinking primary number combinations at the other ship?"

Mary Davis slapped him on the back of his head. "They already know we're an intelligent species."

Michael sat straight up, looked over to Laudrum's two students and back to McStron. "No, that might work." He looked up to the intercom speaker. "Raj, can you hear me?"

"Just a second." McSron fiddled with the controls in front of him. "Now try."

"Raj, can you go and see if there are any identifying marks on the escape pods?"

"Nine on the first one we found and seventeen on the one you brought up from the planet. Why?

"We can blink those numbers at the Torvons." He jumped out of his chair, leaned on the back of it looking around the table at each of the attendees before calling up to the speaker. "Raj, ask Captain Young if she can blink the forward ship lights nine times then pause for a minute and blink them again for seventeen."

"Mr. McStron?" came through the speaker.

"I have to concur, Captain. It can't hurt; they can't mistake blinking lights for aggression."

"Navigation, energize the forward hazard lights and set them to blink nine times."

Michael stood up straight and looked over to where Cowloom was sitting. "Raj, do you think you and Wizen CeSonto could pilot one of those pods over to our mystery ship?"

"I don't have any flying experience, especially with those crafts."

"But I do," Cowloom said. "And it'll be easier with you there to tell me what switch I'm looking at."

The background noise from the bridge disappeared from the intercom feed. Then, "Red Alert! Project the trajectory of that object. Give me a time to impact. All energy defense fields forward. Arm the forward missile batteries."

On the view screen, they couldn't see anything approaching the ship. At least until Commander McStron switched the view to a tactical one and everything was rendered into a computer line drawing. A dot, something, was approaching the *Resolute* very quickly.

And just as quickly the dot disappeared.

"Stand down, Red Alert!

"Mr. McStron, they appeared to have fired on us with those maybe-not weapons, but self-destructed the warheads after we discontinued the lights. Gentlemen, I need some answers."

"Why would they fire on us, then stop their attack?" the ship's Tactical Department head asked.

"Do we have a recording of them firing on us?" Bart asked.

McStron fiddled with his control console and the image right before the launch from the Torvon ship appeared on the view screen. As he ran the recording forward, a bright light appeared on the upper right side of the forward dome, then blinked out of existence.

"They blinked a light at us?" Laudrum asked.

They watched as the light never came back on, but after a minute an explosion appeared and the projectile ceased to exist.

"No, what we saw as a blinking light was them firing their weapon," Bart announced. "If I'm right, once they determined that our blinking lights was not a weapon, they self-destructed theirs."

"Blinking lights may not be a good idea," Martin added.

A few seconds later, Captain Young was on the com. "Mr. McStron, what are they thinking?"

"Michael?" The First Officer stared across the table at the man still standing behind his chair.

"We need to talk with the Torvons, really talk. Without an effective radio for communications, anything we try could look provocative. Raj is the only one who can do that, he's the only one that understands their language. We need to get him over to the Torvons. Maybe if we send over a small party, in one of their pods, he may get close enough to begin a dialogue."

"We could send a portable radio with him to allow ship-to-ship communication after he arrives," Bart Higgins added in.

"And if they fire on the approaching pod?"

"Then we'll know they have hostile intents," Laudrum said.

"They've already fired on us."

"But aborted the weapon, they haven't actually done anything to any of us." Laudrum walked over to the monitor, spun his finger to encourage McStron to cycle through the views until he came to a close-up view of the asteroid, then he squeezed his hand into a fist to hold the image and examined it. "Those shuttles sent over to your science ship haven't been intercepted." He turned back and leaned with both hands on the conference table. "We can't just keep sitting here until one of us decides to board the other. And that's what it'll look like if either side sends their own shuttles or troops over. If you want my opinion, I'm willing to risk going personally."

"McStron, who was that?"

"Dr. Reginald Laudrum of the University of California, captain," he announced. "It's time I contributed something to this mission."

"Captain," McStron replied. "Their plan would be less confrontational than any effort we mounted. I would even go so far as to say, no military escort for the pod."

"Okay, get down to the hanger and see which pod is safest for this trip."

"Thanks, Connie." Commander McStron glared across the table at Michael.

"**Mr.** Harrod," said the voice over the intercom. "Don't take any chances. Bring everyone back alive."

Chapter Forty-Eight

Despite the fact they had used a large quantity of the fuel in the escape pod they'd blasted off of the planet with, it still had a larger amount left in its reserves than the number nine pod they'd recovered from the asteroid field.

"If I had to guess, Lieutenant," the landing bay technician said. "This baby may have been powering its way through the asteroid field until it ran out of fuel. There was nobody inside it to shut things down."

"Can we get the extra tanks off the side of the other one, at least?" Lieutenant Attah asked.

"Why not fuel them back up, rig a wireless control for inside the pod and use them as a backup," the tech said, staring at the engines attached to the side of the pod. "It'll probably take less time than pulling those things off, sir."

"Just get a move on. The Captain wants them to launch before the shuttles get to the *Venture*, in...," he stared at his watch, "fifteen more minutes."

With the installation of the engines on the side of the pod, the hatch to get into number seventeen pod was several feet higher than on the other one. Michael had to climb the steps up into it. Raj and Cowloom were already inside. Raj was translating the controls for Cowloom as best he could.

"I don't recognize a lot of these symbols," Raj said. "We didn't find any kind of Torvon flying device back on Ranklin."

"Like lifting off that planet," Cowloom replied. "All I have to do is launch and point this thing at the Torvon ship. We're counting on them to bring us in."

Michael stepped into the pod as another of the landing bay technicians climbed up the steps with a two foot wide box. "Sir, could you pass that on to Wizen CeSonta. Oh, hello, sir," he said as he found he was high enough to see Cowloom looking back at him.

"That's the control for the engines you guys installed on the side of this baby. Simple mechanism," the tech climbed into the pod since he had gotten Cowloom's attention. "This starts the right engine and this button starts the left one. There's a throttle dial below each and the joystick in the center can be set for either both of them or individual maneuvering." He looked around the inside of the pod. "Seems a bit cramped. Good luck, sir." He walked back onto the steps and climbed down.

He passed Dr. Laudrum as he got off the steps, who quickly climbed into the pod.

"I was really surprised, Reginald. I didn't expect you to volunteer," Michael said, pointing to the seat on the opposite wall directly across from where he was strapping in. In the seat next to Michael was the four-by-two-by-two foot radio link they were taking over to the Torvon ship.

"So was I." He sat down and pulled the straps over his shoulders and connected them with the ones under his seat. "I guess I owe Dr. Pashine an apology, and I wanted to prove my faith in his translations by coming along. By putting my life in his prowess."

"Thank you, Dr. Laudrum. Your acceptance means a great deal to me," Raj said from the seat next to Cowloom.

"I'm closing the hatch now." Cowloom pressed one of the buttons in the panel and the door began to close on its own. He high-fived Raj; on the planet, they had to pull the door closed, only knowing how to seal it.

"How do you know when maintenance is done?"

"Kevin already gave me the thumbs up out there. According to the plan, they should be lifting the pod up. There they go." Cowloom felt the pod rise into the air and begin moving in the direction of where he remembered the hanger doors being. "Once outside, they'll release us and I can fire up the engines. I'm going to start with the externals, this time. Get us aimed in the right direction, then one short burst, and we can float over for the Torvons to catch us."

"And how will you know when they release us?" There was a cession of motion and a thud as one of the cables banged against the hull of the pod. "I see now," Laudrum said.

Cowloom played with the controls on the external engines control box. Michael felt the pod turning as Cowloom and Raj watched a view screen they hadn't had on the flight up. Cowloom corrected slightly for an overshoot then fired the engines for a two-second burst. There still weren't any inertial dampeners but the acceleration was not nearly as violent as the ride up from the planet.

A speaker sounded as they got half way across to the Torvon ship. Raj turned in his chair to Michael, "The Torvon ship is trying to make contact." He turned back to the control panel and spoke towards where the voice had come from.

"Damn, I didn't know this thing had a communications system," Michael said to whoever was listening. Compared to the engine noise they'd experienced lifting from Vaneran, he could almost whisper to anyone in the pod.

"It probably wouldn't have been compatible with the *Resolute* anyway," Cowloom replied.

"They asked us to cut our engines, so I let them know we're on a ballistic glide path," Raj said after responding to another message. "They'll bring the pod in."

Michael saw something grayish blink in the view screen. He undid his restraints and stepped up so he could get a better look. As the pod drifted under its momentum towards the Torvon ship, the tip of that ship began to dissolve. First it was a point of blinding light in the surrounding darkness of space. Once it had opened wide enough, and his eyes became used to the brilliant illumination, Michael began making out details of the interior of the Torvon ship. The opening kept growing until it was over ten times the size of the escape pod.

Something jerked the pod. He staggered but grabbed the back of the two chairs and kept himself upright. He could feel the pod's momentum stop, then jerk again as something pulled it towards the opening in the Torvon hull. He shifted his feet and watched as the

Torvon ship grew closer and angled to accept the pod into the now-open bay.

Inside the massive ship, they came to rest half way across the bay. Cowloom was reaching for the button to open the pod hatch when it began unsealing on its own. A moment later, it swung open and a Torvon in a green tunic and ear muffed cap stood at the entrance looking in. While Michael stared at what had to be a strap running near his mouth, the Torvon said something Michael couldn't understand but Raj responded to.

"He wants us to come out of their pod slowly," Raj translated. "I told him we would. "

"Raj, why don't you go first in case they want to tell us something else." Michael gestured to the hatch for Raj to lead the way. As he made his way to the front, Michael noticed Raj pulling his hand from his pocket to grab the edge of the hatch, steady himself and step down a few inches.

As Michael followed him to the hatch, he saw the Torvons had rolled a three step ramp up to the entrance. At the bottom, Raj had stepped off to the side as Michael made his way onto it and down to a deck swarming with a new, yet familiar, alien race.

Chapter Forty-Nine

The four of them appeared to have stepped into a large hanger bay, similar to the one they'd encountered on the stone segment they'd found floating in the Vaneran asteroid field. Their pod had landed in the center of it. The Torvon who stood before them had slacks the same shade of green as his tunic and cap, though it looked like he had a bulge under those slacks just below his lower back, like something was tucked behind him. Michael had a nasty thought, they were built in seat cushions. That the stone seats on this ship were really uncomfortable. Then he decided they were too high to serve that purpose.

In a line on either side of the four were six Torvons wearing gray uniforms that looked less formal then the green uniform on the man in front of them. They stood exactly one arm's length away from the next Torvon. And each of the gray suited men stared at the four of them holding some kind of rod rock steady in their direction.

The man, whom Michael began thinking of as an officer, kept watch on them while similarly-uniformed Torvon ran up the ramp and into the pod. He emerged a moment later and said something to the first one from the top of the ramp.

Michael tapped Raj on his shoulder. "What's going on?"

"He couldn't find it."

"Find what?"

"Whatever his superior here had sent him for. All he said was 'It's not here'."

The other Torvons inside the hanger didn't have the tunic nor cap the men leading them did, they wore the same slacks but had off-white shirts on. None of them displayed the tails all the mummies had had, but they did have bulges clinging to their lower backs.

Cowloom caught up with Raj and whispered to him, "Those bulges on their backs?"

"Is see them also. I don't understand why they're hiding their tails. On Ranklin, they had extra poles mounted everywhere. We assumed they were using those tails on them."

"You're sure about that," Cowloom replied.

Michael looked around as they walked. The Torvons had discontinued the jobs they had been occupied in and stared at his party. "Any idea where he's taking us?" The aliens didn't approach, just stayed where they'd been working and watched. Michael worried when he saw one of them had completely turned around on the twenty-foot ladder he was on top of. At least until he spotted the blond, furry tail sneaking out of the Torvon's trousers and wrapping around a couple of the ladder rungs.

"Yup," Michael tilted his head towards Cowloom. "Tails."

They came to the hatch leading out of the hanger. Four of the guards went through first, followed by the lead officer, who—according to Raj—instructed them to follow. Cowloom, the tallest of their group, had to duck slightly to get through the hatch, into a corridor that was barely tall enough for him to stand fully erect. The other soldiers followed the second officer through the hatch.

They were escorted down the corridor, with soldiers in front and behind them, several yards before their guide stopped and turned to a door in the wall. He said something and Raj replied to him before turning to his friends. "This is the forward elevator, he taking us down to meet the Captain and the command staff." As the doors opened, Raj led the way into the small room.

"At least it's not like the open air ones we found in the hanger bay of the artifact." Michael remembered having to climb the ladders mounted to the sides of the ones there, as this elevator proceeded down. He could feel it descending.

"No inertial dampeners," Justin observed.

They suddenly zipped past a deck that opened on three sides to what looked like a green space. As the walls enclosed again, Reginald added, "I wouldn't stick my hands out and touch those walls if I were you." He leaned against a hip high rail mounted to the car's sides. "This may be an open air car, but the shaft is enclosed."

The car finally came to a stop, the door opened into a short corridor that led to a large room with an oddly shaped table in the center. The table looked like two smaller ovals that had been attached to the ends of one shaped like a C. There was a single chair inside the circle with all the others on the outside of the table facing the center.

That chair was occupied by another green uniformed Torvon, only he had a red stripe running the length of each of his sleeves. Around the table were several other Torvons with Martin, LeRena, and Aaron between pairs of them. Michael waved at his wife.

The central Torvon stood up from his chair and approached Michael's group. He said something to the leading Torvon, who turned to Michael's group and said something that Michael thought had the tone of an order.

"We're to sit down," Raj relayed.

They walked around the table to the empty chairs. Their guards took up positions against the wall behind them. As they settled into a relaxed watchful stance, their rods disappeared like they'd never been holding them.

As he tried to get comfortable in the short chair, Michael empathized with what his wife and her longer legs had to deal with. As the leader took his seat, Raj stood up, gave him a short bow and said a few words Michael couldn't understand.

At least until, "... be of service?", came through a speaker built into the table.

"They can translate what we're saying?" Michael leaned forward on a table short enough to make it look like he was trying to climb across it and began looking for whatever speaker had broadcast the translation. He could find no indications of one in the stone of the table.

"I've been working with their linguist people," Martin said from further down. Seconds later, Torvon words emanated from the table. "We have a passable translation program, now."

LeRena leaned over the table and looked towards Michael. "They've come for their ship, Michael. We think this is the

Leviathan and that's Captain Ronong. We found a recording of the last minute before evacuation of the *Sparrow* but..."

"*Levolation* and *Spakown*," the Captain corrected. "Mine is the *Levolation* and it was the *Spakown* that was lost about fifty ..." the translator paused, "... ago."

"We've aged this find at around one hundred years." When he heard the translator pause, Michael turned to Martin. "Units. It hasn't got our two sets of units translated. We need to work out a consistent series of units for this thing."

"Something to work on," the Captain said. "We never expected to find a section of her like this. We were close by when we began getting a distress call from one of its escape pods. As we approached this system to investigate, we detected the remains of the *Spakown*. which was a surprise, since the *Spakown* was smashed to pieces by an asteroid storm in another sector of the galaxy. A structural reconstruction of the remains found indicated the entire ship was located there. We had no indication that a chunk of her was laying out here.

"Since the escape pod was approaching us, we decided to check out the *Spakown*. Looking over the remains here poised a real dilemma. How did this section get here when we found the entire ship over five hundred—" The Captain said something that the speaker blanked on before continuing, "—away? And why doesn't it show the same collision damage the rest of the ship did?"

Michael looked down the table at Martin, who responded to the unasked question, "This is news to me. I'd want to be going through whatever records you guys have about the *Spakown's* destruction. That might give us an idea of what to look for out there."

Michael looked back over to the Torvon captain. "Have your people found anything?"

The Torvon officer on the far end began speaking, "The cut, break, or tear on this section of the *Spakown* is right on one of the seams we use in building our ships. It could have been a repair current discharge liquefying that seam and the two sections pulling apart. But since our ships do not carry the correct current generator to release that type of seam, we're classifying that as an improbable scenario.

"To have crashed into one of these asteroids enough to jar loose this hull section, the bond of a seam is often stronger than our building materials themselves, would have taken enough force to have caused other damage to both the fragment and the rest of the ship. We found the *Spakown* adrift about fifty—" again the translator failed, "—ago with all her life pods launched and memory files purged. While it was pulverized and broken into hundreds of pieces, this section shows no physical damage."

The Captain quickly spoke, "We are convinced you did not have a hand in her destruction. It happened so long ago"

"And yet you fired on us." Laudrum sat up straight in his chair with his arms folded in front of him and stared straight at the Torvon Captain.

"We thought your blinking lights were warhead launches. Once we realized our error, we destroyed our warheads."

"Reginald, let them continue," Martin said, to get things back on track.

"The only memory records we could find," the other officer continued, "or rather, you found, was the personal diary of a crewman whose quarters happened to be the point of contact for whatever it was." He turned to a view screen Michael hadn't seen when they walked into the room and leaned back into his chair as a bare-chested Torvon came into view and spoke. Michael waited for the translation but none was forth coming. "Let me tie him into the translator. Keep watching."

A couple of minutes in, a high-pitched whine began. The image bounced around until whatever was recording came to rest. The Torvon then pulled on a shirt and a door closed, shutting off the light from the recorder. From there the image was black with just the sound of people running. As the running sounds decreased, the hiss of air escaping began to be heard. A few seconds later, the recording stopped.

"Unless you keep holding, or pick it up every few—" Again there was a word the translator couldn't handle, "—the recorder shuts itself down. We were hoping one of the escape pods would have recorded what happened after the pods were launched. But the only two we know about are the one currently in our hanger bay and the one you have. The memory rod in pod number seventeen is missing. So we'd like to go over to your ship and examine pod number nine for its memory."

Raj pulled the rod out of his pocket. "That won't be necessary." He handed the rod across to Captain Ronong. "I found this in the shelf below the control console. I didn't want to pull the whole unit out. I assume any of your readers can access the information?"

"Krise, see what's on this?" The captain slid the rod across the table to where his officer was sitting.

Krize caught the rod as it got within arm's reach and turned it upright to stand on the table while he removed the other rod from his reader. He set the removed one next to the other and picked the new one up and inserted it into the reader. The images on the screen showed the interior of the *Resolute* as the pod was launching into space to make its way to the *Levolation*.

"That would be its last recording. Let me reset this thing to its beginning." The screen went blank as Krize played with the reader's controls. After a minute, static filled the screen followed by a brief star field view before the screen went to static again. "It looks like I'm going to have to work with this thing to get a history out of it. Captain, if you'll excuse me, I'd like to work on this in my workshop?"

"So, gentlemen. There is the question. If that hull fragment is from the *Spakown*, and the serial numbers on its components match, how did it get here? Drakan, can you pull up the records on the *Spakown* and see what—" again the translator's speaker went quiet, "—has on its recovery and service history?"

"Aye, captain." Then he got up, walked over to where Krize had been sitting and started working the controls mounted into the table.

"In the meantime, you fellows might as well go back to your researches on that fragment. Specifically, see if you can find out what caused the front section of the *Spakown* to shear off?"

"Captain, how do you know that section out there is the bow and not the stern?" Martin asked.

The captain looked puzzled at the translation. "I don't understand how those actions have anything to do with the end caps."

"How do you know it's the front and not the rear?"

"Oh, the word bow means more than a body gesture and stern more than an expression. As for our ships, whatever end cap is pointed in the direction we want to go is the front section. Otherwise, both ends are identical." He stood up from the chair he'd been sitting in. "If you don't mind, I'd like to embed some of my science officers in your teams."

"I think that's a good idea," Martin replied. "And I'd like to stay here with Drakan to see what we can discover in your records."

"That can be arranged, Drakan." Then the Captain reached down and pressed several keys on his computer station. "My officers will be waiting for you in the landing bay when you get there. Good luck, and keep me informed. And you guys," he waved his hand at the two men still sitting, "work out a system of consistent units we can use."

Chapter Fifty

"This is interesting," Drakan said as he looked up from his monitor screen to find Martin pacing by the windows that overlooked the asteroid with the *Venture* resting atop it and the Torvon ship fragment.

Martin walked over to the chair next to him and dropped into it. "Okay, give."

Drakan had to think for a moment. "I have nothing to give you. I just found this information interesting."

"Translator programs, so literal." Martin complained. "I meant what's interesting?"

"Oh. Well, according to ship repair records from one hundred of your years ago, ninety-five point five years to be precise." Martin had used his and Drakan's chronometers to develop a baseline time measurement and extrapolated that out to the concept of the human year. The Torvon rotar was only slightly longer. "The *Spakown* arrived at the Dolalox shipyards for repairs. Here it says," he pointed to the words on the screen, "that she was missing her end cap. All bulkheads interior of the cap had been sealed and she had a minimal losesof crew, six are listed here. They applied a new cap to her and sent her on her way."

"And you guys didn't know that?"

"The Dolalox shipyards is not noted for meticulous record keeping, nor forwarding records back to Torvo Prime. It is a place where ship captains come when they want repairs made with no questions asked." He called up another file and scanned through its contents. "As I suspected, there is no listing on the shipyard's records of any repair made to any Torvon military vessel in that time period."

"So why would the *Spakown* go there? Doesn't sound like something a reliable captain would do."

"It is the closest shipyard to this location. If he had a system about to go critical..."

"Your Captain would head for the closest repair facility. But how does that explain the duplicate ID codes on the sections? You guys did say the piece out there," Martin pointed out the wall monitor, "had the same ID codes as the corresponding fragments you found in the asteroid field."

"Another reason to go to Dolalox for repairs is they will make it look like nothing ever happened to your ship. They would have to have built an end cap from scratch, meaning they could have given it any code they wanted. They just matched the code for the missing section."

"Wouldn't the Captain of the *Spakown* have reported his repairs and loss of men?"

"He may have been planning to. Records are downloaded whenever a ship returns to Torvo Prime, not while we are out traveling. If she hadn't returned since the incident, the records would not have been transferred. When they found the *Spakown,* all her records had been wiped. Probably from lack of use, like the data rod from your escape pod's recorder."

"We found some of your recordings that were over a thousand years old, still intact enough for Dr. Pashine to work out your language. And you're saying modern recordings of them can't last a tenth that time?"

"When you put it that way, it does sound odd."

Chapter Fifty-One

Raj, Justin, Lieutenant Attah and their Torvon escort walked across the asteroid surface, suited up against the malfunction of the force field holding in the atmosphere around that asteroid. They straddled the line marking the inside of the Torvon hull from the rocky surface so they could examine it.

Pulling off his glove, Justin ran his hand over the surface of the edge of the hull fragment, then along the surface of the outer hull, where he had several inches of air held against it by the field from the *Resolute,* which had pulled up alongside.

"It doesn't feel the same." He looked over to the Torvon officer. "Langlo, that's your name isn't it?"

"Lanlo," the Torvon corrected after the translation came back from the *Levolation.* It was a longer delay than it had been in the conference room. Justin's words had to be radioed to the receiver Michael had brought over in the escape pod, spoken to the *Levolation's* computer, which had to return the translation through the Torvon communication system. Then Lanlo's reply had to reverse the process. It was a long minute's wait for all the signals to get through.

"Sorry, Lanlo. When you guys cast your shells to build things. Is it usually as rough as the outer hull or as smooth as this?" Justin ran his hand over the edge of the shell.

Lanlo pulled off his glove and ran his hand over the edge. "That is way too smooth."

"What's this?" Justin stood up and kept running his exposed hand over the edge. "I've got a ripple or something here."

In turn, each of them ran their bare hand over the spot Justin indicated. "Feels like an uneven cut," Lieutenant Attah remarked. "Like whatever did it had a power fluctuation at that moment."

After a minute, "Fluctuation?"

"A momentary change in the intensity of something, like the flame of a cutting torch," Justin said.

"But a cutting torch wouldn't cut through this stone," Raj said. "Melt it, maybe, if it could get hot enough, but not make this precise a cut."

"If something had melted it there would be droplets of stone on the edges."

"And remember," added the salvage officer from the *Resolute*. "Whatever caused this had to operate in the vacuum of space. Why didn't we notice this before?"

"We weren't looking for what caused this to be here, just what was in it," Raj explained. "I think we had better get back inside and see what Martin has found."

* * *

"We now think we have the pieces necessary to explain what happened here one hundred years ago," Martin began. An archive picture of the *Spakown* was displayed on the conference room's monitor. "We've dated whatever happened to her to one hundred years ago. But based on the wear patterns on the asteroid, we've come to the conclusion she's only been sitting against it for the last seventy years. That means what happened didn't occur here, but in deep space, and the hull fragment came to rest thirty years after the incident."

Around the conference table sat the same *Levolation* officers, *Venture* scientists and Captain Young with her specialist from the *Resolute*.

"And based on the orbital velocity of this asteroid cloud surrounding this system," Drakan added, "It entered this system barely one-tenth of a degree of arc around from here. Less than two thousand —" again the translator paused, "— from where we are now. If needed, we could work out where it entered the system, but not the velocity it had when it entered it seventy years ago."

"What we've concluded in our analysis of the edge of the hull segment is that it has been cut from the *Spakown* by some kind of high powered energy device." Justin stood next to Martin while Drakan sat at the monitor's controls.

262

Lieutenant Attah looked from Captain Young to Captain Ronong. "What they're not saying is that it was some kind of energy weapon. All the weapons we have amongst our fleets are kinetic weapons; missiles, rail guns, mass driven bombs. Somewhere out there is another intelligent race of beings that have developed weaponry that can attack us at a distance at the speed of light."

"And in their first contact with us, proved themselves hostile," added Captain Ronong. He looked over to his UEF counterpart.

"We have to track them down." Connie stared right back at him.

The End

More books by John Lars Shoberg:

De-Evolution - Two colony children lost in a violent storm leads to first contact with a sentient native race, and a mystery that must be solved if the colony is to survive.

The Waste Gun - Dr Von Scorio has developed a way to permanently dispose of radioactive waste. Others see it as a threat to the Earth. 247 pages

The Stone Builders - Tension simmers in a colony shared by 2 races. It explodes when they discover the remains of an earlier colony by a third, unknown race. Even worse, something on the planet seems to have declared war on this colony. 273 pages

All available in hard copy from MoonPhaze.com

MoonPhaze.com

has more than just genre books.

We have a variety of cosplay prosthetics, as well as

Handcrafted items such as:

Pillowcases

Keychains

Teddy Bears

Knick Knacks

Coasters

Billfolds

And much more!

Check us out!

www.ingramcontent.com/pod-product-compliance
Lightning Source LLC
Chambersburg PA
CBHW070552120726
47909CB00007B/2317